BODIES
AND
SOULS

Fourteen chilling, thrilling tales, worldly and other-worldly, each with Catholic setting, mood, or characters. Here are such favorites as G. K. Chesterton's Father Brown, Agatha Christie's Hercule Poirot, stories by MacKinlay Kantor and Shane Leslie, a splendid chiller by Ernest F. Miller, a Redemptorist priest. Here are tales of murder, hauntings, exorcism, stories of saints and of sinners, of found bodies and lost souls . . . guaranteed to delight catholic, as well as Catholic, mystery fans in search of something different.

BODIES
AND
SOULS

edited by

DAN HERR and JOEL WELLS

DOUBLEDAY & COMPANY, INC.
GARDEN CITY, NEW YORK

Copyright © 1961 by Doubleday & Company, Inc.
All Rights Reserved
Printed in the United States of America

Grateful acknowledgment is made to the authors and also to the copyright holders, magazines, publishers and agents named below.

THE DARK CORNER, by Frank Ward. Copyright © 1958 by Frank Ward. Reprinted by permission of the author and the author's agent, Scott Meredith Literary Agency, Inc.

THE BODY IN THE BASEMENT, by Ernest F. Miller. Reprinted by permission of the *Liguorian.*

"A Diabolic Intervention," by Shane Leslie, from SHANE LESLIE'S GHOST BOOK. Published in 1956 by Sheed and Ward, Inc., New York and reprinted with their permission.

"The Chocolate Box," by Agatha Christie. Copyright 1925 by Dodd, Mead & Company, Inc. Renewal Copyright 1953 by Agatha Christie. Reprinted by permission of Dodd, Mead & Company, Inc.

HEAVEN CAN WAIT, by C. B. Gilford. Copyright 1953 by Davis Publications, Inc. (Formerly Mercury Publications, Inc.) Reprinted by permission of the author and the author's agent, Scott Meredith Literary Agency, Inc.

"The Finger of Stone," from THE POET AND THE LUNATICS, by G. K. Chesterton. Copyright 1929, published by Sheed and Ward, Inc. Reprinted by permission of Miss D. E. Collins and Cassell & Co., Ltd.

"The Patron Saint of the Impossible," by Rufus King, from THE STEPS TO MURDER. (First published in *Ellery Queen's Mystery Magazine.*) Reprinted by permission of Rogers Terrill Literary Agency.

TOO MANY COINCIDENCES, by Paul Eiden. Copyright © 1958 by Fosdeck Publications, Inc. Reprinted by permission of the author and the author's agent, Scott Meredith Literary Agency, Inc.

THE GREEN SCARF, by A. M. Burrage. Reprinted by permission of Stephen Aske, London.

ROGUES' GALLERY, by MacKinlay Kantor. Copyright 1935 by the Crowell Collier Publishing Co. Reproduced by permission of the author.

"The Apples of Hesperides," from THE LABORS OF HERCULES, by Agatha Christie. Copyright 1940 by Agatha Christie. Reprinted by permission of Dodd, Mead & Company and Wm. Collins Sons & Co. Ltd.

THE VIGIL OF BROTHER FERNANDO, by Joan Vatsek. Reprinted by permission of Story Magazine. Copyright by Story Magazine, Inc., 1943.

"The Secret Garden," from THE INNOCENCE OF FATHER BROWN, by G. K. Chesterton. Copyright 1910, 1911, by Dodd, Mead & Company. Copyright renewal 1938 by Frances Chesterton. Reprinted by permission of Dodd, Mead & Company and Messrs. Cassell & Co. Ltd.

MURDER FOR FINE ART, by John B. Price. Reproduced from The London Mystery Magazine and reprinted with their permission.

All of the characters in this book
are fictitious, and any resemblance
to actual persons, living or dead,
is purely coincidental.

CONTENTS

CONTENTS

INTRODUCTION

If you are the querulous type you may feel obliged to complain about a collection of stories seeming to imply that Catholics take an unnatural delight in bloodthirsty reading, or are themselves especially prone to committing mayhem. We know from experience of at least one irate Catholic who is passionately concerned with this very problem. Not long ago he called at our bookstore to deliver a heartfelt protest against our advertisement for a murder mystery.

"Don't you people know," he thundered, "that murder is against the Fifth Commandment? You're encouraging murder by passing it off as entertainment. And you call yourselves Catholics!"

Just in case he's still around and hasn't been taken by the apoplexy that almost felled him that day, and in case there may be others like him, we will state unequivocally that we are in favor of all the Commandments, and certainly not excepting the Fifth. To make sure that we do not unjustly incriminate our fellow Catholics, we would also wish to make clear, though with slightly less emphasis, that not for one minute do we hold to any theory which would show Catholics to be more homicidal by nature than Southern Baptists. We are proud to say that up to this moment not one Catholic of *our* acquaintance has been convicted of murder. As for ourselves, we wouldn't harm a rhinoceros.

Actually, this collection of stories should tend to allay fears of this nature; because it just happens that most of the victims, rather than the murderers here, are Catholics. With that major issue patly and primly dealt with—to our satisfaction, at least—we can proceed to the business of this introduction, which is to

9

tell you that we have tried to select stories which we believe will be of particular interest to Catholic readers. These tales of suspense, murder, mystery and ghosts will have a heightened meaning for Catholics, either because of the viewpoint of the author, or because of the background of the story. Just as we believe there is no reason to apologize for reading stories grisly and grim, we hold that no excuse is necessary for presenting to you this collection of what we consider outstanding examples of the literature of violence and horror.

If you are already a mystery buff, you will recognize some of your favorite authors, but we hope you will find in these pages new authors to rank with them. For those who are not yet addicts of this form of escape reading, we hope that the quality and variety of the stories we have mined from likely and unlikely sources will endear you to this noble form of writing. As for our standards of selection, we picked these stories of Catholic interest because we liked them.

We hope you will like them, too.

Your kind and gentle editors

THE DARK CORNER

BY FRANK WARD

TO MRS. PURCEY, THIS ONE HOUR OF SATURDAY NIGHT, SHROUDED in gloom, was the fulfillment of her entire week. She moved on creaking legs down the long centre aisle, her eyes fixed on the altar, hurrying a little because she was late.

All about her the church seemed to hold its breath, as it always did on Saturday nights. She moved in a sea of deserted pews, like a chunky little tugboat swinging toward the anchor chain of the sanctuary light. Above her, marbled pillars lost their heads in the dark dome of the church, and fastened to one of them, the clock pointed out her error. It was then eight-forty, and later than she had thought.

She arrived at the main cross-aisle breathless, her composure shaken. But the light was still on over the door of the confessional in a dark recess to her left, and her sigh of relief whistled in the still air.

She trundled down the side aisle, her eyes fixed on this light. It flung a jarring brilliance like a challenge into the softer gloom beyond it, and in its reflection she could discern the form of the priest, the glimmer of his white surplice, the vague outline of his listening face as he inclined his head toward the grating that separated him from the box on his right. Mrs. Purcey averted her eyes, feeling obscurely ill at ease.

She rustled her way into a pew, not so close that the murmur of voices would be audible to her. She did not look again toward the confessional, which was a great pity. Instead, she let her mind slide into the old, familiar path her sins had worn across the years of her conscience.

They were small, insignificant sins, and very dull. At sixty-five she had long forgotten the ones that had brought her to this place in shame and remorse twenty or thirty years before. Now she clung to her transgressions as if they were old and friendly ghosts of their former selves.

Her fingers caressed the worn pages of her missal, which fell open almost resignedly at the Examination of Conscience.

A small sound, as if someone had sighed heavily, filled the alcove where the confessional stood. Mrs. Purcey blinked rapidly, curbing the urge to turn her head and pry, and sank her eyes into the printed page.

"Oh, God," she read, the words blurring a little in the dim light, "grant me the grace to be truly sorry . . ."

She shifted on the hard kneeler and lifted her head in irritation. Her attention had been drained from this one, comforting ritual, and she resented it. She resented it so deeply that when the confessional door opened and the soft whisper of footsteps moved in the aisle behind her, she did not so much as bother to look around.

The footsteps paused. She heard a soft intake of breath, a breath that shivered, and still she did not look up. She was aware, somehow, that the candles on the small side altar had fluttered, as if an uneasy wind had brushed their wicks. And then the footsteps slithered away into the obscurity of another aisle, and she was alone. Mrs. Purcey raised her head, as if emboldened by the sudden quiet.

From the corner of her eye she could make out the figure of the priest, barely discernible beyond the grilled door of his cubicle. His face had a smooth pallor, cast in the shadow by an upraised hand, and it struck her foolishly that he looked as if he were still listening. She stirred uncomfortably, rustling her skirt, intentionally touching her toe against the kneeling bench. But still he did not move.

Somewhere a clock chimed the quarter-hour. She squeezed out of her seat, collecting the pattern of her faults into one tight knot in her mind, and moved slowly toward the box. It was set in a dark corner, and the curious sensation of watching eyes followed her into the darkness. The sensation was still with her, although the church was deserted, as she sank heavily to her knees. Before her a crucifix stood out starkly from the wall of the box, ivory figure on black wood. Still the priest did not stir. It struck her then that he might be asleep.

But his eyes were open when she peered at him through the small grating, and they were not looking at her. The door, of its own accord, closed behind her with a distinct click, vibrant in the stillness, but still Father McKay remained motionless, his face partly in shadow.

Mrs. Purcey opened her mouth to speak the first words, "Forgive me, Father . . ." but she never uttered them.

In the flickering light from the altar she saw his hand move, as if to acknowledge her presence. His head slid slowly sideways, touching the grating, and for one terrible moment his eyes stared directly into hers.

Mrs. Purcey's shriek of terror followed her down into eternity.

To Father Brett, the hours between seven and nine always passed too quickly, so that at the big clock's chime he was left with a sense of loss, as if something important had slipped through his fingers. Some scrap of evil left alive to haunt for another week, some word of kindness not spoken, some opportunity missed, these were the things that always sent him to his bed on Saturday nights tense and unrelaxed.

Of late he had even taken to striding up and down the dingy street behind St. Mark's when confessions were over, a tall black figure, time-bent, like a tree. But tonight a cold wind blew a colder rain against the vestry windows, and his spare frame shivered at the sight. There was no escape for him in that direction.

He turned away from the unfriendly glass. The black cord of a hearing aid dangled unnoticed on his shoulder, his one concession to self. By merely disconnecting it he could step beyond the reach and demands of all men. Because of this one indulgence on this one particular night, he did not hear Mrs. Purcey's cry. When he sighed and reluctantly put himself back into communication, it was too late.

Nine-thirty had come and gone, but as he stepped into the church the tiny white finger of light still beckoned from Father

McKay's box. Father Brett frowned. It was a rule of St. Mark's that confessions ended at nine o'clock, and no one in his recollection had ever stayed beyond that time. The sacristan, in fact, had already locked the church and gone home.

The elderly priest moved across the church, pausing before the altar to genuflect, and continuing on his silent way like some tall shadow of doom. He could see that one door of the confessional was tightly shut; and he could see the bent head of Father McKay. But he could hear nothing, and this was all wrong.

Even the most timid sinner must make himself heard. Father Brett paused, within an arm's reach of the box, and checked the connections on his hearing aid. He coughed, experimentally. The cough echoed off into the shadows and beat back at him reproachfully from a dozen hidden corners.

He put his hand out, touching the knob. His fingers closed on it, hesitantly, but already a dreadful premonition was growing in his mind. He had seen death too often to mistake its slack, shapeless form. His hand tightened and turned, and the door moved toward him.

Father McKay moved, too. He slid even further down the side of the box, and one white hand, outflung, fell into view. The fingers were curled tightly, but even as Father Brett stared in horror, they opened.

For a long time the two priests faced each other, the one rigid and stunned, the other beyond all shock.

Then Father Brett put one hand out and touched the dead fingers, and to his imagination, it seemed already that they were growing cold.

To Archer, Saturday night was a time of trouble, and it kept no particular hours. At nine o'clock he walked into the Thirteenth Precinct station house, glancing up at the clock and hurrying, because he was a little late.

He went directly into his office, shaking the rain from his coat, and hung it on a rack in one corner of his cheerless room. He put his hat on top of the filing cabinet. He wiped the rain off his face, pulled the chair out from behind the desk, and sat down.

So far, so good. This was routine, the refuge he had found, and to be effective, it must be followed every inch of its tedious way. When he paused, when he hesitated or strayed, Alma's presence rushed in to capture the wall he had left unguarded, and although she had been dead for two years, he still had found no defence against her.

He lit a cigarette and reached for the stack of reports on his desk. He had worked his way down to the third one when the phone rang in the squad room. He heard the sergeant's heavy voice tramping across the stillness, and yawned. He felt leftover tonight, like something that had been packed away from the day before, and his eyes hurt. They felt gritty when he blinked.

The smell of the office sank into his pores, a combination of used-up air and used-up emotion. Depression these days walked a twenty-four hour beat with him, but always one pace behind, and he had to keep it there.

The light on the phone extension glowed and Archer reached for the receiver. The sergeant's voice said, "There's a call from St. Mark's, Lieutenant. One of the priests is dead, they say, and an old woman, too."

"How?" Archer asked.

"The doctor doesn't know yet. But he sounds worried."

"Send a car," Archer instructed, and deliberately did not ask which priest had died.

He put the phone down and went on to the fourth report, but the words seemed to be arranged in the wrong order. When he looked up again, the sergeant was standing in the doorway, watching him.

"So," Archer said.

The sergeant coughed. "It was Father McKay, Lieutenant."

Archer stared at him. He could feel the blood heating the skin over his cheekbones, and an elation he could barely conceal gave his eyes a high polish.

"Thanks for telling me. You sent the car?"

"On its way."

The sergeant cleared his throat. "He was hearin' confessions when it happened, sir."

Archer put down the reports and folded his hands into one

big fist on top of them. The sergeant moved uneasily. He looked at Archer's thin, almost hostile face, at the steady dislike in the grey eyes, and dropped his own gaze.

"I just thought you might like to know, Lieutenant."

"All right," Archer said evenly. "Now I know. Is there anything else you'd like to say?"

There was, but the sergeant just shook his head and walked out of the room.

Archer blew out his breath. He got up and walked around the office. He smoked another cigarette without tasting it, waiting. And when he had waited long enough, the phone rang again.

He stretched a long arm and picked it up.

"Archer, Thirteenth Precinct," he said. "Yes? What is it?"

"Foyle here, sir."

"Where are you?"

"St. Mark's, Lieutenant. You've heard about Father McKay, sir? And the old woman?"

Archer's lips tightened. "I've heard. What about them?"

"I'd rather not say on the phone, Lieutenant. But there's something wrong about this. Something very strange. I think you'd better come and have a look."

Archer spoke sharply. "Is there a doctor there?"

"Yes, sir. Doctor Angelus. He doesn't like it either."

"What's he think?"

"He says heart attack for the old woman. Her name's Mrs. Purcey. He isn't sure about Father McKay, but he thinks it might be brain hemorrhage. He doesn't know why it should be."

"Any marks on him?"

"None we can see, sir. Only a little blood in his right ear. Just a drop of it."

Archer looked at the clock. It was nine-forty. He said, "All right, Foyle. I'm coming right over. And don't let anyone touch either of them."

Foyle's voice stuttered. "But it isn't decent, sir. . . ."

Archer smiled like a vicious grey wolf. "I said nobody is to touch them—under any circumstances. Is that understood?"

He re-cradled the phone before Foyle could say yes or no, got into his coat, snatched up his hat and walked out into the rain. Behind him, the sergeant put one finger along his nose and treated the palm of his hand to a little smile of satisfaction.

It was still raining when Archer arrived at the church.

The doctor was a small, round man with a shiny head and a worried mouth. He was talking to a tall, elderly priest when Archer came in a side door and walked across the church toward them.

His heels made a deliberate mockery of the silence, and his face bore the stiff, haughty imprint worn by so many men who hide aching emotions. His hair, almost silver, gleamed in the candle-light. As he came up one of the patrolmen stepped back, and the two ambulance men who had been leaning against the confessional sighed with relief and went out for a smoke and a walk around the block.

Archer stopped in front of the side altar. He looked at it blankly for a moment, and then turned his head toward the body of Father McKay. At the sight, he stopped breathing. Then he dropped to one knee and turned the head toward him. He knew this face well. It had been a broad, mobile face, touched with asceticism, tempered with good humor, and the eyes that stared into his now had always held a deep twinkle, as if Father McKay was keeping back one great eternal joke.

But there was no laughter in the dead face now, only a mild expression of surprise. Archer stood up. He stepped over Father McKay's body and shone a flashlight into the dark box of the confessional.

Mrs. Purcey still knelt there, her hands clasped together, but her face was a nightmare. There was a sharp, biting odor in the confined space. Archer snapped off the light and turned to the doctor.

"I'm Archer," he said, and despite himself, his voice was trembling.

"Angelus," the doctor said. He wiped his hand over his bald spot.

The tall old priest stepped forward. "Mr. Archer," he said quietly, "I must insist that you allow me to do my duty, too."

Archer smiled. "And that is?"

"You know very well what it is."

"I do. But perhaps you've forgotten what mine is."

"Your duty I know," Father Brett said tightly. "About your motives I'm not certain."

"Then I'm entitled to the benefit of the doubt, according to your standards. Isn't that so?"

"If there were doubt," said Father Brett. "Do you propose to stop me, Mr. Archer?"

"I'm surprised you waited so long," Archer said. He touched the doctor's arm and drew him down the aisle, while Father Brett stepped into the alcove and sank down on his knees beside the dead.

"All right, Doctor," Archer said. "Let's have it."

Dr. Angelus fidgeted. "I understand one, but not the other. I knew Mrs. Purcey. Her heart was running down, like an old clock, you understand. The shock of finding Father McKay dead would be too much for her. That is my opinion. Her appearance bears it out."

"And the other?"

Dr. Angelus seemed to be haggling with himself. He wiped his bald spot again, and frowned into the dimness of the church. "I don't understand that. He was a comparatively young man. About forty, would you say?"

"Forty-three," Archer said softly.

"And in good physical condition, I should think."

"The best," Archer said, just as quietly.

"You see? Too young, nothing organically wrong with him. Father Brett told me that he had never complained of feeling ill while he was here. And that's how long?"

"Eight years." Archer's eyes had a lost, distant look. "What are you getting at?"

"I wouldn't like to say, exactly. But I think your medical examiner should have a look at him."

Archer moved his hand. "The blood in his ear?"

"Yes. Only a drop, but still, you see what I mean?"

"I think I do. You mean he was murdered."

Dr. Angelus nodded. His eyes were very dark.

Archer turned around slowly and looked toward the altar. It hadn't changed. The curving rail gleamed like brown satin in the yellow candle-light. A star of red twinkled in the sanctuary. There was a smell of incense in the air. Incense . . . and something else that might be death.

He walked back the way he had come, skirting the knot of people huddled in the alcove where Father McKay had heard his last confession, and went out into the night air.

Later, there would be the men with their black bags and their cameras and their sharp, technical glances. But now, at least, he was alone. It was still raining. He closed the church door and leaned his back against it, and the rain trickling down his face gave him the look of a man crying, silently, dumbly.

He knew he should feel hate, a hate eased by this last of all retributions. But the emotion stuck in his throat. He could feel nothing but pity, and perhaps a little remorse.

He sighed and slogged down the path toward his car and, with a cold hand, picked up the radio transmitter and gave his orders.

It was early afternoon before Archer awoke, with the insistent droning of the door buzzer in his ears. He groaned, and rolled over on his face, but the droning went on spasmodically until he admitted defeat and got out of bed.

He shuffled to the door, wrapped in a faded dressing gown, unhooked the night lock, and opened the door, still vigorously protesting inwardly.

A girl stood facing him, her gloved finger poised above the button.

"Spare it," Archer said thickly. "You've flushed your prey. What do you want?"

"You're Michael Archer?"

"I am."

"I'm Helen McKay."

Archer scrubbed his eyes with the back of one hand and examined her. He wasn't surprised to find her there, because nothing surprised him these days. But he was surprised to see how shabby she looked. Her face seemed almost nondescript, a face that could fit a thousand girls and never make their fortune. But the resemblance to Father McKay was there nevertheless. She had the same broad mouth, grim now and unsmiling. Her eyes were the same dark shade of blue, set wide apart and accepting no sham. There was the same hair, black with a blackness that is almost midnight blue, and crisply curled.

"Are you all through examining me?"

He flushed then, recognizing the instant defence in her voice, the defence of poverty that makes an attack of every glance and every remark.

"Sorry," he said. "I didn't know I was staring."

"You were."

"And you don't like it."

"I don't care," the girl said, but her cheeks were red. "It really doesn't make any difference. Are you going to invite me in, or not?"

Blunt, direct, uncompromising. Despite himself, Archer smiled, because this girl could be no one else but Father McKay's sister.

He said, "Come in, by all means."

She walked past him, but there was no perfume to tantalize the sense or arouse male interest. She wore a loose brown coat with the collar turned up and walked with a free, steady swing. He followed her into the living room.

She stopped beside the fireplace and turned to face him. Her hands were folded over her bag, her chin was up, and she was obviously in no mood for anything Archer would have to give her. Or any man, for that matter.

"I didn't know you'd be asleep," she said.

"Don't apologize. Most people don't."

"I wasn't apologizing, Mr. Archer. Frankly, I couldn't care less about what you do."

Archer laughed outright. "Fair enough. What do you care about, then?"

"It's what you're going to do I want to know about," she said.

"Then I'll tell you. I'm going to make some coffee. I'm going to wash my face and get into some clothes and smoke a cigarette. After that, perhaps I'll give you ten minutes or half an hour, depending on what you have to say. And after that . . ." He shrugged. "Sit down. I won't be long."

He made coffee and went into the bathroom and splashed cold water over his face and head. In the cold grey light of afternoon his features had a blurred look, as if too much rough experience had worn down the clean, sharp outlines.

He was an old man of thirty-six, wearing a face that had seen fifty hard years, and the eyes that watched him soberly in the mirror were red-rimmed and weary. There was a little black in his close-cropped grey hair, but very little. He smiled at his reflection, a savage smile, and went back into the bedroom reaching for a sportshirt and a pair of slacks. Then he returned to the living room, stopping on the way to collect the coffee.

He stopped dead in the living room archway. Helen McKay was standing with her back to him, examining a picture on the mantelpiece . . . the picture of a woman. It had been lying face down, as it had done for two years, but she had propped it up and was standing before it with her head cocked very slightly to one side.

"Put that down," Archer said in a grating voice.

The girl turned her head without moving her body. Her eyes were very grave.

"Put it down," Archer whispered. The coffee cups were shaking in his hand.

Her mouth tightened. She put the photograph face down.

He walked over to a table and set the cups on a tray. His whole body was shaking and his mouth was so dry he had difficulty in moistening his lips.

When he straightened up, Helen McKay was still staring at him. Her face had fallen into a soft, almost pitying expression, and her eyes were large and nearly black.

"I'm sorry," Archer said. He cleared his throat. "I shouldn't have used that tone to you. You couldn't know."

"You don't have to say you're sorry, Mr. Archer. I had no right to touch your personal property."

He sat down, and when he held out his cigarettes, his hand had steadied.

"That's a leading remark, Miss McKay, and you know it. It gives me the opportunity of pouring my own personal troubles into your sympathetic ear."

"I didn't mean it that way . . ."

"It doesn't matter," Archer said evenly. "What you mean isn't important to me. It's what you do when you're in my home that matters. I don't want your pity, Miss McKay. I don't want a soft shoulder to cry on. Or is it something more? Is it the fact that if it hadn't been for your brother's stupidity, that picture would be standing upright?"

He drew a deep breath and made an abrupt motion with his hand.

"Sit down, will you? You make me nervous, standing there as if you were trying to make up your mind how to judge me."

She sat down facing him.

"Now," Archer said, drinking coffee that was too hot, "why did you come here today?"

"My brother . . ."

"What about him?"

"He . . . died last night. As you know."

Archer smiled brutally. "As I know. He died hearing confession, which should come under the heading of strange coincidences, Miss McKay. My wife died while he was hearing hers. Would you say that made us even, Miss McKay?"

"Nothing," the girl said in a shaking voice, "will ever make you even. You're quite right. I know all about you. Everyone in this neighborhood knows all about you. Everyone has heard your story, because you took good care to see that they knew it. You're an object of interest to everyone, even the poor people who live in my neighborhood and look as shabby as I do."

"I'm flattered."

"You needn't be. You don't fool us, Mr. Archer. We call you poor Mr. Archer, but it isn't because we feel sorry for you. It's because you are poor . . . poor in everything that counts. You're the most poverty-stricken person I know, a man with nothing in his pocket but revenge and nothing in his heart but hate."

Archer leaned back, the cigarette hanging from his lower lip. He smiled, but for some reason, the smile hurt his face.

The girl's quiet, even voice went on as if he hadn't moved. "I didn't come here to tell you that. It just fell out. What I did come to say is that I know how my brother died and I want to know what you're going to do about it. If you know yourself."

"If you know that much, you're one up on me."

"More than one up. I have the advantage of being alive, all the way through, and not just on the surface."

Archer drew on his cigarette and let his eyes stray insultingly over her clothing. The insult was implied and obvious, but it gave him little satisfaction to see her wince.

"Your family has a certain trait I don't admire," he said thinly. "The trait of judging others before they judge themselves."

"Not judging, Mr. Archer. Just seeing straight."

His mouth had a scraped look. He made a gesture with the cigarette. "I think you've worn out your welcome, Miss McKay. You've got me out of bed to tell me nothing."

She paused and looked down at her hands.

"I want your help," she said quietly. "I have to have it."

"And this is the way you go about it?"

"I'm not begging you for it, if that's what you mean. I have the right to expect it . . . and demand it."

She leaned toward him. "Doesn't it mean anything at all to you that a man was murdered last night? That he was killed by someone who knelt in the confessional next to him, someone he was trying to help? He had no chance at all."

"I'm touched," Archer said. "If it had been someone else, I'd have been touched a little more." He held up his hand, as if in warning. "My personal feelings don't enter into it. I'll do what I can."

He got up and walked around the room, aimlessly. It had once been a warm and cheerful room, a place for flickering firelight on cold nights, a haven from crime and sordidness and deceit . . . a refuge. It was now a cold and neglected trap.

He stopped by the window and looked down into the street, but there was nothing to see.

"All right," he said. "Let's get down to it. How did your brother die?"

"I think you'd better talk to your medical examiner, Mr. Archer."

He nodded. "I'll talk to him. How does that help you?"

Her voice shocked him with its cold, driving intensity, and he knew then that he was not the only one in this room who could turn all the energy of living into the one narrow channel of hate.

"I want you to find whoever did it," she said in her whispering voice, "and take him out and kill him."

He swung about. She had half-risen from her chair, so that she seemed to crouch, and her face bore an expression he had never seen before . . . and didn't want to see again. It was deathly pale and the wide, pleasant mouth, made to smile and curve in amusement or happiness, was tight with anger, and an almost savage, a completely unwomanly bitterness. In the stillness, he could hear her breathing, like a small animal trapped in a cage.

She was not looking at him but completely through him, and for once, he had run out of words.

Then she turned, gathering up her coat, and almost ran toward the door. It slammed behind her.

Archer stared down at his hands. They were clenched into fists. He opened them with an effort and walked back to the coffee table, and his glance fell on the picture lying face down on the mantelpiece. But strangely enough, it was a passing glance, and had he thought about it then, he would have remembered that for the first time in two years the sight of that long-dead face had no terror for him.

He tasted the luke-warm coffee and found it bitter. He exchanged the cup for the phone and dialed a number.

When he had been connected with the coroner's office he asked a question and was given an answer. He listened for perhaps three minutes.

When he replaced the receiver in its cradle his face was curiously slack, as if some inner cord had been cut.

Someone had taken a long, sharp instrument, perhaps a thin ice-pick, or a hat-pin, and driven it into the ear of Father McKay as he leaned against the grating in his confessional. That was the manner of his going; that was the explanation for the terrible hurt in Helen McKay's eyes.

Archer shivered. For the first time in two years he began to think of Father McKay as a human being and not as an instrument of loss and torture to himself. He sank down in his chair and looked at the far wall.

The priest had died without having been given the slightest chance to defend himself. And his killer had stepped from the confessional with head down, a mockery of repentance, and disappeared into the night as if he had never been there at all.

Father Brett walked slowly down Vincent Street, ignoring the children who cannoned off his legs, and the protesting screams of their mothers. He walked as a man walks who has no intention of coming back, although he knew that this was a dead-end street, a place where people huddled together to lead dead-end lives. There was no escape for any of them, including himself.

Voices yelled at him. A street peddler raised his hat and smiled at him. And like a long black destroyer, Father Brett sailed through it all, his smile fixed firmly in place, one hand partially raised, so that no one who watched him would have known where his thoughts lay.

He came at last to the high brick wall of the factory, and turned to look back over his course. The return trip stretched before him, littered with old-model cars, the emblems of social prestige on Vincent Street, and here and there that greatest of all blessings, a television aerial. It was a street of time payments, but in Father Brett's mind there was only one question: how could anyone pay for what had happened to Father McKay?

Was there an installment plan in eternity, a purgatory with no cash down and all the years beyond reckoning in which to total up the payments for one lifetime? Curiously enough, he was not concerned for Father McKay, beyond the ordinary sense of loss. Father McKay had been a man in a dangerous profession, and he had gone prepared . . . or should have. But the other, the one who knelt and whispered the parody of confession while busy fingers fumbled with the pointed steel . . . that one was another question. For that one Father Brett could feel real terror.

The old priest shook his head and took a deep breath to see if that would ease the pain that had been growing steadily more apparent in his chest. He looked cautiously around him and reached for the switch on his hearing aid, shutting out the bellow and chaos of this place, and walked back the way he had come in a strangely peaceful silence.

He had almost reached his starting point when he saw the plain black car pulling up to the rectory door. He paused as Archer got out, and a tentacle of suspicion reached into his mind to torture him. There was hatred here, and motive, and opportunity, but even his keen old eyes could make nothing of the detective's grim, secretive face.

Father Brett winced at the thought. He knew what this man had been through, he found himself considering extenuating circumstances. But even as he walked toward Archer, his mind threw the image of the dead Father McKay before his eyes, and he could find no excuse. He touched his little switch and tuned himself back to humanity.

Archer nodded curtly, but Father Brett smiled, although it was almost a timid smile. His sudden suspicion had thrown him out of touch with this man, and with his own ability to look impartially at his fellow man.

He said, "Hello, Michael. It's almost nice to see you again."

Archer grinned crookedly. "I'll believe the *almost*, at any rate. Where can we talk?"

"You've no objection to my study?"

"I'm on duty," Archer said, but his words lacked bite. "Your study will do."

They went in silence into the locked church. It had a stained grey look on this day, a look of desertion. It no longer waited for the stray footstep. It was a desecrated place, because murder had been done here, and the killing had left its own dark imprint.

Archer looked toward the alcove. The door of the confessional hung slackly open. A photographer's flash bulb lay near it, almost concealed by a kneeling bench. Archer frowned. He walked over to the place where Mrs. Purcey had died and put his head into the box.

The strange smell was no longer there. It had gone with Mrs. Purcey, and he made a mental note to check into it later. It could mean something . . . or nothing. It could be as meaningless as the smears of fingerprint powder on the old wood. Hundreds of sweaty hands had rested there; he could expect nothing from that.

He glanced into the priest's cubicle, but nothing remained to remind him of Father McKay. Archer grunted, and went back to Father Brett, and together they walked into the vestry.

The door was opened for them by a thin, grey-haired woman who smiled mechanically at Father Brett and stared at Archer. She had a time-washed but somehow ageless face, the face of a spectator who has never taken part. Her mouth was thin and close-lipped, the eyes set in a network of wrinkles. The eyes themselves had a curiously vacant look, as though Mrs. Randolph had drawn a dull grey curtain over her thoughts. She was at once efficient, uninteresting and unfathomable.

She closed the door behind them and said, in her whispering, anonymous voice, "Will there be anything you'd like, Father Brett?"

"Yes," he said. "See if you can find us a cup of tea, will you, Mrs. Randolph?"

"I will," she said, and went away.

"A curious woman," Archer said as they walked up the stairs toward the priest's study.

"Why so?" asked Father Brett, smiling. "Why more curious than others?"

Archer shrugged. "I don't know. Her eyes, perhaps. They don't tell you anything."

"Perhaps there's nothing to tell. She leads a secluded life here. She seldom goes out, she has no friends . . . and for that matter, no enemies."

"Strange," Archer said, "to be so easily satisfied with life."

"Better, perhaps, than to find no satisfaction at all."

Father Brett led the way into his study. It was a small, square room, very much like a cell. Books lined one wall. A desk faced the door, and there was a faded leather armchair behind it, and a straight kitchen chair. Father Brett chose the latter.

"Well, Michael?"

Archer spread his hands. "I know how he died, I know when—within half an hour, anyway. But I don't know why. The murder weapon is no help to us. It could have been a hat-pin, wielded by a respectable lady parishioner with a twisted mind. Or an ice-pick, used by a kill-crazy punk, or a homicidal maniac with a knitting needle. The *how* doesn't really matter, except that it was silent. The *why* does, and it's beyond me."

Father Brett's eyes contracted with pain. "So you have nothing? No clue at all?"

"Nothing but the angle of motive."

"No one could have a motive to do a thing like that, Michael."

"No?" Archer took his pipe and loaded it. He sat quietly, holding the pipe with both hands, staring at Father Brett. "How can you be so certain?"

"I was only praying out loud. I'm not certain at all."

"That," said Archer with a thin smile, "is more like it. Unless we decide on the homicidal maniac, we have to assume that there was a good reason . . . something he knew, something someone thought he might tell."

"Everyone knows he would tell nothing he heard in that box."

"You're wrong," Archer said. "You were proved wrong last night. Someone killed him."

Archer leaned back. "It's just possible, you know, that not everyone believes all you tell them from the pulpit."

Father Brett touched his old cheek with an unsteady finger. "Do you hate us all that badly, my son?"

"I don't hate anyone," Archer said tightly. "I just don't buy everything you and people like you try to sell me. Some things I just can't take."

"There are so many things you can't take."

"Perhaps because I've had to take too much." Archer threw his pipe on the desk with a clatter. "My wife would be alive today but for Father McKay and his meddling. You know that. He knew it too. If he hadn't touched her, if he'd left her alone and waited for a doctor. I wouldn't be . . ." He let the words trail off.

Father Brett nodded.

"You've put your finger on it, haven't you? *You* wouldn't be . . . You wouldn't be what? You wouldn't be alone today, isn't that it? Isn't that your real trouble, Michael? You found a tragedy and you've taken nothing from it but bitterness and hatred."

"I didn't come here for a sermon on psychology."

"And I don't preach them." Father Brett's eyes were gleaming and almost hard. "I preach that man has a dignity of his own, that he has an obligation to uphold that dignity. I preach that he owes not only to God, but to other men and to himself. What have you given to anyone for two years? The sharp edge of your tongue?"

"No one's ever given me anything."

"Because you've never asked for it. Why? Isn't it because you're afraid that someone will find out that you're actually a fraud? That you don't really want anything but the sour loneliness you have now?

"You blame Father McKay because he did what anyone would have done. He saw a woman lying in the street and he went to help her. How could he know that her neck was broken, that the slightest movement would kill her? What would you have done if you had been there yourself?"

The old priest put his trembling hand on the desk. His voice had become almost a whisper. "Or is it that you think you have deceived everyone, Michael? That we all believe you walk alone because of a lost love . . . and not remorse?"

Archer got slowly to his feet. He picked up his pipe and the stem snapped between his fingers. He let the two pieces fall on the carpet.

Then he walked out of the room without a word and blundered down the short staircase and along the passage toward the front door. His face was an unseeing mask.

He almost ran down the housekeeper, who was waiting for him in the vestibule.

"Mr. Archer," she whispered, "a word with you."

Archer stopped. He was breathing thinly and he saw the woman as if through a curtain of smoke. He blinked, clearing his vision. "What do you want?" he demanded.

"Just a word." She glanced over her shoulder, but the rectory lay wrapped in silence, broken only by the distant racket of children playing in Vincent Street.

"It's about poor Father McKay," she said then.

Archer frowned. "What about him?"

She moved closer. Her thin mouth was quivering with what

might have been eagerness, but her voice still ran across a flat vista of sound, neither rising nor falling.

"About his death."

Archer closed the inner door, shutting them both into the small vestibule.

"I'm listening."

"He had a visitor the other night."

"Where?"

Her mouth tightened even more, the lips almost disappearing.

"It was in the church. On a Thursday night. She came in by the side door just as Father was passing down the centre aisle. But he was expecting her. I know he was."

"A woman?" Archer said.

"Oh, yes." Mrs. Randolph snuffled. He could smell the odor of an unwashed body, thinly disguised with cheap toilet water. There was another smell, too, but it eluded him. He tried to back away.

"Oh, yes," she said again. "It was a woman. A young woman, too, but I could not see her face."

Archer lit a cigarette, partly to kill the nearness of the woman.

"Well, what's so unusual about that?"

"She was no member of this parish, that I'll have you know."

"You just said you couldn't see her face."

"I know them all, each and every one. I know them, the fancy ones with their fine coats and their whispering in the church and their poor mouths when anything's asked of them."

She stopped, as if short of breath. A little color had seeped into her grey face, giving her skin a mottled look. She was breathing rapidly.

"Go on," Archer invited. "Tell me more. She wasn't anyone you knew."

"Not that one. They don't dress like that, not even the best of them at St. Mark's. She gave him something, and they whispered for a long time."

"Would you expect them to shout in church?"

"Don't waste your sarcasm on me," Mrs. Randolph said shortly. "I'm only doing my duty as I see it."

"All right," Archer said wearily. "Go on doing it. What kind of a package was it?"

"Thin and flat and wrapped in dark paper with string around it."

"You saw all this, yet you couldn't see the woman clearly?" Archer said.

Mrs. Randolph smiled. The flesh around her mouth creased and her false teeth peeped out. "I found the wrapping paper in Father's waste-basket the next day. And the string." She wrinkled her nose. "It smelled of perfume. A hussy's smell, it was."

"And expensive," Archer said.

"Bought with the devil's money, you can rest assured."

"And you did what with the paper?"

A small sound that might have been a chuckle escaped her. "It's in my dresser now, Mr. Archer."

"Just in case I wanted to see it."

"Just in case . . ." she said. "You never know, do you?"

She came closer, until she was almost touching him, and her eyes looked into his.

"It might be a case of retribution, mightn't it, Mr. Archer. The hand of God, reaching out for the unworthy. Have you thought about that, Mr. Archer?"

"I've thought about a lot of things," Archer said. "That one had escaped me."

"About Father McKay, now. What do we know about him? Really? They say he was a chaplain in the army, but what do we know?"

"I know one thing," Archer said.

"And what's that?"

"You're a malignant old woman. Now find that paper for me."

She gave him a long, blank stare out of her filmed eyes. If she had heard his remark, she gave no notice of it. Instead, she nodded and led the way up the stairs and along the hallway, past Father Brett's study and up another flight to the top floor.

"Wait here," she said, and disappeared into her room.

When she re-appeared, she had a fold of paper in her hand.

"Here it is. And get the smell of it, will you?"

"I'll smell it later," Archer said. He took it from her and folded it into his pocket.

"Now," he said, "we'll talk about this a bit more. What time on Thursday night did this happen?"

"At nine o'clock. It was just before the first Friday, you know, and confessions were over. They stood beside the box jabbering away for at least five minutes. And then she left."

"I thought the church was locked every night at nine."

"Not that night it wasn't. He kept it open just for her." Spite shone in her eyes. "There are privileges for some, and insults for others."

"Can you describe her at all?"

Mrs. Randolph lowered her eyes. "Not so it would help. She was medium height, with a fine coat and one of them Russian things around her head."

"Did you see Father McKay again that night?"

"Only for a moment on his way up." She raised her head. "But he seemed upset."

"How?"

"What do you mean, how?"

"In what way was he upset?"

"He dropped his pipe on the stairs and when I went to pick it up he snapped at me."

"Where was the package then?"

"Under his arm, it was. He tried to hide it from me."

"How did he do that?"

"He turned away so I wouldn't see it. I know he did that deliberately."

Archer turned his hat over in his hands and looked at the lining. There was a foul taste in his mouth, and he wanted nothing more but to get beyond the range of this creature.

"One thing more," he said. "Did Father McKay object to you entering his room?"

"Why should he object? The Lord knows I worked hard enough keeping it clean. He was an untidy man."

"All right," Archer said. "Thanks for telling me."

He turned away from her and paused. "Have you cleaned up there since he . . . died?" he asked.

33

"I wouldn't go in there," she said vehemently, and he believed her.

"Then don't change your mind about it until I tell you."

He walked down the stairs, conscious of her gaze on his back. When he turned his head she was leaning over the balustrade, staring after him, but at that range her eyes had lost any power to tell him anything, if they ever had possessed a knowledge that wasn't a blend of maliciousness and lies.

On the front stoop he paused, drawing in the fresh air, or what passed for it on Vincent Street. He thought for a moment that he should have told Father Brett of this latest development; but he didn't want to see the old priest just then. His mind had closed on the words spoken in that small, book-lined room, like raw flesh closing around an open wound.

He started down the walk and saw Helen McKay coming across the street toward him.

Two people watched Archer go, and two people saw him meet Helen McKay.

In his study window, Father Brett stood looking out on the street. His thoughts had turned from the dead to the living and he was glad, in a way, that Archer had used the words that still seemed to stain the small room in which he stood. It was the first time in two years that the man had spoken his mind.

It was perhaps the first link in a chain that could, in time, draw Michael Archer back into a world where human beings met their problems and lived with them. But his was the tortuous path of escape, and he must run his course along it before he started to learn that there was never any escape. Nothing was ever free. In one way or another, at one time or another, everything must be paid for, every bill met.

In her own room, Mrs. Randolph was at her favorite post, behind one wing of a curtain. Only her face showed, an expressionless moon hung in space, but her eyes were busy. She noted the clothes that Helen McKay wore, and was satisfied that they were no better than her own.

She sought out the young body beneath them, the vigorous stride of the girl's walk, the slim ankles, the proud head, and her satisfaction died. Somewhere deep inside her a devil whispered words that made her squirm. But the sight of Archer gave her some relief, and the thought of her conversation with him took her to her rocking chair, placed so that she could see the tops of the dingy buildings and, perhaps, what went on inside the rooms.

She sank into the chair, folding her hands in her lap, and began to rock. As the chair moved, so did her lips, and she began to croon an old hymn.

Archer stopped the girl as she was crossing the sidewalk.

"Can you spare me a little time, Miss McKay?"

She hesitated, and then she shrugged. "If you wish."

They walked in silence for two blocks, gradually shedding the district and with it, the air of impoverished living, the dirty gutters, the rundown shops. At a cafeteria not far from the precinct station, he said, "Let's have some coffee and talk this over. I promise not to bite."

She smiled at him doubtfully. "You do have pretty sharp teeth, you know."

"And a poisonous disposition. I know. I'll curb it."

They found a table in a deserted corner, and without preamble, Archer repeated to her the story told him by Mrs. Randolph.

The girl shook her head. "You make it sound so . . . sordid."

"Correction," Archer said. "I'm repeating, not inventing."

"But you believe it?"

"Let's say I believe the general outline. She'd have no reason to make it up. The details you can take or leave."

"I'll leave them, thanks. I knew my brother pretty well, Mr. Archer. It isn't that he just wasn't that kind of a priest. He wasn't that kind of a man, either."

Archer frowned. "Just what kind of a man was he, Miss Mc-Kay? I've often wondered."

"I don't think you have, Mr. Archer. I don't think you've wondered about that at all. I think you may have been puzzled by your own reaction to what happened, but my brother was always the same."

Archer lit a cigarette. He said, with great care, "Let's get one thing straight. My personal problems have nothing to do with this. Whether I liked your brother or not means nothing now."

"Do you expect me to believe that?"

He had a reply to that, quick and cutting, but it died in his throat. She was looking at him with an expression of great concern in her eyes, as if his answer meant a great deal to her, and for once, his sarcasm failed him.

"I hope you will believe it. I'm a policeman, Miss McKay. I'm not paid to have personal emotions or feelings of any sort. And even if I did have anything against him, I guess it's wiped out now. I don't know any more just how I do feel. It seemed so important to hate him and all his kind."

He pressed his fingers against his temples. "Now I'm not so certain. But I am certain of one thing. If everyone involved in this case treats me like some kind of a curiosity, I'll never get anywhere. Can you see that?"

She bit her lower lip. "I . . . yes, I can see that."

"Good. Now let's get down to business. First, I don't think that Father McKay was murdered because he was a priest. I think he was murdered because as a priest he had learned something. Whoever killed him believed that he would not keep his secret."

"You mean someone who went to him in the confessional?"

He shook his head. "I don't think so. Anyone doing that would rely on the seal of confession or he wouldn't go there in the first place. No, this is something he learned outside the confessional, something he could reveal if he wished. But for some reason, he didn't—or didn't get the chance to."

Helen McKay drank some of her coffee and made a bitter mouth. In the soft light, the contours of her face had softened, and Archer studied her with a new interest. Her chin was buried in the upturned collar of her coat, and she wore a cheap beret at an angle that seemed almost jaunty. She looked up and caught his eyes and smiled wearily.

"You're suggesting that he was involved in some intrigue, aren't you? The mysterious woman, the whispered conversations, the unknown package. It sounds so cheap."

"And so plausible?"

"Am I supposed to take offense at that? Why should I? My brother was never anything but what he wanted to be, Mr. Archer. He had no . . . past, if that's what you'd call it. He had no reason to want anything else. He was a happy man, and happy men don't need secrets or motives or double lives. They don't need pasts. They have the present."

"Leaving the past to others, perhaps?"

She spread her hands and examined them closely. Then she straightened up in her chair.

"All right, Mr. Archer, let's have it out. Once and for all. For two years you've blamed him for what happened to your wife. Can't you understand that it was an accident? How many people have to tell you that before you'll believe it? What he did was a natural thing. . . ."

"And it killed her," Archer said in a low growl. "It was that natural."

The girl picked up her gloves.

"You're hopeless. You can't see anything because you won't look. What are you afraid of, Mr. Archer? That someone will finally work their way through that hard crust and discover just what kind of a man hides behind it? You're nothing but a cheap edition of a human being, living in a tawdry little world of your own. Oh, you're tragic, all right, but not because you've lost your wife. You're tragic because you haven't got the courage to live without her."

She stood up. Her voice was shaking.

"And now let's take a look at the evidence you talk about so much. Just who did hate my brother enough to kill him, Mr. Archer? Who had the biggest motive of all, the motive of a man soaked in hate and self-despair? Who has the least reason to mourn him?"

She turned away from him and walked unsteadily toward the door, leaving Archer slack in his chair. People at other tables turned to watch her go, and then stared pointedly at Archer.

For quite some time he sat there, unmoving, while the girl's words burned their track across his mind. The enormity of her suggestion shocked him as nothing had since his wife's death. He felt a small hard core of physical sickness in the pit of his stomach. This, then, was the way people thought of him. The picture of the lonely man carrying his burden crumpled in front of him. For an awful moment he looked into his own heart. What he saw there turned him cold.

He reached for the check on the table and stared at it unseeingly. His hand brushed against the folded mauve paper Mrs. Randolph had slipped into his hand. Something seemed to have snapped in his head, releasing a flood of emotion that bewildered him. He stared at the paper, frowning, trying to concentrate his vision on it. Pale mauve in color, it was shot through with fine threads of gold, and woven into its texture was the name of a nationally famous jeweller, visible only at a certain angle and in a certain light.

He put money on the table, gathered up the paper and string, and walked out into the street. It was raining again. He stood there, hatless, letting the coolness soak into his skin. Then he got into his car and drove downtown.

The jeweller touched the paper with a refined finger, smiled, and nodded his head.

"Indeed, sir, there can be no mistake. This is certainly ours."

"And you wrap everything in this?"

The jeweller gave Archer a pitying look that included the cut of his suit and the knot in his tie.

"Of course not, Mr. Archer. This is, I may say, a most expensive paper. Only our very best objects are wrapped in this. It is presentation paper."

"Then there's some hope of tracing it?"

The jeweller spread his hands. "How can I say? It is comparatively new, this paper. Within the last six months. Not much has been used, but we have many of the elite on our books. I don't see how that would help you."

"But you could look them up?"

The jeweller sighed, a man over-taxed.

"If it is necessary, I could do so."

"It is necessary," said Archer.

An hour later, he walked out of the store with a list of seven names. His headache, which had been growing ever since his discussion with Helen McKay, had gone. He almost smiled as he drove toward the precinct station.

The sergeant noticed this as Archer walked in, and was puzzled. Archer was not a man known for his sunny disposition.

But he made no comment. He merely said, "Good evening, Lieutenant. Any luck?"

Archer shook his head and went into his office and sat down. He put the list on the desk before him and stared at it. Seven names of people who could, if they felt like exerting the effort of raising one hand, make life very difficult for an obscure detective lieutenant. Yet somewhere on this list, if his reasoning was sound, lay a connection between the city's most prominent socialites, and a priest working in a rundown parish on the fringe of the slums.

Archer put a cigarette in his mouth and waggled it. His parcel was not more than four inches long, not less than three inches wide. But it was fairly thick. A jewel box? But what reason would any woman have for handing a jewel box to Father McKay? The police had been through his room at the rectory and there was nothing of value to anyone there, except to the dead man.

Archer lit the cigarette. He watched the smoke curling upward. It made no sense at all, unless . . . He leaned back, the cigarette hanging forgotten. Conscience money. Atoning payment for some guilt, gift-wrapped.

He reached an arm for the phone and called the rectory, but Father Brett was out. Mrs. Randolph answered in a tone of voice that asked prying questions, but Archer hung up before she had a chance to put them into words. He glanced at the clock on the wall. It was just after seven.

He pushed a button on his desk and the sergeant materialized.

"Yes, Lieutenant?"

"Who was working the Vincent Street district on Thursday night?"

The sergeant pondered.

"O'Shea, for the last two weeks."

"Can you find out where he'd be between quarter to nine and nine-fifteen on Thursday?"

"Without even asking him, I can, sir."

Archer looked up. "How's that?"

The sergeant smiled. "I used to have that shift myself. And at nine o'clock I always had a moment or two to drop into Skelly's for a cup of coffee and a little chat. That's directly across from St. Mark's."

"And O'Shea does the same?"

"If he's in a uniform, Lieutenant, he's no different from the rest of us."

"Where's he now?"

The sergeant glanced at the clock.

"He checked in at six-thirty. He's due in from Vincent in ten minutes, perhaps less."

"Fine," said Archer. "I'll pick him up."

It was a two-minute drive to the corner of Vincent Street. At eight minutes past seven he was parked just beyond the intersection, waiting, and at ten minutes past he saw the wet gleam of a policeman's rain cape moving toward him through the drizzling darkness. He got out of his car.

O'Shea came up and touched his cap. "A filthy night, Lieutenant," he said.

"Get into the car," Archer said. "And rest your feet."

O'Shea climbed in and looked at him expectantly. Archer offered him a cigarette.

"Now," he said, "let's see if that stimulates your brain cells. You've already turned in a report on what you saw Saturday night, which was precisely nothing. Go over that again for me. I want to know about everything that moved from the time you arrived here Saturday evening."

"At five to nine, sir."

"Until you left."

"At exactly ten past, Lieutenant."

"That's fifteen minutes."

O'Shea looked embarrassed. "Well, sir, it was a wet night. . . ."

"And you stopped for coffee."

The officer cleared his throat and said nothing.

"Go on," Archer growled, "I know how it is."

O'Shea opened his mouth and shut it again. He tried not to stare at Archer, but every muscle in his face wanted to.

"Well, thank you, Lieutenant." He stepped nimbly on the thin ice and got into thicker detail. "I'll swear to it that no one came out of St. Mark's from the time I arrived until after I left. And they couldn't come out after nine, because the doors are locked then. I know. I've tried to get in myself, when I was late. In this district, they have to be careful."

"Never mind that," Archer said. "I just want to be certain . . . as certain as you say you are."

"No one," O'Shea said positively, "came out. Or went in, for that matter. It was a foul night. I would have seen anyone walking around in that weather."

"Okay," Archer said. "We'll go back to Thursday. You were here when?"

"About the same time, Lieutenant."

"Did you see anything unusual?"

O'Shea paused. "Well, nothing happened, Lieutenant, if you mean was there any trouble. But there was one thing. I had to speak to the driver about it."

"What driver?"

"The chauffeur in the big car. He'd parked it right where we are now, and there's a fire hydrant two feet away, although you probably didn't see it."

"What make of car?"

"Some foreign job, sir. About two blocks long and not in my class."

"You didn't by any chance take a note of the license number?"

O'Shea wrinkled his brow. "I'm afraid not, Lieutenant. You see, he hadn't really done anything wrong. All I saw was the initials on the door."

Archer blew out his breath.

"Tell me, O'Shea, can you remember what they were?"

"Sure," said O'Shea. "A C. and an M. interwoven sort of."

"And you didn't bother putting any of this in your report?"

"I was asked about Saturday, sir, not Thursday."

Archer nodded. He looked at O'Shea and his smile was not fatherly.

"Go back to your beat, O'Shea. Walk it slow. You'll probably spend most of your life on it."

When O'Shea had gone off into the rain, Archer took out his list of seven names. Only one of them corresponded with the initials on the door of the car that had parked outside St. Mark's on Thursday night. It was Cecellia Marlowe.

Archer got out of the car and walked up the path to the rectory door.

Mrs. Randolph opened it. She stood framed against the yellow light, squinting into the darkness, clutching a small black book in her hand.

When she recognized Archer she stepped back, contriving at the same time to look over her shoulder.

"It's you," she said in her hushed voice. "Come in. But if you're wanting Father Brett, he's over at the bishop's palace. It's about the re-consecrating. He'll be late."

Archer stepped inside out of the rain. "You'll do," he said. "Where can we talk?"

Her face lit up. "You've found the hussy, then? Come up to my room. No one can bother us there."

"I thought you said Father Brett was out."

"He is," she said shyly, "but there are others, you know. It's best to be cautious, I always say."

"So let's be cautious," Archer growled, and followed her up the stairs to the room under the eaves. It was a long, narrow room, and as bare as an old man's future. A bed was half-hidden behind a curtain that closed off an alcove. There was a table, the rocking chair that faced the window, a chest of drawers and a closet door, half-ajar.

"Take the chair," she invited. "I'll stand."

He shook his head and walked over to the window. But there was nothing to see except the cheerless night. He turned and looked at her.

"About this woman you saw," he prompted.

She licked her thin lips. "I'll tell you all about it, Mr. Archer. They think I'm a dull stick here, but I'm sharp, a lot sharper than they think. I use my eyes."

"I'll bet you do," Archer said. "Now's your chance to use your mouth, too."

She sank into the rocker and began moving back and forth, as if lulling herself. But there was nothing sleepy about her eyes.

They peered at him cunningly from the dead flat expanse of her face.

"It's a crying scandal," she said, grinning at him. "If it was only the one night I might overlook it. But it's been more than that. Oh, yes. He thought I didn't know, but I seen it all. Every Thursday night I went down and waited. But she only came once a month, and they always talked in a corner, so I couldn't hear."

"But not for want of listening."

"What are you trying to say? It was my duty."

Archer nodded. "Go on."

"I know your kind. You, that's known for the way you hate them all. You still don't want to believe, do you? You think I'm making it all up, about him and that hussy?"

"No," Archer said softly, "I don't think you're making it up."

Somewhere in the house a phone rang, and Mrs. Randolph gave an exclamation of impatience. She got to her feet, threw him a sharp glance, and trotted over to the door.

"Don't go away," she said. "I'll be back in a minute."

"I'll be here," Archer said, and waited until her footsteps had receded down the stairs.

Then he walked over to the chest of drawers and went through them with practiced fingers, disturbing nothing but examining everything. It was a pitiful array, with only one exception. Buried under some old sweaters in the bottom drawer was a neat stack of the best silk stockings money could buy. The price tags were still on them. He straightened up, the feel of the silk still soft and seductive on his fingers.

He had found this woman's one secret vanity, and he felt slightly ashamed. He closed the drawer and wandered around the room, finally opening the closet door and looking inside. Rows of plastic bags were suspended from hangers, plastic that crinkled when he touched it. He could see a coat, two or three dresses, the usual odds and ends. But his nose wrinkled and he felt the desire to sneeze. Then he recognized the smell and grinned ruefully. Mothballs. The tattered treasures of the years, packed in plastic and guarded against rot and corruption.

Archer walked back to the window and stood looking out.

There was nothing for him here but the scurrying sound of this woman's voice, an eager terrier yapping at his heels and begging for scraps of information he didn't have himself. He felt weary and disgusted, not only with Mrs. Randolph and her evil prying habits, but with himself.

He walked to the door. In the distance, he could hear a phone conversation dragging on. He descended the stairs to the next floor and sauntered along the corridor until he came to the room that had been Father McKay's.

He put out his hand and touched the knob. There was a stillness in the rectory now, a waiting silence. He opened the door and stepped into a musty darkness.

Even without light, he knew this room as well as he knew his own home. The desk, set against the solitary window; the shelves of books, the bed. He turned on the light and closed the door behind him.

He walked over to the desk and stood looking at it. At this piece of furniture had sat a man who had plunged him into his own peculiar sort of hell, but for the first time in many aching months he could not stir to active life his old, passionate hatred. It lay dead, buried under the weight of time, dissolved by the thing that had happened to Father McKay. For the first time he wondered how the priest had felt, and suddenly, it seemed important that he should know. He sat down at the desk and began pulling out drawers.

In the second one, he found the diary.

He picked it up and laid it on the desk, spreading it open. It had been kept until the day of Father McKay's death. There was even a note on the Saturday morning. But Friday was missing, torn bodily from the book, as was Thursday before it—the Thursday on which Father McKay had gone down into the church to meet Cecellia Marlowe.

There was another significant gap. From April 4, two years before, until two months later, no entries had been made. The pages stared blankly at him. For two months after his wife had died in the priest's arms, Father McKay had written nothing. He had made no appointments.

Archer closed his eyes and tried to picture how it must have been for Father McKay, but he could no longer put himself in the place of others. He had spent too much time thinking only of his own sorrow.

He turned back to the previous Friday and sat staring at the book. What had happened on that Friday, only twenty-four hours before the murder, that made it so important no one should see those entries? What had Father McKay written in his book on that day? And who could even know that he had written it?

Archer slipped the book into his pocket and sat there, thinking about it. Distantly he heard a door close, and remembered that he had told Mrs. Randolph he would wait for her. But she was only a waste of time. Everything she would have to say had already been uttered or was implicit in the twist of her mean mouth or the sideways glance from her secretive eyes. She was a type he knew only too well.

He became aware that footsteps were slowly climbing the stairs. In a moment the door opened and Father Brett looked into the room.

"Back again?" he said pleasantly. "What a lot of time you're spending with us these days, Michael. Have you found what you're looking for?"

"I don't quite know how you mean that."

"You have a mind that sees two sides to every question, I take it."

"And to most answers. No, I haven't found what I'm looking for." He lit a cigarette, and leaned forward, his arms on the desk. "But perhaps you can help me. Do you know a woman named Cecellia Marlowe. She has been coming here for quite a long while."

"Why?"

Father Brett frowned.

"I don't think I can answer that for you."

"Then answer this, if you can. Was she paying some sort of conscience money to Father McKay?"

"You put that rather crudely, Michael. I wouldn't call it conscience money. But then, I wouldn't discuss it at all."

"Even if it had a direct bearing on Father McKay's murder?"

"What are you saying?" Father Brett sat down slowly. His eyes were curiously bright and there was anger around his mouth. "Are you accusing a fine girl . . ."

"I'm not accusing anyone."

"I don't think it has any bearing on this terrible business. None at all."

"We differ," Archer said dryly, and added, "as usual. Unfortunately, I do. Did you know that she had seen Father McKay on Thursday night?"

"I knew," the old priest said. "He told me about it on Friday."

"She gave him money, didn't she?"

Father Brett sighed. "You seem to have an accurate source of information. Yes, she gave him money. Quite a good deal of money."

"And she came on the third Thursday of every month, didn't she?"

"Yes. She came."

Archer crushed out his cigarette, holding his thumb on it until the heat seared his skin.

"But this time you didn't get it, did you? The money was gone the next day?"

The priest nodded slowly. There was the dawning of a new pain in his tired old eyes.

"Yes," he said, "this time it was gone."

"How much was it?"

"Quite a good deal, Michael. Two thousand dollars."

"And it just vanished?"

Father Brett looked down at his hands. "No. It was stolen."

"Why did she bring it here?"

"This time? For an orphanage she thought needed help. Last month, it was for another good cause."

"And it was delivered?"

Father Brett looked up. "Would you like to see the receipt, Michael?"

"I didn't mean it that way. What I was getting at was this: the money was brought here on a fairly regular schedule, but it varied in amount. From what you tell me, she must have had a pretty delicate conscience. She was paying off pretty high."

"I said it wasn't conscience money, Michael. It was just some-

46

thing she felt she had to do, and she did not wish to appear in it publicly. For one thing, she is not a Catholic and her husband might disapprove. For another . . . well, it gave her more peace of mind to know that someone else was sharing in her good fortune."

Archer looked at Father Brett steadily.

"Thanks for telling me that. It gives me a lead. And I think you can see which way it's leading, can't you?"

Father Brett nodded unhappily. "I do," he said. "Someone knew he had the money, and stole it. Father McKay must have discovered this person's identity."

"Yes," Archer said. "He found out who it was. And instead of coming to the police, he decided to handle it his own way. Because of that, he was killed." He paused. "Did he tell you who it was, Father?"

The old priest looked at him. "No, my son, he did not."

"That," said Archer, getting to his feet, "is too bad. If he had, he would probably be alive today."

"Would you want him to be?"

Archer hesitated. The lines about his mouth were deeper, and his shoulders sagged.

"You all think me pretty low, don't you? Let me tell you this. Father McKay went into that box knowing that a desperate person went with him. Perhaps he felt that he could handle the situation. Perhaps this person had pretended repentance, and had offered to give the money back. I don't know, and I probably never will. But he went in there cold, offering one last chance, the chance to repent, to return, and to forget. He was willing to risk that much to offer help to another person. I can't hate a man like that, Father Brett. I can only be sorry he offered so much to the wrong person."

At the door he looked back at the old priest.

"On the night it happened, did you have that hearing aid connected?"

Father Brett looked up. His eyes were warm.

"You remember my old trick. No, not at the time it happened."

"Then if Mrs. Purcey had cried out—and I think it's more

than likely she did—you wouldn't have heard it. How about the other priests here?"

"No," said Father Brett. "Father Donaldson is on vacation. There would be no one else besides Mrs. Randolph."

"And she was in all night?"

"Oh, yes. She brought me some warm milk at seven o'clock, and she was in her room after that."

Archer nodded. He closed the door behind him, leaving Father Brett to his own thoughts, and walked downstairs.

The parlor door was open. Mrs. Randolph was sitting before the empty fireplace, reading her little black book. It was a copy of the New Testament.

She looked up as he passed by, but gave no sign of recognition. Her eyes were curiously blank and indrawn, as if all her attention had gone into the printed page before her.

Archer went out into the night. It was still raining. A chill wind blew from the north. Vincent Street was deserted, a glistening stretch washed almost clean.

Archer went down the walk toward his car.

At eleven o'clock that night Archer keyed open his apartment door and walked into the cheerless living room. He hung up his hat and coat and walked around aimlessly, touching this object and that, until he arrived finally at the picture on the mantel-piece.

He picked it up and turned the beloved face toward him. Then he propped the photograph where he could see it from the armchair beside the fireplace, and sank down, sighing with weariness.

There was only one small light on, casting a dim glow. He put his empty pipe between his teeth and stretched out his legs, relaxing his muscles. But nothing could relax his mind.

Somewhere in the apartment a clock chimed the hour, but he heard it with only half an ear. The face on the mantelpiece watched him, the eyes wide and honest, the mouth soft and inviting. There had been a time when those eyes held reproach, if only in his imagination, but he realized tonight that they had never held anything but love captured by a camera.

The reproach had been in his own mind. Only he, and perhaps Father McKay had known why Alma had gone to the church on the night she was killed. Now the secret was his own, and for the first time in two years, he looked it in the face without trying to hide his own. There had been nothing left between them, only the withered husk of an emotion that had died from neglect. She had walked out, saying she would never come back, and she had been right.

She never had the chance. And it was the thought of her running from him, into the path of a speeding car, that had brought the grinding remorse to him. She had run to her death, and she had died, not because of Father McKay, but because of him. Archer covered his eyes with his hand. A coldness was creeping over him, drying out his blood. He moved uneasily, hunching his shoulders, and it was not until he heard the creak of the kitchen door that he knew where the coldness came from.

He started forward in his chair. He heard the explosion, deafening in the small room, and felt the bullet kiss his cheek in passing. The picture on the mantelpiece dissolved in a shower of glass and noise. He went down on his knees, cursing with fear, as the gun exploded again and again, tearing the room to shreds. From the corner of his eyes he saw the muzzle flame blooming in the kitchen doorway behind him. Then he was flung forward, almost into the fireplace, and all the sound of death exploded in his ear, and was finally silent.

On Monday night at eight o'clock Father Brett opened the vestry door and entered the church. He was wearing his white surplice and he walked with his head down, but his step was slower than it ever had been and his face was haggard.

He paused at the centre aisle and made a painful genuflection, remaining on one knee for almost a minute. The church, following the re-consecration ceremony, was almost empty, but there was still work for him to do.

He approached the confessional where Father McKay had died and hesitated. There were other confessionals in the church, one with his own name above it, but for some reason he felt drawn to this box. He opened the door and the light above it glowed on, indicating that he was waiting—although tonight, he wondered just what there was to wait for.

Father Brett sat down and tried to pray, but his mind was numb with what he had discovered. Outside in the church, footsteps were approaching the box, a reluctant shuffle that hesitated and then resumed their pace. The door on his left creaked open. Father Brett inclined his head and then waited.

The voice declared itself, and Father Brett drew in a shuddering breath. This was not the one. He forced himself to listen impartially, but it was with relief that he heard the door open and close. The footsteps walked away, a little more springily, he hoped, on perhaps a straighter path . . . even if only for tonight.

The clock rang eight-thirty, as from a great distance. He moved stiffly, and was about to turn on his light so that he could read his office, when other footsteps approached again.

The sound ceased. There was a long pause. He heard the main door of the church creak shut, and knew, without glancing out, that he was alone with his last penitent. A hand touched the door of the box on his left. He settled the hearing aid more comfortably in place, and bent his head, his hand half-raised to support his cheek.

He waited.

The door opened. Clothes rustled and a peculiar smell came to him through the small grating. He closed his eyes as the door clicked shut. The kneeling bench creaked.

Father Brett opened his eyes, and they were sick with the misery of knowledge.

The voice whispered in his ear, without personality or even true reality. It was like a disembodied spirit of evil, floating in a black pit.

"Bless me, Father," it said, "for I have sinned . . . I must have your blessing."

There was a pause.

"You know who I am, Father?"

"I know," the priest said heavily.

"You know what I have done?"

"Yes."

"I didn't mean to do it. You must forgive me."

"It is not for me to forgive you," Father Brett said. "I have nothing to do with forgiving or condemning. That is for God."

"But you are His minister."

"I am. But what you have done is not for me to forgive."

"God will forgive me," the voice whispered. "I know that."

"Then why do you come to me?"

"I wanted to talk to you." It seemed to him that part of the voice was missing, that part of it had gone with the mind that once controlled.

"Then talk," he said, "if it will help you. But there is only one ending to all this."

"One ending?" The voice whispered. "You mean the police. I can never go to them. They wouldn't understand."

"Nevertheless, to them you must go. Otherwise, I cannot give you absolution."

"That's what *he* said," the voice whispered. "I must give it back. All that money. Do you know how much that money meant to me? All to myself, everything I ever wanted, an escape, fine clothes, beautiful things. Can you understand that, Father?"

"I have understood it all my life. I have never been able to understand stealing it."

"Because you've never really needed it," the voice lashed out. "Because you've never wanted for anything. You and your kind, well-fed, waited on hand and foot, you with people to bow and scrape. What do you know about it? You've never gone without food or watched other women laughing or died inside because no man would look at you."

The voice choked off, smothered by its own impassioned breathing.

There ensued a silence.

Father Brett wet his lips, for his mouth had become very dry.

"Do you want to tell me anything else?"

"I want you to promise that you won't tell anyone. You can't. You can't tell what you hear in this place."

"No," said Father Brett. "I can't tell what I am told in this box. But I knew about you before I came here, and you are a danger to yourself and to others. I promise you nothing."

The silence had weight and shape. Father Brett could feel the painful thump of his heart, and he was suddenly and terribly afraid that it would stop at any moment.

He had faced death before, as any man faces it who lives long enough, but he had never thought that it would come like this, in a tiny box hot with his own fear and the passion that hung almost unleashed on the other side of that fragile grille.

He opened his mouth to pray, not only for the deranged mind so close to him, but for his own courage. But the prayer was never uttered. His head was thrust sideways by a terrible blow. He tried to cry out, but all power of speech was lost in the agony that seemed to split his very head open. He fell sideways in the box, gasping for one last breath. And in those few remaining seconds of awareness he saw the shadow of a woman dart across the grille directly in front of him.

For one second her face peered in at him, the eyes wide, the mouth curved in a grimace that might have been a smile. He tried to unlatch the door of his cubicle, but his entire head was one great wall of pain and sound that tottered his very reason.

And then the pain and the sound stopped and he fell forward against the door.

In the stillness of the church, the owner of the voice moved on hushed feet along a side aisle. The emptiness of this place reached out to her, but it found no answering peace in her heart. She was shaking with her hatred and with an exultation that exceeded anything she had ever known. She paused, and replaced the long hat-pin under the lapel of her coat.

Then her head jerked up, listening.

The main door of the church had opened and a man stood there, hatless, his eyes fixed on the shadow that surrounded her. He was a tall, gaunt man with a face like death, and his trench-coat hung cloak-like over his shoulders.

The woman whimpered in fear. She pulled the bandanna tighter around her head, and looked around the church for one avenue of escape. But there was none. The vestry door was too far. The side doors were locked. She turned and ran on silent feet toward the stairway that led to the choir loft, and Archer, his eyes blurred by the pain of a broken collar-bone, watched her go without moving.

He listened, his head cocked to one side, and at last the scurrying sound stopped. Then he walked slowly down the centre aisle, holding onto the backs of the pews, and behind him a uniformed policeman stepped into the doorway, filling it with his bulk. Archer limped on until he came to the alcove, and what he saw there sent his teeth savagely into his lower lip. The warm blood ran down his chin as he opened the door and caught Father Brett in his arms.

The old man groaned. One side of his face was covered with bright blood, and the hearing aid was a ruptured ruin, hanging by its black cord. But the old heart beat faintly under Archer's hand, and he whispered, "Thank God."

He straightened up painfully. With every movement he could feel the broken collar-bone scraping together, and the pain of it made him dizzy. The strapping put on by the doctor had come loose, but there was no time now to repair the damage. He beckoned to an officer and said in a low voice, "Get Dr. Angelous over here. But no ambulance. No publicity. Understand?"

"Yes, sir," the policeman whispered. "At once."

Archer looked up toward the choir loft. There was no movement there, and no sound, but for all he knew the hand that had gunned him down the night before, and left him for dead, might still be pointing the same weapon at him. He started down the side aisle, reeling on his feet. He had been conscious for only four hours, and it felt like four years. He reached the foot of the stairs and called out, in a cracked voice, "You might as well come down. There's no way out for you. If you don't, I'll come up and get you."

Silence. Somewhere a board creaked. Archer took a shallow breath and even that hurt. He thought about the gun she had stolen from his desk drawer the night before, and tried to remember how many shots had been fired. But his mind refused to function. There was only one thing to do. He started up the stairs.

At the first bend he stopped, listening. In the body of the church a man coughed once, sharply. A door opened below him and footsteps hurried down the aisle. But up here it was quiet and dark, a remote vastness of space, held by one defender.

Archer gathered his strength and climbed the next flight, and heard another board creak. He froze in the shadows, waiting.

Beyond him in the darkness there was a faint click, and the protest of wood. He took one last step and the organ loomed before him. The creaking started again, and was followed by a sigh, as if life had grown too much to bear.

His mouth was dry and when he called out, his voice was barely audible. But there was no answer, only the faint creaking.

He took out his flashlight and aimed it at the sound, his thumb on the button.

The light sprang out eagerly, eating into the darkness, carving its own way.

Archer made a small, sick sound in his throat.

The body of Mrs. Randolph swung from a beam, moving slowly in a diminishing circle. One shoe lay on the floor below her, and one of her fine silk stockings was wound around her neck.

At ten-thirty that night Archer stood up to go. His chest was a mass of pain, and he could hardly keep his eyes open.

But he managed a smile for Father Brett and Helen McKay, and said, "Don't bother seeing me off. I know the way."

"Do you think you know the way back in, Michael?"

Archer shook his head.

"There's no answer to that one for me yet. Perhaps there isn't even enough time to find an answer."

Father Brett smiled, despite the bandage on his ear and cheek. "I'll wait," he said, "just in case you do."

Archer looked at him for a moment, and smiled. "You never give up, do you?"

The old priest shook his head. "At my age, I really can't afford to. Good-bye, Michael, and thank you."

The girl got to her feet. "I'll see you out."

He nodded and they walked in silence down the corridor together. At the front door she put a hand on his arm.

"You will come back . . . to see us, I mean?"

He looked down at her.

"An undesirable type like me, Miss McKay? That's a strange question, coming from you."

"Perhaps I'm a strange person, Mr. Archer."

"Not as strange as some I've known lately."

"Perhaps not." She hesitated, and then met his eyes. "When did you first know about . . . her?"

"I haven't got an answer for that. When I woke up this afternoon with her bullet in me, I think. I remembered the smell then."

"The smell?"

"The mothballs. It was there in the confessional on Saturday night, but very faintly, and I didn't think anything about it. It was in her clothes closet, when I glanced in there yesterday. It was in my apartment last night, when she waited for me. You see, she had only the one coat and she never went out, or practically never. But if anyone saw her leaving the confessional, she had to be dressed for the street. So she wore a bandanna around her head and bundled herself up in the old coat. But she never left the church. I know, because a policeman told me so. It was her biggest mistake, but she couldn't know that he would be watching on that particular night."

He lit a cigarette and coughed.

"If only she'd left it at that, I probably would never have known. But she had to be clever. She had to tell me about the mysterious woman, and lead me right to her own front door." He smiled, almost sadly. "The funny thing is, she probably never would have spent all that money. She'd bought a dozen pairs of silk stockings with it, and hidden the rest, only God knows where. But there was really nothing against her, if she'd only kept her head."

"Nothing but what Father Brett would call the hand of God, perhaps?"

"I don't know about that," Archer said. "I don't know how she could kill a man to keep that kind of money. She had no use for it. Yet she killed your brother, and tried to kill me because she heard me talking to Father Brett and thought I had found her out. And she tried to kill an old man who wanted to help her."

55

Archer shook his head. "He knew about it even when he walked into that box. Yet he still went."

"He didn't really have much choice, Mr. Archer. But he did have one thing she lacked, and I think he wanted to give her that much."

"Such as what?"

The girl frowned. "Love, I think. Perhaps that's why she took the money. To have something of her own to love. She had nothing else."

Archer opened the door. Rain had flooded the gutters and hung in the night air like spun glass.

He shivered. Behind him the air was warm and soft with yellow light and the smell of home, and the presence of the girl beside him touched a longing he had thought dead. He touched her cheek lightly and smiled at her.

"A lot of us have nothing else."

"I know," she said gravely, but offered him no invitation. He understood then that if he wanted anything this woman had to offer him, he would have to come back in his own way and earn it.

He turned and plodded through the rain to the end of the path.

When he looked back, she was still standing there with one hand raised, as if in salute . . . or blessing.

He hunched his shoulders and walked off into the darkness.

THE
BODY
IN
THE
BASEMENT

BY ERNEST F. MILLER, C. SS. R.

I AM A PRIEST. BEFORE I BECAME A PRIEST I WAS A DOCTOR. IT WAS during my first years of practicing medicine that I met a girl, fell deeply in love with her and almost married her. It was strange that I never succeeded in learning much about her background: where she came from, who were her parents and so forth. All I knew was that she was decidedly in love with me as I was with her. I also knew that she was the loveliest girl whom I had ever met and that it would be next to impossible for me to live without her.

And then I found out that she was already married.

I must confess that this news was as great a shock to me as would have been the news of her death. For months I could not get back to work. She pleaded with me not to abandon her, to go off with her either with or without the blessing of a judge or a minister. She said that she would die if I left her.

The struggle I went through was of such violence that I cannot begin to describe it. We had a final scene, a terrible scene. My only resort was flight. But before I departed I made a promise that I would never forget her in my prayers before God, and I added a kind of prophecy that some day we would meet again and that when we did, I would be able to help her as I was unable to help her now.

I never saw her again. I heard of her on several occasions—she was out on the West Coast—she had married again and had left her faith completely. But I did not meet her or speak to her. And the years went on.

Now I am a priest. There has not been a morning when I said Mass during the past twenty-five years that I did not mention this girl's name, Mary, along with the names of my mother and father. During all those years my prayers seemed to go unanswered. But God has His ways. Only too well was I to learn that at the end.

For two decades I have been teaching philosophy in a Midwestern major seminary. During the week I give my lectures to my classes and over the weekend I drive out to a parish nearby or relatively far away to help a pastor who cannot do all of the work of the parish alone or to take the place of a pastor who is away and will not be back in time for Saturday confessions and Sunday Masses.

The latter was the case in my most recent assignment—a country parish in northwestern Minnesota, whose pastor had been taken suddenly ill and carried off to a hospital a hundred miles away. I was to take care of the parish Friday evening, Saturday and Sunday. I would return to my classes on Monday.

A blizzard was beginning to gain momentum as I got under way. It grew worse as I drove along. Few places in the country can boast of more furious winter storms than northwestern Minnesota. The winds of these storms seem almost alive, at one moment wailing and moaning as though in pain, and the next moment screaming and crying as though mad with grief and anger. They sigh and scold and whistle and whisper. In fact, every sound that is the property of the human voice is duplicated by the snow-laden, blinding, freezing gales that come pounding across the prairies of the Dakotas for a rendezvous just under Canada in upper Minnesota.

It was fortunate that I arrived at my destination when I did. Already it was beginning to get dark. An hour later might have found me out on the highway in serious trouble. Thank God, I said to myself, that I had succeeded in gaining the security of the rectory. I parked my car in the empty garage and ran as fast as the attacking wind would allow me for the nearest door. It was the back door of the house. I did not pause to knock. I opened the door and rushed in, carrying with me a veritable landslide of snow.

Momentarily blinded by the snow and the wind I was unable to make out what kind of a room I was in or any of the objects that made up its furnishings. Gradually my eyes came back to normal. The first thing that I saw was a man, dressed in somber black, standing silent in the middle of the room. He made no effort to help me remove my coat or to brush off the snow that clung to me. He waited until I had done these services myself. Then he spoke. His first words explained the reason for his funereal black.

"I am the local undertaker," he said. "I came here to the rectory to be sure to catch you before you retired so that you would know about the body in the basement."

Did I hear the man aright? "Body in the basement?" I asked. "In the basement of the rectory? How come? Whose body?"

Yes, I had heard aright. The story unfolded. The woman, whose body was in the basement, had died the night before. The pastor of the parish had been spoken to about the burial. But then the pastor of the parish had been taken sick before the final arrangements could be made. It wasn't known that there'd be another priest to take the pastor's place so soon. So, that morning, Friday, he, the undertaker, had tried to bury the woman in the parish cemetery which was right next to the church.

"Why so soon?" I asked. "If she died last night and you intended to bury her this morning, she would almost be warm when you put her in the ground. Why the haste? Why no wake, no Mass, no prayers?"

"The woman had been a shiftless individual," answered the undertaker, "dirty and ragged in her person and appearance, a confirmed drunkard; in short, a misfit member of the human race. Who would there be to mourn for her if a customary wake were held? She had no relatives. She could claim no friends. She wouldn't have wanted any more attention than she was getting if she were in a position down there in the basement to express a preference."

"But don't you think that a Mass ought to be said for her soul even though there were nobody present at it except herself and the priest who said it? I mean it just doesn't seem right to bury a human being like an animal."

"She wouldn't have wanted any Mass. She died as she lived. The doctor said it was a heart attack. They found her dead on the floor of her shack in a stand of trees outside of town. She had no sacraments, no priest, no prayers. She had nothing. Why bring her into a church? The priest of the parish said that that was the way she was to be buried. I furnished her with a coffin for the shelter of her body. And I intended to bury her just as the priest said. But when I came to do it, I found that it was impossible."

"Why?"

"The weather had been so cold for so long a time that the ground had become as hard as concrete. Even a pickaxe couldn't make a dent. And the blizzard was blowing so hard that the gravediggers quit work. What was I to do? There was my hearse at the gate of the cemetery and the body in it ready to be buried. But no grave. I couldn't take the body back to my place because the storm might last a week. And I couldn't keep it in the hearse. Then I thought of the rectory cellar.

"On the side of the rectory facing the graveyard there is one of those old-fashioned basement stairways on the top of which are slanting doors that open upward and outward from the middle. There is no heat in the basement. It is ice-cold from front to back. I thought that that would be an ideal place to keep the body until it could be buried. I believe that the same thing had been done years before on a similar occasion.

"So, we carried the coffin into the basement and left it on the floor. In the morning I'll be back with a neighbor farmer from up the road, and we'll blast out a grave with dynamite. This farmer is an expert with dynamite. I hope that you are not angry because I turned your house into a morgue."

"Of course not," I responded. "I have no fear of corpses in or out of basements. But how about you? Do you feel safe in going out in this storm? Shouldn't you stay here in the rectory for the night?"

"No, I can't. I have all the arrangements made to stay with the farmer. I'll be O.K. The house is straight down the highway. I'll make it." With that he bundled up tightly, bent down to buck the wind head-on and disappeared into the dark and the swirling snow.

No sooner had he gone than the storm fell upon the house

with a fury unreached until then. The rectory was old to begin with and poorly put together. The boards on the walls and floors were thin and loosely fastened in their places. Doors were not hung straight. Window panes were rattly. The winds made their attack on all these imperfections at the same time. Windows rattled, boards sighed exactly as though a group of people were walking over them, and doors gave off noises like the knocking of human knuckles upon them. To top it all off, in one sudden and fierce blast of power that sounded like a thunderclap, the storm swooped down upon the house—and the lights went out. I found myself in total darkness.

I should have been afraid in view of the fact that the dead woman in the basement lay directly beneath the chair in which I was sitting when the lights went out. I was afraid. I had dissected many cadavers and should not have allowed one more to disturb me even though I was alone with it in a pitch-black house. But it did disturb me. There is no point in my denying it.

Fortunately I had brought along with me a flashlight. I felt my way to my satchel, took out the flashlight and began a search for a candle. My search was soon rewarded. The remnants of a thick Easter candle stood on the mantelpiece—enough of the remnants to last me though the night. I lit the candle, put it alongside my chair and once more sat down to say my breviary.

My prayers were finished about eleven o'clock. I closed the book. There was a lull in the blowing of the wind. I was about to proceed to the icebox in the kitchen for something to eat when I heard the voice. It seemed to be coming from afar off. And it held a note of great urgency. It was a human voice. I listened more closely. It was a woman's voice. For a moment I stopped breathing. Where was it coming from? What was it saying? And then I knew. It was coming from right beneath me— from the basement where lay the dead woman in her coffin! And its words were, "Let me out of here! Let me out of here!"

I was sure now that I was afraid. Was I to become involved with the supernatural? With the world of spirits? What was down there in the basement? A chill came over me. But chill or no chill, it was my duty to investigate.

I put on my overcoat, my scarf, my gloves and hat. In one

hand I carried a bottle of holy water and the ritual. In the other hand I held the candle. So armed and with a prayer on my lips I began my descent. The coffin was in the middle of a low-slung raftered room, surrounded by the accumulated trash of many years. I approached it cautiously.

The voice that I had heard upstairs was now silent. But the closer I came to the coffin, the more it seemed to me that a noise was escaping from a spot in the general area of the front part of the lid, a noise not unlike the scratching of fingernails over the surface of a piece of wood. I looked around for a tool of some kind to remove the lid. On a bench over in a corner I found a large screwdriver. I put down my candle, secured the screwdriver and quickly, lest my nerve depart from me entirely, pried open the top of the coffin.

It was unnecessary for me to lift the lid from its place once I had pried it loose. Unseen hands pushed it away and sent it clattering to the floor. And there, before my very eyes, the body of a woman sat up, her eyes opened wide and she spoke. The moment the first word was uttered, the moment my eyes beheld her, I knew who she was. My heart seemed to stop beating in my body. The woman was my Mary, the girl whom I had almost married, the girl whom I said that I would meet again and whom I was certain I would be able to help. Her body was worn and wasted almost beyond recognition. There was hardly anything left to it but skin and bone. But life was present, I was sure of that. Her being alive may have been due to supernatural agencies. It must have been due to supernatural agencies. How else could the phenomenon be explained? Whatever the explanation, there she was, sitting up before me.

For a reason I cannot understand, all fear left me. I put my hand over the hands that I had held so often when I was a young man in the world. They were not cold as in death. They were rough and wrinkled but warm with the life that was in them.

She called out my name. I said simply, "Mary!" She went on. "You told me years ago that always throughout your life you would speak of me to God, that someday we would meet again, that when we did you would help me even as you were unable to help me then when I needed you so badly. Well, now you have your chance to help me. I know that you are a priest. Hear my confession."

She folded her hands, leaned against the back of the coffin and began, "Bless me, Father, for I have sinned." Through all the sordid and sinful adventures of the past she led me—down the path of the broken commandments, through the tragedies of a thousand despairs, into the poisoned areas of satanic arrogance and pride. She skipped nothing. Never in all the years of my priesthood had I heard so thorough a confession. And never had I witnessed such sorrow. Tears poured from her eyes and flowed down her withered cheeks. The words of her act of contrition were said as though they were drawn from the very bottom of the heart.

I said nothing when she finished. I only raised my hand and gave the absolution. *Ego te absolvo a peccatis tuis*—I absolve you from your sins." And then, "God bless you." The confession was over. Sweat stood out on my brow.

The moment I said, "God bless you," the strangest thing of all happened. "Thank you, Father," she said. And then she called me again by my name, lingering over it lovingly, caressing it, as though she were loath to let it go. But even as she did so, her eyes began to close and her body to slump down once more into the coffin.

In fascination and by the flickering light of the candle I saw the pallor of death come over her face and the stiffness of death take command of her limbs. Her breathing stopped. Her body seemed to shrink and shrivel up. I felt like a doctor signing the death certificate of a total stranger. I knew that she was dead. I also knew that a moment before she had been alive. But without a doubt now she was gone. Her soul was before God. Her body was ready for the grave.

For a long moment I stood there not moving, hardly breathing. Then I rested my hand on her forehead and imparted a final blessing, after which I retrieved the cover of the coffin and put it in its proper place. It is impossible to describe my feelings at that moment. I was certain that God had walked through that cellar as once upon a time He had stood outside the tomb of Lazarus and cried out, "Lazarus, come forth." Was it possible for a miracle to happen in the twentieth century that had happened in the first? Yes, I knew that it was possible. Was it possible for the prayers of a man, by no means a holy man, even though he was a priest, to be heard by God in heaven and to be answered by an act that demanded divine intervention? I knew that it was possible. As sure as I was that I lived, I was sure that the girl whom I had known so many years before and for whom I had said so many prayers was eternally safe.

I knelt down alongside the coffin and prayed in thanksgiving. The cold did not touch me. I hardly heard the howling of the wind. How long I remained there I do not know. But finally the cold began to penetrate my flesh and bones so deeply that I could stand it no longer. I took my candle and returned upstairs.

The next morning I had hardly finished Mass when the undertaker and his friend arrived. The storm had abated sufficiently to allow them to work on the grave.

"Father," asked the undertaker, "did anything happen during the night?"

"Not much," I answered. "However, in spite of the storm I had a guest. Nobody you would know. A person who had been a close friend of mine years ago. But she couldn't stay. In fact she was here only a few minutes. She's gone now. I don't think that she'll be back."

"That is strange. I wonder where she came from and where she went in this kind of weather. Oh, well! We'd better get to work."

He led his friend to the cemetery. They began their work of digging a grave.

A
DIABOLIC
INTERVENTION

BY SHANE LESLIE

THE FOLLOWING STORY IS INTERESTING IN THAT THE CHIEF EVENTS described are of recent date, and are fully documented with statements made at the time by many of the witnesses who underwent various experiences. Moreover, at least in the earlier stages of the alleged manifestations, individual witnesses were unaware that others had previously seen, heard or felt anything untoward. The case is unsatisfying in that any attempt to explain it in "scientific" terms, to suggest the cause or purpose of the manifestations, or to draw a moral from them seems impossible. The refusal of most of the participants to allow their identity to be disclosed and the legal obligation of concealing that of the property affected enforces the strictest anonymity. At the same time, the present writer has had the opportunity not only of reading the official dossier of the case, which comprises documents covering a period of over two years, but of cross-questioning a number of the witnesses to what seems to have been an authentic intervention in human affairs by a spirit, and an evil one at that.

The scene is a house in the English countryside, a rather large house according to modern ideas, standing in its own grounds, with over a dozen bedrooms. It presents anything but that aspect of mystery and gloom traditionally associated with ghost-stories. Built on mediaeval foundations with traces of Tudor architecture in the cellars, the greater part of the house, added by the succeeding generations, is Georgian in style, with large windows, light, airy rooms, wide passages with no dark corners, and is lit abundantly with electricity. The garden is large and modern with flower beds and lawns, in one of which, somewhat over-close to the house, there is a small but deep pond, presumably fed by underground springs. This is believed to be an old quarry, the stone from which may have been used for building the original house. It features later in the tale, though the earlier manifestations seemed at the time to have no connection with it.

At the date the story begins, a newly married couple, both Catholics, owned the house which had been in continuous occupation previous to their purchase. They had lived in it happily for about ten years. No rumour was heard in the countryside that there was anything queer about the house, nor is that part of England greatly given to stories of ghosts, bogles, pixies or things of that type. One day, in midsummer, a young man staying in the house called on a local doctor, asking for a full medical examination. As both his appearance and the necessary tests showed him to be in bounding health, the doctor asked bluntly for an explanation. This was given, and, after promises of professional secrecy, put into writing then and there. It appears that on a sunny June day, just after lunch, the young man and the lady of the house were walking through a room leading by French windows to the lawn, when the young man suddenly fainted. There was a commotion. When he came to, he let it be understood that his heart might be slightly strained. This explanation was accepted on his promise to go and see a doctor at once. The truth was quite otherwise. He said that on glancing back over his shoulder as he followed his hostess out of the house, he had seen close behind him a figure with its hands covering its face. Since he was of a decidedly husky masculine type, the doctor, who knew him well, suggested this was insufficient reason for his patient's faint. The young man agreed, saying that really why he had fainted was a strong intuition that should the figure withdraw its hands and disclose its face he would inevitably die of shock. No hint of this unpleasant event was given at the time to any one apart from the doctor who took down the statement.

One evening while it was still broad daylight about two months later, a housemaid, going about her legitimate business in a room—actually the same one in which the young man had had his experience and fainted—was surprised to see by the window opposite a figure which for a moment she took to be that of the owner of the house whom she had just seen elsewhere. On the instant she recognized this figure to be that of a stranger, it seemed to her to move slowly through a solid wall and disappear. Being a woman of considerable courage and character, she said nothing to anyone at the time, but told her doctor, whom she visited next day, and who happened to be the same doctor to whom the young man had previously related the story told above. Under a similar pledge of professional secrecy the housemaid also agreed to make a written declaration, which included a detailed description of the figure, as did the story of the young man. The two descriptions tally, though the housemaid felt no undue sense of fear since, to use her own words, "it did not seem as though the figure was interested in me."

The figure seen by the young man and the housemaid in broad daylight was opaque in the sense that light did not pass through it. Nevertheless it did not give a three-dimensional impression; while its outline was curiously vague. Both witnesses saw the figure for a few seconds only, but under cross-questioning proved to be excellent observers. The figure seemed to be draped or composed of a dirty brown substance—if "substance" is the right word to use. It cast no shadow nor were any feet visible. When it moved, the figure seemed to ripple or undulate in a manner difficult to describe, as though the undulations took place in the substance itself. Neither observer saw a face, but the clear suggestion of hands described by the young man as covering the face showed them to be apparently of the same substance as the rest of the figure or its other coverings or draperies, or whatever word can best describe the apparent surface seen. The figure was somewhat less than the medium height of a man and gave a squat and ungainly impression. In both cases it seemed to be hunchbacked or hunched up, whether still or in movement.

These are the only two occasions during the whole two years and more on which this, or for that matter any, figure was seen by anyone. On the other hand, from that time onwards various other curious events took place in the house with increasing frequency. For example, a priest staying in the house was awakened by heavy knocks on his bedroom door. He turned on the light, sat up in bed and said, "Come in." The door did not open, but, as the priest put in the written declaration which he himself drew up a few days later, something did come in, accompanied by a sense of abject terror. This something was invisible but not inaudible. For two hours it was as though a large animal perambulated the room, grunting and gasping, paying no attention to the Reverend Father's adjurations to depart. The priest said nothing to the owners of the house at the time.

Again, an army officer visiting the house for a week-end and who incidentally was not sleeping in the room previously occupied by the priest, was found to have departed before breakfast on Sunday morning, leaving a lame note of excuse and apology for his host. On being asked by a mutual friend a day or two later why he had behaved so strangely, the army officer told in confidence an extraordinary story. This too was committed to paper. It appeared that on going to bed on the Saturday evening at about half past eleven, he had just turned out his bedside lamp when he suddenly felt fingers stroke his face. He naturally turned on the lamp again at once but nothing was to be seen. Thinking he must have been the victim of delusion, he turned out the lamp once more when immediately the same thing happened. Yet a third time fingers touched his face soon after the light was extinguished. This was unpleasant but the officer declared he was only a little disturbed and in no sense terrified. He got up, searched the room after turning on all the lights, and, feeling anything but sleepy, began to read a book in bed. He soon found he could not concentrate on what he was reading; terrible ideas, wholly foreign to his nature, pressed in upon him. These gradually developed into an urge to kill himself for no logical reason save a black wall of hopeless despair. For an hour or more he fought this notion with his common sense. There was nothing in his normal life or mind even faintly justifying so dreadful and desperate an act, but the idea grew like a fog thickening. There came a desire that he should go and drown himself in the pond outside the house, which up to that moment he had hardly noticed. This officer states that at one moment he found himself actually climbing out of the bedroom window. Suddenly all pressure was removed, leaving the unfortunate victim so weak and shaken that he felt he could not face remaining in the house.

On another occasion the lady of the house and a woman friend were going upstairs to bed having turned out the lights on the bottom floor. The stairs themselves were brilliantly lit and yet both women heard heavy footsteps coming up behind them, which they described as like those of a man wearing carpet slippers soaked in water. While they shrank against the wall, the footsteps passed up the stairs beside them and disappeared down a lighted corridor. Nothing was seen. This event, which took place some twelve months after the figure had twice been seen in daylight, made it no longer possible, or even desirable, to maintain secrecy. The owner of the house, who had himself experienced nothing and heard no stories of alleged mysterious happenings in his house up to that time, sought the counsel of two friends, one of whom happened to be the doctor who had been consulted by the two witnesses of the brown hunchbacked figure. Permission was obtained to disclose their stories, and by one means and another there came to light not only the experience of the priest and the army officer described above, but a number of others which different persons associated with the house had undergone at various times during the previous months.

Amongst other experiences described was that of a visitor who had slept in yet a different room, and who, like the priest, had been woken up by a heavy rapping on his door. He did not bid the visitor come in but switched on his bedside light, and was astonished to see "the hearthrug fly up the chimney." This somewhat ludicrous performance lost its humour when the bewildered observer remembered clearly that the fireplace had no hearthrug. He got up, opened the door and found nothing in the passage. He then examined the chimney, which was painted white, and having assured himself that no sort of optical illusion would account for what he had seen, he noticed that the register was already in place and the chimney thus completely closed. He is firm in putting down his terrifying nightmare, when he got to sleep again after making a careful note of the affair, to ordinary reaction from his disturbing experience. This may have been so, but it is interesting that the vague recollection of his dream in the morning showed it to have been connected with drowning, hatred and horror.

Several people made declarations of being woken up in the night by knockings and one other daylight experience was recorded, though this took place after the private inquiry into the business had been set on foot. The owner of the house, having up to that date experienced absolutely nothing unusual, was engaged one morning hammering a large nail into the wall of the staircase for the purpose of hanging there a big family portrait. He had ascended a few steps of a solid, new and firm stepladder, set squarely on a broad flat landing. A friend standing below had his hand lightly resting on the stepladder and was looking at the hammering operation taking place only some four feet above his head. The friend was startled to see the owner of the house apparently throw the hammer violently back over his shoulder and make a decidedly athletic and dangerous backwards leap from the step to the stairs. Beyond a slight vibration inseparable from an exercise of this type, the stepladder did not budge and the friend, after ensuring that the owner of the house was unhurt, not unnaturally asked him what he thought he was playing at. The latter said that just as he was about to hit the nail with the hammer for the first time while holding the six-inch wire nail in his left hand, he felt the hammer wrenched out of his right hand by some terrific force. His subsequent jump had been purely instinctive.

There is no need in this account of apparent hauntings to catalogue the many varied and odd experiences which came to light during the inquiry, some of which duplicate the experiences of others, while some were rejected as of doubtful accuracy or authenticity. One other story must however be told. Although it was not recorded at the time, it was recollected that about three months before the first appearance of the figure, a child sleeping in the house kept on having bad dreams which were foreign to its nature, and complained to its mother that "mice" ran over its face after it was dark. There were no mice in the room the child occupied, though traps were set as an assurance. When the child was moved to a room in a different part of the house both dreams and "mice" ceased. This recollection is of particular interest in connection with the later recorded story of the army officer who felt fingers stroke his cheek in the dark, and also in that the particular room of which the child complained had not previously been slept in. Research showed that for at least thirty years, and probably longer, it had been used only as a storeroom.

Once all these stories were put together and examined a few possibly significant facts seemed to emerge. No trace existed in living memory of anything untoward prior to the bad dreams and "mice" of the child, after which the inexplicable events had taken place with increasing frequency. In so far as concerned manifestations at night, it was at once apparent that, wherever the time had been recorded by the witness it was always almost exactly two o'clock in the morning. So far as could be ascertained the same hour fitted the experiences of others who had not thought to look at a clock. Again, no manifestation was recorded or reported by night or day save on one or two days either side of a full moon, though what such a terrestrial event could have to do with apparently spiritual disturbances was clear to no one at the time. However the priest who eventually exorcised the ghost, as recorded below, said that he had once come across a similar phenomenon and was impressed by the coincidence.

Despite the varied nature of the manifestations, it was found that all had taken place in only one part of the house, curiously enough the newest, where every room, with one possible exception, the staircase and all passages were connected with at least one sinister event: the smaller part where were located the kitchens, offices and bedrooms used by the servants, with one or two spare rooms, had nothing recorded against them. The possible connection was noted between the child's tale of mice and fingers stroking a face in the dark, together with the impressed ideas of suicide, wet feet and despair, for there were stories of dreams and depressions available other than those recorded here.

This inquiry, which was kept as confidential as possible and of which for practical reasons the servants in the house learned nothing, with the exception of the maid who had seen the figure some eighteen months earlier but had had no other unpleasant experience, was interrupted by a terrible event. One afternoon another maid quietly put down her dustpan and brush, walked straight out of the house and jumped into the pond on the lawn. She was dead when her body was recovered. The subsequent inquest, both official and unofficial, disclosed no sort of reason why this poor woman should have committed suicide. Her life contained no apparent sorrow or dread secret, and though the official verdict of suicide while the balance of her mind was upset received some support from vague stories of a far-off relation in a home for the feeble-minded, private inquiry never identified the latter.

This sad occurrence naturally caused talk in the village, but without producing any stories of ghosts or hauntings. At the same time an elderly and taciturn farmer of the neighbourhood, whose grandfather had been the village schoolmaster, hinted one day to the owner of the house that he might find the Record Office interesting. Papers in the Record Office were duly searched and the Inquisitiones post Mortem for the Hundred disclosed a remarkable state of affairs. It appeared that from some time during the reign of James I there had been irregular periods of a year or so during which a shocking number of suicides had taken place in or on the edge of the quarry pond in the garden. These batches of suicides were separated from one another by irregular periods of up to fifty or sixty years during which nothing happened. There was no regularity in the length of any of the periods or in the number of suicides which took place in any group. It was noticed however that, for example, a farmer living seven or eight miles away, who had evidently decided to take his own life for certain reasons of his own which were disclosed at the inquest, had walked eight miles to the edge of the pond and shot himself there with a gun instead of doing so on his own farm. Others had hung themselves on trees near the pond, while others seem to have jumped into its waters.

Armed with these sinister facts and the full documentation of recent happenings, the owner of the house, a Catholic, as has been said earlier, consulted the bishop of the diocese, who at first adopted an attitude of reserve until he had studied the dossier. Immediately thereafter he sent for the owner of the house and with the utmost gravity told him that he had decided on the evidence to use his episcopal powers and permit a full solemn exorcism of the house.

For those who have little knowledge of such matters, it may here be mentioned that permission for a solemn exorcism of this kind is very rarely granted: in fact, it is not easy to lay hands on the text or directions for the rite. The priest authorized by the bishop has to be specially selected or approved by him. Before performing the rite, which involves a Mass to be said anywhere in or near the haunted precincts, as the priest may choose, the latter is bound to observe an absolute fast for twenty-four hours beforehand, during which period he must be as far as possible in a state of prayer, in accordance with the statement of Our Lord that this kind goeth not out save by prayer and fasting. The episcopal authority allows the selected priest to perform the rite more than once for the same haunting in the event of the first exorcism apparently proving ineffective. This is in accordance with the Apostolic command to go on praying and not to faint. It also indicates the Church's recognition that we know little and are indeed not meant to know much in this world about the affairs of the next. It is not a question of science but of faith.

The main part of the exorcism consists, after special prayers, of a command in the name of Our Lord to the spirit to betake himself to the place appointed. The language used is terrific in its authority, unlike the usual quiet dignity of the Church's rites.

Before the exorcism could take place a further experience was recorded. The witness knew about the previous phenomena, being a member of the small unofficial committee of inquiry, but, though a frequent visitor to the house, he had never previously experienced anything himself. For these reasons he was personally inclined to disregard his own story as being of purely subjective origin. Ecclesiastical authority thought otherwise and directed that it should be included in the dossier.

This observer spent a night in the house over an Easter weekend. He occupied a bedroom in the newer portion, but one in which no phenomenon had been recorded as occurring up to that time. On the Saturday evening he went to bed shortly before midnight after a very cheerful party and, according to his own account, with no thought of the hauntings in his mind. He went to sleep but was woken some time during the night with the notion that somebody had called him by name. The impression was so strong that he got out of bed and opened the door into the passage, although the call was not repeated and the whole house seemed quiet. He did not turn on the lights since the room was nearly as bright as day with moonlight streaming in through the uncurtained windows. This witness observes that it was not until next morning that he remembered a connection between Easter and the full moon. After a moment or two looking up and down the passage he went back to bed, glancing at his watch as he did so. The time shown was exactly two minutes past three. This is of particular interest, since on using this argument to convince others that the affair was unconnected with the ghost, he found his argument turned against himself, since he had forgotten that Summer Time was in force, so that the true Greenwich Mean Time was two minutes past two and his awakening must have taken place almost exactly at two o'clock.

This witness's statement records that he lay down in bed and tried to turn over preparatory to going to sleep again when, to his great disquiet, he found himself paralysed. Not only was he unable to turn over but he could not move his head or his limbs, although he found he could open and shut his eyes. His first thought was that he must somehow have ricked his back or done himself some other physical damage. Before he could decide what to do, if anything, whether to call out for help or wait to see if the apparent paralysis passed off, he became aware, without sight or sound, that something indescribable, a personality, but one utterly repugnant and hostile to himself, was arriving from a very great distance at a very great speed. The "thing" seemed to arrive and the witness confesses that he was frankly terrified. Invisible and inaudible though it remained, the thing seemed nevertheless in some way to dart at the witness, whereupon something else, of which the witness had in no way been conscious up to that time, seemed to intervene and throw the first thing off. The witness states that he prayed hard and went on doing so. Not once, but many times, the unpleasant thing hovering around seemed to make sudden darts at the witness, only to be repulsed each time by the intervention of the other thing. This very unpleasant experience went on until suddenly the witness heard a cock crow. The phenomenon ceased instantly. The witness, finding he could move, got up and looked at his watch. Three hours had elapsed; the sun was just rising, but he did not go to bed again although all sense of fear had left him, so that until called officially that morning, he slept peacefully in a chair, discovering that his mattress was wringing wet with the sweat that had poured from him during his dream or ordeal.

The exorcism was duly performed; the selected priest being one who had made a certain study of alleged occult happenings. He chose to say Mass in the room wherein the child had complained of the "mice," giving as his reason, which he insisted must be taken as purely experimental, first that the child's experiences were possibly the earliest of the series, and secondly that the room itself might be, in picturesque terms, the "gateway of the monster," and the fact that any human had slept there might have provided the means of unlocking that gate. In view of the apparent connection between the strength of the manifestations and the lunar cycle, the priest elected to say his Mass and perform the rite on a day on which the moon was full.

Nothing happened during the Mass or the rite, which naturally took place in the morning before breakfast. That night however two people sleeping in the house in rooms overlooking the lawn with the pond were woken by a noise which they likened to the howling of dogs, apparently coming from the lawn outside. The moon was full and the night was cloudless; whence it was apparent that there was nothing visible on the lawn which could be held responsible for the sounds, though the spot they were apparently coming from could be identified with certainty. The time was exactly two o'clock in the morning. As the watchers gazed in horror at the empty lawn, the sound of the howling began to recede in jerks, as though something was being thrust farther and farther away. It faded into the distance and could no longer be heard. Since that date there has been no trouble in the house.

THE
CHOCOLATE
BOX

BY AGATHA CHRISTIE

IT WAS A WILD NIGHT. OUTSIDE, THE WIND HOWLED MALEVOLENTLY, and the rain beat against the windows in great gusts.

Poirot and I sat facing the hearth, our legs stretched out to the cheerful blaze. Between us was a small table. On my side of it stood some carefully brewed hot toddy; on Poirot's was a cup of thick, rich chocolate which I would not have drunk for a hundred pounds! Poirot sipped the thick brown mess in the pink china cup, and sighed with contentment.

"*Quelle belle vie!*" he murmured.

"Yes, it's a good old world," I agreed. "Here am I with a job, and a good job too! And here are you, famous—"

"Oh, *mon ami!*" protested Poirot.

"But you are. And rightly so! When I think back on your long line of successes, I am positively amazed. I don't believe you know that failure is!"

"He would be a droll kind of original who could say that!"

"No, but seriously, *have* you ever failed?"

"Innumerable times, my friend. What would you? *La bonne chance*, it cannot always be on your side. I have been called in too late. Very often another, working toward the same goal, has arrived there first. Twice have I been stricken down with illness just as I was on the point of success. One must take the downs with the ups, my friend."

"I didn't quite mean that," I said. "I meant had you ever been completely down and out over a case through your own fault?"

"Ah, I comprehend! You ask if I have ever made the complete prize ass of myself, as you say over here? Once, my friend—" A slow, reflective smile hovered over his face.

"Yes, once I made a fool of myself."

He sat up suddenly in his chair.

"See here, my friend, you have, I know, kept a record of my little successes. You shall add one more story to the collection, the story of a failure!"

He leaned forward and placed a log on the fire. Then, after carefully wiping his hands on a little duster that hung on a nail by the fireplace, he leaned back and commenced his story.

That of which I tell you, (said M. Poirot), took place in Belgium many years ago. It was at the time of the terrible struggle in France between church and state. M. Paul Déroulard was a French deputy of note. It was an open secret that the portfolio of a Minister awaited him. He was among the bitterest of the anti-Catholic party, and it was certain that on his accession to power, he would have to face violent enmity. He was in many ways a peculiar man. Though he neither drank nor smoked, he was nevertheless not so scrupulous in other ways. You comprehend, Hastings, *c'était des femmes—toujours des femmes!*

He had married some years earlier a young lady from Brussels who had brought him a substantial dot. Undoubtedly the money was useful to him in his career, as his family was not rich, though on the other hand he was entitled to call himself M. le Baron if he chose. There were no children of the marriage, and his wife died after two years—the result of a fall downstairs. Among the property which she bequeathed to him was a house on the Avenue Louise in Brussels.

It was in this house that his sudden death took place, the event coinciding with the resignation of the Minister whose portfolio he was to inherit. All the papers printed long notices of his career. His death, which had taken place quite suddenly in the evening after dinner, was attributed to heart-failure.

At that time, *mon ami*, I was, as you know, a member of the Belgian detective force. The death of M. Paul Déroulard was not particularly interesting to me. I am, as you also know, *bon catholique*, and his demise seemed to me fortunate.

It was some three days afterward, when my vacation had just begun, that I received a visitor at my own apartments—a lady, heavily veiled, but evidently quite young; and I perceived at once that she was a *jeune fille tout à fait comme il faut.*

"You are Monsieur Hercule Poirot?" she asked in a low sweet voice.

I bowed.

"Of the detective service?"

Again I bowed. "Be seated, I pray of you, mademoiselle," I said.

She accepted a chair and drew aside her veil. Her face was charming, though marred with tears, and haunted as though with some poignant anxiety.

"Monsieur," she said, "I understand that you are now taking a vacation. Therefore you will be free to take up a private case. You understand that I do not wish to call in the police."

I shook my head. "I fear what you ask is impossible, mademoiselle. Even though on vacation, I am still of the police."

She leaned forward. "*Ecoutez, monsieur.* All that I ask of you is to investigate. The result of your investigations you are at perfect liberty to report to the police. If what I believe to be true *is* true, we shall need all the machinery of the law."

That placed a somewhat different complexion on the matter, and I placed myself in her service without more ado.

A slight color rose in her cheeks. "I thank you, monsieur. It is the death of M. Paul Déroulard that I ask you to investigate."

"*Comment?*" I exclaimed, surpised.

"Monsieur, I have nothing to go upon—nothing but my woman's instinct, but I am convinced—*convinced* I tell you—that M. Déroulard did not die a natural death!"

"But surely the doctors—"

"Doctors may be mistaken. He was so robust, so strong. Ah, Monsieur Poirot, I beseech of you to help me—"

The poor child was almost beside herself. She would have knelt to me. I soothed her as best I could.

"I will help you, mademoiselle. I feel almost sure that your fears are unfounded, but we will see. First, I will ask you to describe to me the inmates of the house."

"There are the domestics, of course, Jeannette, Félicie, and Denise the cook. She had been there many years; the others are simple country girls. Also there is François, but he too is an old servant. Then there is Monsieur Déroulard's mother who lived with him, and myself. My name is Virginie Mesnard. I am a poor cousin of the late Madame Déroulard, M. Paul's wife, and I have been a member of their ménage for over three years. I have now described to you the household. There were also two guests staying in the house."

"And they were?"

"M. de Saint Alard, a neighbor of M. Déroulard's in France. Also an English friend, Mr. John Wilson."

"Are they still with you?"

"Mr. Wilson, yes, but M. de Saint Alard departed yesterday."

"And what is your plan, Mademoiselle Mesnard?"

"If you will present yourself at the house in half an hour's time, I will have arranged some story to account for your presence. I had better represent you to be connected with journalism in some way. I shall say you have come from Paris, and that you have brought a card of introduction from M. de Saint Alard. Madame Déroulard is very feeble in health, and will pay little attention to details."

On mademoiselle's ingenious pretext I was admitted to the house, and after a brief interview with the dead deputy's mother, who was a wonderfully imposing and aristocratic figure though obviously in failing health, I was made free of the premises.

I wonder, my friend (continued Poirot), whether you can possibly figure to yourself the difficulties of my task? Here was a man whose death had taken place three days previously. If there *had* been foul play, only one possibility was admittable—poison! And I had had no chance of seeing the body, and there was no possibility of examining, or analyzing, any medium in which the poison could have been administered. There were no clues, false or otherwise, to consider. Had the man been poisoned? Had he died a natural death? I, Hercule Poirot, with nothing to help me, had to decide.

First, I interviewed the domestics, and with their aid, I recapitulated the evening. I paid especial notice to the food at dinner, and the method of serving it. The soup had been served by M. Déroulard himself from a tureen. Next a dish of cutlets, then a chicken. Finally a compote of fruits. And all placed on the table, and served by Monsieur himself. The coffee was brought in a big pot to the dinner-table. Nothing there, *mon ami* —impossible to poison one without poisoning all!

After dinner Madame Déroulard had retired to her own apartments and Mademoiselle Virginie had accompanied her. The three men had adjourned to M. Déroulard's study. Here they had chatted amicably for some time, when suddenly, without any warning, the deputy had fallen heavily to the ground. M. de Saint Alard had rushed out and told François to fetch a doctor immediately. He said it was without doubt an apoplexy, explained the man. But when the doctor arrived, the patient was past help.

Mr. John Wilson, to whom I was presented by Mademoiselle Virginie, was what was known in those days as a regular John Bull Englishman, middle-aged and burly. His account, delivered in very British French, was substantially the same.

"Déroulard went very red in the face, and down he fell."

There was nothing further to be found out there. Next I went to the scene of the tragedy, the study, and was left alone there at my own request. So far there was nothing to support Mademoiselle Mesnard's theory. I could not but believe that it was a delusion on her part. Evidently she had entertained a romantic passion for the dead man which had not permitted her to take a normal view of the case. Nevertheless, I searched the study with meticulous care. It was just possible that a hypodermic needle might have been introduced into the dead man's chair in such a way as to allow of a fatal injection. The minute puncture it would cause was likely to remain unnoticed. But I could discover no sign to support that theory. I flung myself down in the chair with a gesture of despair.

"*Enfin*, I abandon it!" I said aloud. "There is not a clue anywhere! Everything is perfectly normal."

As I said the words, my eyes fell on a large box of chocolates standing on a table near by, and my heart gave a leap. It might not be a clue to M. Déroulard's death, but here at least was something that was *not* normal. I lifted the lid. The box was full, untouched; not a chocolate was missing—but that only made the peculiarity that had caught my eye more striding. For, see you, Hastings, while the box itself was pink, the lid was *blue*. Now, one often sees a blue ribbon on a pink box, and vice versa, but a box of one color, and a lid of another—no, decidedly— *ça ne se voit jamais!*

I did not as yet see that this little incident was of any use to me, yet I determined to investigate it as being out of the ordinary. I rang the bell for François, and asked him if his late master had been fond of sweets. A faint melancholy smile came to his lips.

"Passionately fond of them, monsieur. He would always have a box of chocolates in the house. He did not drink wine of any kind, you see."

"Yet this box has not been touched?" I lifted the lid to show him.

"Pardon, monsieur, but that was a new box purchased on the day of his death, the other being nearly finished."

"Then the other box was finished on the day of his death," I said slowly.

"Yes, monsieur, I found it empty in the morning and threw it away."

"Did M. Déroulard eat sweets at all hours of the day?"

"Usually after dinner, monsieur."

I began to see light.

"François," I said, "you can be discreet?"

"If there is need, monsieur."

"*Bon!* Know, then, that I am of the police. Can you find me that other box?"

"Without doubt, monsieur. It will be in the dustbin."

He departed, and returned in a few minutes with a dust-covered object. It was the duplicate of the box I held, save for the fact that this time the box was *blue* and the lid was pink. I thanked François, recommended him once more to be discreet, and left the house in the Avenue Louise without more ado.

Next I called upon the doctor who had attended M. Déroulard. With him I had a difficult task. He entrenched himself prettily behind a wall of learned phraseology, but I fancied that he was not quite as sure about the case as he would like to be.

"There have been many curious occurrences of the kind," he

observed, when I had managed to disarm him somewhat. "A sudden fit of anger, a violent emotion—after a heavy dinner, *c'est entendu*—then, with an access of rage, the blood flies to the head, and *pst!*—there you are!"

"But M. Déroulard had had no violent emotion."

"No? I made sure that he had been having a stormy altercation with M. de Saint Alard."

"Why should he?"

"*C'est evident!*" The doctor shrugged his shoulders. "Was not M. de Saint Alard a Catholic of the most fanatical? Their friendship was being ruined by this question of church and state. Not a day passed without discussions. To M. de Saint Alard, Déroulard appeared almost as Antichrist."

This was unexpected, and gave me food for thought.

"One more question, Doctor: would it be possible to introduce a fatal dose of poison into a chocolate?"

"It would be possible, I suppose," said the doctor slowly. "Pure prussic acid would meet the case if there were no chance of evaporation, and a tiny globule of anything might be swallowed unnoticed—but it does not seem a very likely supposition. A chocolate full of morphine or strychnine—" He made a wry face. "You comprehend, M. Poirot—one bite would be enough! The unwary one would not stand upon ceremony."

"Thank you, M. le Docteur."

I withdrew. Next I made inquiries of the chemists, especially those in the neighborhood of the Avenue Louise. It is good to be of the police. I got the information I wanted without any trouble. Only in one case could I hear of any poison having been supplied to the house in question. This was some eye drops of atropine sulphate for Madame Déroulard. Atropine is a potent poison, and for the moment I was elated, but the symptoms of atropine poisoning are closely allied to those of ptomaine, and bear no resemblance to those I was studying. Besides, the prescription was an old one. Madame Déroulard had suffered from cataract in both eyes for many years.

I was turning away discouraged when the chemist's voice called me back.

"*Un moment*, M. Poirot. I remember, the girl who brought that prescription, she said something about having to go on to the *English* chemist. You might try there."

I did. Once more enforcing my official status, I got the information I wanted. On the day before M. Déroulard's death they had made up a prescription for Mr. John Wilson. Not that there was any making up about it. They were simply little tablets of trinitrin. I asked if I might see some. He showed me them, and my heart beat faster—for the tiny tablets were of *chocolate*.

"It is a poison?" I asked.

"No, monsieur."

"Can you describe to me its effect?"

"It lowers the blood-pressure. It is given for some forms of heart trouble—angina pectoris for instance. It relieves the arterial tension. In arteriosclerosis—"

I interrupted him. "*Ma foi!* This rigmarole says nothing to me. Does it cause the face to flush?"

"Certainly it does."

"And supposing I ate ten—twenty of your little tablets, what then?"

"I should not advise you to attempt it," he replied dryly.

"And yet you say it is not poison?"

"There are many things not called poison which can kill a man," he replied as before.

I left the shop elated. At last, things had begun to march!

I now knew that John Wilson held the means for the crime—but what about the motive? He had come to Belgium on business, and had asked M. Déroulard, whom he knew slightly, to put him up. There was apparently no way in which Déroulard's death could benefit him. Moreover, I discovered by inquiries in England that he had suffered for some years from that painful form of heart disease known as angina. Therefore he had a genuine right to have those tablets in possession. Nevertheless, I was convinced that someone had gone to the chocolate box, opening the full one first by mistake, and had abstracted the contents of the last chocolate, cramming in instead as many little trinitrin tablets as it would hold. The chocolates were large ones. Between twenty or thirty tablets, I felt sure, could have been inserted. But who had done this?

There were two guests in the house. John Wilson had the means. Saint Alard had the motive. Remember, he was a fanatic, and there is no fanatic like a religious fanatic. Could he, by any means, have got hold of John Wilson's trinitrin?

Another little idea came to me. Ah! You smile at my little ideas! Why had Wilson run out of trinitrin? Surely he would bring an adequate supply from England. I called once more at the house in the Avenue Louise. Wilson was out, but I saw the girl who did his room, Félicie. I demanded of her immediately whether it was not true that M. Wilson had lost a bottle from his washstand some little time ago. The girl responded eagerly. It was quite true. She, Félicie, had been blamed for it. The English gentleman had evidently thought that she had broken it and did not like to say so. Whereas she had never even touched it. Without doubt it was Jeannette—always nosing round where she had no business to be—

I calmed the flow of words, and took my leave. I knew now all that I wanted to know. It remained for me to prove my case. That, I felt, would not be easy. *I* might be sure that Saint Alard had removed the bottle of trinitrin from John Wilson's washstand, but to convince others, I would have to produce evidence. And I had none to produce!

Never mind. I *knew*—that was the great thing. You remember our difficulty in the Styles case, Hastings? There again, I *knew*—but it took me a long time to find the last link which made my chain of evidence against the murderer complete.

I asked for an interview with Mademoiselle Mesnard. She came at once. I demanded of her the address of M. de Saint Alard. A look of trouble came over her face.

"Why do you want it, monsieur?"

"Mademoiselle, it is necessary."

She seemed doubtful—troubled.

"He can tell you nothing. He is a man whose thoughts are not in this world. He hardly notices what goes on around him."

"Possibly, mademoiselle. Nevertheless, he was an old friend of M. Déroulard's. There may be things he can tell me—things of the past—old grudges—old love affairs."

The girl flushed and bit her lip. "As you please—but—but—I

feel sure now that I have been mistaken. It was good of you to accede to my demand, but I was upset—almost distraught at the time. I see now that there is no mystery to solve. Leave it, I beg of you, monsieur."

I eyed her closely.

"Mademoiselle," I said, "it is sometimes difficult for a dog to find a scent, but once he *has* found it, nothing on earth will make him leave it! That is, if he is a good dog! And I, mademoiselle, I, Hercule Poirot, am a very good dog."

Without a word she turned away. A few minutes later she returned with the address written on a sheet of paper. I left the house. François was waiting for me outside. He looked at me anxiously.

"There is no news, monsieur?"

"None as yet, my friend."

"Ah! *Pauvre* Monsieur Déroulard!" he sighed. "I too was of his way of thinking. I do not care for priests. Not that I would say so in the house. The women are all devout—a good thing perhaps. *Madame est très pieuse—et Mademoiselle Virginie aussi.*"

Mademoiselle Virginie? Was she *"très pieuse?"* Thinking of the tear-stained passionate face I had seen that first day, I wondered.

Having obtained the address of M. de Saint Alard, I wasted no time. I arrived in the neighborhood of his château in the Ardennes but it was some days before I could find a pretext for gaining admission to the house. In the end I did—how do you think—as a plumber, *mon ami!* It was the affair of a moment to arrange a neat little gas leak in his bedroom. I departed for my tools, and took care to return with them at an hour when I knew that I should have the field pretty well to myself. What I was searching for, I hardly knew. The one thing needful, I could not believe there was any chance of finding. He would never have run the risk of keeping it.

Still when I found a little cupboard above the washstand locked I could not resist the temptation of seeing what was inside it. The lock was quite a simple one to pick. The door swung open. It was full of old bottles. I took them up one by one with trembling hand. Suddenly, I uttered a cry. Figure to yourself, my friend, I held in my hand a little phial with an English chemist's label. On it were the words: *"Trinitrin Tablets. One to be taken when required. Mr. John Wilson."*

I controlled my emotion, closed the little cupboard, slipped the bottle into my pocket, and continued to repair the gas leak! One must be methodical. Then I left the château, and took train for my own country as soon as possible. I arrived in Brussels late that night. I was writing out a report for the *préfet* in the morning, when a note was brought to me. It was from old Madame Déroulard, and it summoned me to the house in the Avenue Louise without delay.

François opened the door to me.

"Madame la Baronne is waiting for you."

He conducted me to her apartments. She sat in state in a large armchair. There was no sign of Mademoiselle Virginie.

"M. Poirot," said the old lady. "I have just learned that you are not what you pretended to be. You are a police officer."

"That is so, madame."

"You came here to inquire into the circumstances of my son's death?"

Again I replied: "That is so, madame."

"I should be glad if you would tell me what progress you have made."

I hesitated.

"First I would like to know how you have learned all this, madame."

"From one who is no longer of this world."

Her words, and the brooding way she uttered them, sent a chill to my heart. I was incapable of speech.

"Therefore, monsieur, I would beg of you most urgently to tell me exactly what progress you have made in your investigation."

"Madame, my investigation is finished."

"My son?"

"Was killed deliberately."

"You know by whom?"

"Yes, madame."

"Who, then?"

"M. de Saint Alard."

The old lady shook her head.

"You are wrong. M. de Saint Alard is incapable of such a crime."

"The proofs are in my hands."

"I beg of you once more to tell me all."

This time I obeyed, going over each step that had led me to the discovery of the truth. She listened attentively. At the end she nodded her head.

"Yes, yes, it is all as you say, all but one thing. It was not M. de Saint Alard who killed my son. It was I, his mother."

I stared at her. She continued to nod her head gently.

"It is well that I sent for you. It is the providence of the good God that Virginie told me before she departed for the convent what she had done. Listen, M. Poirot! My son was an evil man. He persecuted the Church. He led a life of mortal sin. He dragged down other souls beside his own. But there was worse than that. As I came out of my room in this house one morning, I saw my daughter-in-law standing at the head of the stairs. She was reading a letter. I saw my son steal up behind her. One swift push, and she fell, striking her head on the marble steps. When they picked her up she was dead. My son was a murderer, and only I, his mother, knew it."

She closed her eyes for a moment. "You cannot conceive, monsieur, of my agony, my despair. What was I to do? Denounce him to the police? I could not bring myself to do it. It was my duty, but my flesh was weak. Besides, would they believe me? My eyesight had been failing for some time—they would say I was mistaken. I kept silence. But my conscience gave me no peace. By keeping silence I too was a murderer. My son inherited his wife's money. He flourished as the green bay tree. And now he has to have a Minister's portfolio. His persecution of the Church would be redoubled. And there was Virginie. She, poor child, beautiful, naturally pious, was fascinated by him. He had a strange and terrible power over women. I saw it coming. I was powerless to prevent it. He had no intention of marrying her. The time came when she was ready to yield everything to him.

"Then I saw my path clear. He was my son. I had given him

life. I was responsible for him. He had killed one woman's body, now he would kill another's soul! I went to Mr. Wilson's room, and took the bottle of tablets. He had once said laughingly that there were enough in it to kill a man! I went into the study and opened the big box of chocolates that always stood on the table. I opened a new box by mistake. The other was on the table also. There was just one chocolate left in it. That simplified things. No one ate chocolates except my son and Virginie. I would keep her with me that night. All went as I had planned. . . ."

She paused, closing her eyes a minute, then opened them again.

"M. Poirot, I am in your hands. They tell me I have not many days to live. I am willing to answer for my action before the good God. Must I answer for it on earth also?"

I hesitated. "But the empty bottle, madame," I said to gain time. "How came that into M. de Saint Alard's possession?"

"When he came to say goodbye to me, monsieur, I slipped it into his pocket. I did not know how to get rid of it. I am so infirm that I cannot move about much without help, and finding it empty in my rooms might have caused suspicion. You understand, monsieur"—she drew herself up to her full height—"it was with no idea of casting suspicion on M. de Saint Alard! I never dreamed of such a thing. I thought his valet would find an empty bottle and throw it away without question."

I bowed my head. "I comprehend, madame," I said.

"And your decision, monsieur?"

Her voice was firm and unfaltering, her head held as high as ever.

I rose to my feet.

"Madame," I said, "I have the honor to wish you good day. I have made my investigations—and failed! The matter is closed."

He was silent for a moment, then said quietly: "She died just a week later. Mademoiselle Virginie passed through her novitiate, and duly took the veil. That, my friend, is the story. I must admit that I do not make a fine figure in it."

"But that was hardly a failure," I expostulated. "What else could you have thought under the circumstances?"

"Ah, *sacré, mon ami,*" cried Poirot, becoming suddenly animated. "Is it that you do not see? But I was thirty-six times an idiot! My gray cells, they functioned not at all. The whole time I had the true clue in my hands."

"What clue?"

"The chocolate box! Do you not see? Would anyone in possession of their full eyesight make such a mistake? I knew Madame Déroulard had cataract—the atropine drops told me that. There was only one person in the household whose eyesight was such that she could not see which lid to replace. It was the chocolate box that started me on the track, and yet up to the end I failed consistently to perceive its real significance!

"Also my psychology was at fault. Had M. de Saint Alard been the criminal, he would never have kept an incriminating bottle. Finding it was a proof of his innocence. I had learned already from Mademoiselle Virginie that he was absent-minded. Altogether it was a miserable affair that I have recounted to you there! Only to you have I told the story. You comprehend. I do not figure well in it! An old lady commits a crime in such a simple and clever fashion that I, Hercule Poirot, am completely deceived. *Sapristi!* It does not bear thinking of! Forget it. Or no—remember it, and if you think at any time that I am growing conceited—it is not likely, but it might arise."

I concealed a smile.

"Eh bien, my friend, you shall say to me, 'Chocolate box.' Is it agreed?"

"It's a bargain!"

"After all," said Poirot reflectively, "it was an experience! I, who have undoubtedly the finest brain in Europe at present, can afford to be magnanimous!"

"Chocolate box," I murmured gently.

"Pardon, mon ami?"

I looked at Poirot's innocent face, as he bent forward inquiringly, and my heart smote me. I had suffered often at his hands, but I, too, though not possessing the finest brain in Europe, could afford to be magnanimous!

"Nothing," I lied, and lit another pipe, smiling to myself.

HEAVEN
CAN
WAIT

BY C. B. GILFORD

"AGE AT TIME OF DEATH?" ASKED MICHAEL, WHO WAS AN ARCH-angel. "Fifty-two. Correct?"

"Correct," said Alexander Arlington wearily. It seemed to him that he'd been answering questions ever since he arrived.

"Immediate Cause of Death?" continued the archangel.

"Heart attack. That is, I think so," Alexander replied.

"Hmmm." The archangel seemed embarrassed. "Now, this last blank. Contributing Circumstances, If Any. Check one, it says. Self-immolation, Foolhardiness, Stupidity, Murder, et cetera. There's a check-mark after 'Murder.'"

Alexander sat up. "Murder?"

"Yes," said Michael. "That's the information I have from my work-sheet. Correct me if I'm wrong. You *were* murdered, weren't you, Mr. Arlington?"

"Well, I didn't think so. I . . ."

"Do you mean," asked Michael kindly, "that you didn't know you were murdered?"

"Why, I never dreamed it!"

Michael sighed. "That sometimes happens, of course. Most people know when they're being murdered, however. Not till the last minute, naturally, but they usually know. I never have learned how to break news like this gently."

"I can't believe it," Alexander repeated to himself several times.

"I regret that you're taking this so hard, Mr. Arlington. You must realize that such things make no difference whatsoever here."

"I was in my study. I think I must have been asleep. I seemed to awaken with a sort of bursting pain . . . in my chest . . . I didn't have time really to think about it."

"There's a note added here," Michael said, consulting his record. "It was your heart, all right, Mr. Arlington. You were stabbed with your own letter-opener . . . in the back."

"Why, that's positively fiendish," exclaimed Alexander. "My letter-opener was really an ivory-handled dagger. . . . Who did it?"

"I beg your pardon? Who did what?"

"Who murdered me?"

"Why, I don't know that."

"You don't know! I thought you had all the information on that infernal work-sheet of yours."

"It's not an infernal work-sheet!"

"All right, whatever it is. Who murdered me?"

"Mr. Arlington!" The archangel looked stern. "Ideas of revenge and recrimination are, as you should already know, forbidden here."

"Okay, okay. I just want to know."

"I don't know who murdered you, Mr. Arlington. I'm an archangel, but I don't know everything. We don't find out such things until the perpetrator of the deed has met his own demise. I'll have a work-sheet on him then, and I'll let you know."

"How long will that take?"

"If the murderer is apprehended and hanged, let us say, it may be relatively soon. If the murderer has been smart and is not found out, it may be years."

"I can't wait! I want to know *now.*"

"Mr. Arlington, I'm sorry—"

"Is there anyone here who *would* know?"

"Well, of course, He would. He knows everything."

"Then ask Him."

"That's impossible. I can't bother Him with such trifles. . . . Mr. Arlington, sit down!"

But instead of sitting down, Alexander continued his pacing. "You told me I should be happy and contented in this place," he complained.

"Absolutely," said Michael with great assurance.

"How can I be happy and contented if I don't know who murdered me?"

"I don't see how that makes any difference, Mr. Arlington!"

Alexander, making a distinct effort to compose himself, sat down again in the golden chair. "Sir," he began more calmly, "what does it say about my profession on your work-sheet?"

"You were a writer of mystery stories."

"Correct. Under the pen-name of Slade Saunders, I was the author of seventy-five mystery novels—more than a dozen of them purchased by the movies—assorted short stories, and articles too numerous to mention. Does that have any significance for you, sir?"

"Not exactly."

"Don't you understand?" Alexander almost lost his temper again. "Here I am, the famous mystery author, who for twenty years asked and answered the question, 'Who did it?' and now—now!—I myself have been murdered and I don't know who did it!"

The archangel smiled. "I see your point, Mr. Arlington," he said. "But the information you're after will come through in good time. Now, if you'll just be patient and compose yourself—"

"I must know the identity of my murderer," Alexander insisted. "I'll never be happy until I do. Stabbed in the back! Really!"

"Come now, Mr. Arlington," soothed the archangel. "Wait till you see our Establishment here. The facilities for enjoyment are quite—"

"I don't want to see it." Alexander slumped in his chair, staring at the floor. "I don't want to see *any* of it."

"Mr. Arlington!"

"It's a fake. It's all a fake. Happy and contented! I'm not happy. I'm miserable."

"You *can't* be miserable up here," Michael said, something like panic rising in his voice. "It's utterly impossible for you to be anything but happy. You're in Heaven."

"I'm miserable."

The archangel rose; his large, bare feet padded noiselessly on the beautiful marble floor. "This is ridiculous," he mumbled several times. "Preposterous! Mr. Arlington, won't you reconsider?"

"I'm miserable."

"Be reasonable, Mr. Arlington," the archangel pleaded. "You simply can't imagine the embarrassment, the loss of prestige it would entail, if you went about Heaven proclaiming that you weren't happy."

"I'm miserable," Alexander insisted, and he looked it.

"I'd ask Him," said Michael; and he was beginning to look miserable, too. "Really I would. But He has so many things on His mind these days. . . . On the other hand, if He knew there was somebody up here who wasn't happy, I'm sure he'd blame me. I'm a department head, Mr. Arlington, which puts the responsibility squarely on my shoulders."

"I'm miserable."

The archangel winced and resumed his pacing. Now and then through the open windows came the gentle sounds of laughter and music. But within the room, Alexander Arlington sat brooding.

Suddenly Michael's expression lightened. He strode back to his desk and sat down again.

"Mr. Arlington, you are a writer of mystery stories," he said briskly. "You are reputed to be clever at devising clues, trapping murderers, and all that sort of thing?"

"Yes."

"What I have in mind," continued Michael, "is completely irregular, of course. But the situation demands swift action. Do you think, Mr. Arlington, that you could solve this mystery to your satisfaction if you were allowed to go back to Earth?"

"Well, I suppose . . ."

"It's as far as I can go," Michael said austerely.

"I could certainly try. But how—?"

"Simple," interrupted Michael. "You are now existing in Eternity, quite independent of the element of Time. So we repeat a certain period of Time, as it were . . . let us say, one day. You would return to earth and relive the last day of your mortal life. Let's see. . . . Here! You died precisely at midnight.

You would have from the moment you awakened on that last morning until midnight of the same day."

"One day?" frowned Alexander. "That wouldn't give me much time."

"If you'd rather not try . . ."

"I'll do it," Alexander said hastily. "When do I start?"

"Immediately. But first, Mr. Arlington, a reminder. That last day of your life is down on the records, so it is not technically subject to change. However, you *will* have to do a little investigating, some few things you didn't do the first time you lived that final day . . . I can make some minor erasures on the Books, but I should be extremely embarrassed if there had to be any major ones."

"But—"

"You will simply have to manage without important changes. It should present no difficulties. You will have, remember, a gift seldom granted to mortals."

"The gift of foresight," exclaimed Alexander.

"Yes. However, Mr. Arlington, I must remind you that you'll have to submit to being murdered all over again."

The gleam in Alexander's eye went out. "I suppose I shall have to be stabbed in the back again. . . ."

The archangel nodded. "That's the way it is in the records," he said, and his voice was like the tolling of a bell. "Do you care to reconsider?"

"No . . . I'll go through with it. I've got to know who killed me."

"Very well, Mr. Arlington. I wish you luck. We do want all our souls to be happy."

"Thank you," said Alexander unhappily, and he walked out through the golden door . . .

. . . And awoke in his own bed, in his own room, in the dark and drafty old mansion in which he had always thought it so fitting and proper for a mystery writer to reside. The ancient grandfather's clock in the hallway was striking twelve. He counted the strokes, and for a horrible moment—before he could collect his wits—he imagined that it might be midnight already. But no, there was the sunshine just beyond his drawn blinds.

Noon, the rising time of a successful author. But it gave him so little time. . . .

There was an insistent knocking at his door.

"Come in," Alexander said.

The door opened and his secretary, Talbert, appeared. "The mail has arrived," Talbert announced.

"Well?"

"There's a letter from Fenton." Talbert was a thin, scholarly man of thirty-five. He seldom smiled, but at the moment the ghost of a smile played at the corners of his mouth. "I opened it, thinking it was routine. But you'd better read it yourself."

Alexander took the letter. "Dear Alex," it began, "I must be candid. It was with some hesitation that we decided to publish that last novel of yours, *Murder of a Mannequin*. Perhaps it will do all right, but if it does, it will only be because of your name and reputation. Frankly, it's the opinion here that you have been slipping. Each book has been a little weaker than the one before. Is the well running dry? Perhaps you should take a long rest. As we've still got a contract with you for your next five books, this is of great concern to us. So I'm coming out to talk things over with you. I'll arrive on the nine o'clock train Thursday morning. Yours, Walter Fenton."

Talbert was still standing there.

"I have a suggestion," he said.

"Oh, you have!" said Alexander savagely.

"Fenton suggests that you need a rest. I agree with him. But while you're resting, the public need not be deprived of the enjoyment of reading mystery novels by the famous Slade Saunders."

"Just what do you mean?" Alexander leaped out of bed.

"I," said Talbert calmly, "will continue to write the books under the pen-name of Slade Saunders. Fenton need never know. Or our public, either."

"*Our* public! Do you imagine for one moment that *you* could imitate my style?"

"I could do more than imitate your style, Alexander. I could improve on it."

"You insolent—you presumptuous—"

"Do I have to remind you, Alexander, how large a part of your last few books was mine, anyway? I worked on the plots, made corrections, did rewriting—"

"Get out of here!"

"It's your only chance to rescue the reputation of Slade Saunders. I'll split fifty-fifty with you."

"You're fired!"

"Alexander—"

"Fired!"

"You'll never be able to replace me. And what's more, you'll never be able to finish another book without me."

"Pack your things and leave, Talbert, or I'll have you thrown out!"

"You'll regret this." And so saying, Talbert stalked out of the room.

Yes, that was the way Alexander's last day had started. The letter from Fenton and the quarrel with Talbert. What an odd feeling to be repeating one's actions precisely! Just as if the incident had occurred before, in a dream—

The thought shocked Alexander. A dream? What if his entire experience with the archangel had been a dream?

The ringing of the telephone interrupted this interesting line of thought. The bedroom extension was at his elbow. Alexander reached for it automatically.

"Hello?"

"This is Michael."

"What? Well . . . uh . . . Where are you calling from?"

"That's a silly question, don't you think, Mr. Arlington?"

"What . . . do you want?"

"Just checking to find out if you made the trip safely. How are things coming?"

"Give me a chance, will you, sir? I haven't even got started!"

"Well, you'd better get to work, Mr. Arlington. You haven't much time, you know. Goodbye for now."

"Goodbye."

That settled that. It was no dream, so it was indeed time to get down to business. But to have to work with Someone looking over one's shoulder, as it were . . .

For the next half-hour Alexander occupied himself with shaving and dressing. He thought about Talbert—timid, shrinking Talbert, who chose today of all days to show his fangs. Yes, Talbert coveted the name and reputation of Slade Saunders, Alexander's most prized possession. Talbert had a motive for murder, all right.

What had happened next?

Alexander discovered that he didn't remember. He was to be murdered at midnight, in his study, stabbed with his own ivory-handled letter-opener. But he remembered nothing else. He should have picked up more information from that archangel.

On the other hand, it might be better this way. Foreseeing *every* detail might be a little too eerie. And this way, too, he'd have a freer hand.

Walking downstairs, Alexander realized that he was hungry. In the dining room, Annie the cook was ready with his usual afternoon breakfast. Alexander studied Annie's broad, empty face as she served him. Besides Annie there was her daughter Agnes, his wife's maid. But neither Annie nor Agnes had any earthly reason to murder him. Anyway, they both went home every night. Alexander decided that he could dismiss both of them from his calculations.

"Better hurry with your breakfast, Mr. Arlington," Annie said to him when she brought in his poached egg. "I've got to have lunch ready on time, because there's going to be a guest."

"Who?"

"Mr. Armbruster."

Now he remembered! This, too, had happened the first time. Armbruster, the big young man with the dark curly hair.

"Good morning, darling."

A quick cool kiss on his left cheek turned him around. The thought shot through his mind—a kiss of betrayal. But he said, quite pleasantly, "Good morning, Ariel."

Alexander abandoned the poached egg for a moment to survey his wife. Twenty-eight, scarcely more than half his age. She was beautiful because he had been able to afford a young, beautiful wife. Blonde, slim, graceful, a creature of light and air. His Ariel.

"So Armbruster's coming for lunch?"

"Do you mind, darling?"

"Yes, I do mind. I mind having that penniless young athlete hanging around my house, devouring my wife with his eyes."

"What an imagination you have, darling!"

"Has he ever made love to you?"

"Of course not."

"That's a lie, my dear. I saw it all yesterday."

Alexander Arlington was amazing himself. Now that the words were out of his mouth, he suddenly remembered what he must have, in the excitement of being murdered, temporarily forgotten. This had all happened once before.

"I saw you, my dearest, out in the arbor. And I might add that I wasn't particularly stunned. Neither of you has been very discreet."

Ariel had paled, and sat down weakly.

"Surprised, my dearest one? Well, now, let me tell you something. It's perfectly all right with me, young Mr. Armbruster's coming here to lunch today. In fact, I think that after lunch you and he should have a long talk. You might tell him that I know everything. And then you can both decide what to do. You personally have two choices. The first is to leave me and go away with Armbruster. Of course, he doesn't have a cent and you can't expect me to subsidize a little love-nest for you. If you get tired of starving with Armbruster, however, you cannot return here. Your second choice is to stay. In that case, I would demand loyalty and fidelity from you, and Mr. Armbruster would have to look for his handouts elsewhere."

That, Alexander reflected, should settle Mr. Armbruster's hash. Ariel was not the sort who could live on love alone. She had been accustomed to the finer things for too long.

But then—and it hadn't, of course, been the first time he had delivered this ultimatum—another thought dawned.

Here was another motive for murder. Ariel was down in his will for half the tidy fortune he had accumulated in a lifetime of writing. If Armbruster knew that, he might prefer Ariel as a moneyed widow rather than as a dispossessed wife. Or if Ariel herself wanted the young man badly enough . . .

"Will you be lunching with us?" Ariel was asking.

"I think not," Alexander answered grandly. "I'd only be in the way. Besides, I've just had breakfast. Also, I've more important things to do."

She went away then, and Alexander watched her trim figure as she departed. Then he returned to his egg, finished it quickly, and left the dining room to Annie's preparations for the luncheon guest.

He went to his study, the scene of the crime.

Alexander felt awe as he entered his own death-chamber. The blinds were drawn, making the room a shadowy place. Uneasily Alexander let the sunlight in. Then he looked around.

There was his desk, of massive mahogany. He surely must have been sitting in his chair, at this desk. And he must have dozed off, as he often did, with his arms spread on the desk and his head on his arms. An inviting target. And there was the letter-opener. He picked it up gingerly, half-expecting to find dried blood on its blade.

But of course there wouldn't be . . . yet.

The thing made a nasty murder-weapon, Alexander reflected. Its handle was four inches long, of smooth and heavy old ivory. It would take fingerprints nicely, if the murderer were careless. The blade was even longer—neither razor-sharp nor needle-pointed. But quite adequate, if thrust with reasonable strength and accuracy, to impale a man's heart.

Alexander shuddered.

A knock interrupted his cogitations. The knocker entered without waiting to be invited. "Busy, Uncle Alex?"

"No, no. Come in, Andrew."

Andrew threw up one fat leg and hoisted himself to a perch on the desk. His weight caused the sturdy mahogany to creak. Andrew's small piggish eyes stared from behind thick-lensed glasses.

"How's finances with you, Uncle?"

"How much this time?" asked Alexander Arlington.

"Five hundred."

Alexander leaned back in his swivel chair and considered the huge lump on his desk. "I told you last time, Andrew, there'd be no more squaring of your debts. At least not until you show some signs of helping yourself—which means getting a job. So my answer, Andrew, is no."

"My situation is pretty desperate, Uncle Alex."

"That's your affair."

"What am I going to do?"

"That's also your affair."

"I'll have to do something . . . drastic."

The remark startled Alexander. This conversation, as well as his argument with Talbert and his talk with Ariel, had also happened before. Andrew was heir to the other half of his estate—not because Alexander had ever liked Andrew, but simply because Andrew was his one and only blood-relative. And now the worthless nephew needed money.

Still another motive for murder.

"Just what would something—er—drastic be, Andrew?"

"I don't know. But if you won't help me, whatever happens will be your fault."

The great mass slid off the desk, walked to the door, and went out. Despite his size, there was a certain grace and quickness in Nephew Andrew's movements. Strangely, Alexander had never noticed this before. But then he was discovering so many things of which he had once been oblivious.

The sunshine, filtering through the curtained windows, looked suddenly inviting. At the moment, Alexander wasn't feeling particularly fond of this room.

He decided that he needed fresh air—and a chance to think.

In the garden, instead of solitude, he found Harry. Old Harry was gardener, caretaker, handyman, chauffeur and, in the evenings when Annie and her daughter had gone, he was the butler. Harry was also an admitted ex-convict. Here he had been especially useful to Alexander. Under the influence of alcohol supplied by his employer, Harry often reminisced of his past exploits in the world of crime for the benefit of Alexander's notebook. Some of these exploits, Alexander had gathered, had never been discovered or penalized. Doubtless there were at least a dozen cities in which Harry was wanted.

At the moment Alexander was in no mood for plot material. But Harry had something on his mind.

"I've been hearing things, Mr. Arlington."

"What things?"

"About your books."

"My books? What about my books?"

"Maybe there won't be any more."

Talbert had talked! The gist, if not the complete text, of Fenton's letter was probably known throughout the household by this time. Then Ariel and Armbruster knew, too. And Andrew.

"How does that concern you, Harry, even supposing it were true? Afraid of losing your job?"

The old man squinted up at him. Harry was remarkably ugly. "Not worried about my job," he answered. "But I've been thinking, Mr. Arlington, about all the things I've told you about myself. That was okay while you were writing your books. But now that there maybe won't be any more books, you might start talking to the cops."

"Why should I do a thing like that, Harry? What does it matter to me what your past is? You've reformed, and you're earning an honest living now."

"The cops don't care about that."

"Well, I'm not going to say anything to the cops. . . . Harry, don't you believe me?"

It was obvious that he didn't. The old fellow turned away and started digging with the hoe again. The strokes were strong, swift, accurate. And his face was dark and grim.

This, too, Alexander remembered with the same strange feeling that it had all happened before. In his garden he had unearthed another potential murderer. . . .

Back at the desk in his study, Alexander sat down heavily. Why, when he had first lived through this fateful last day of his life, hadn't any of these things occurred to him? Why hadn't he realized that he was literally surrounded by people who would profit by his death? Everyone in this house, except old Annie and her daughter Agnes, had a motive to kill him. And at least one of them must also have the nerve.

The telephone rang, and without thinking Alexander picked up the study extension.

"This is Michael."

"Oh . . . Good afternoon."

"Something wrong, Mr. Arlington? You don't sound very chipper."

"This has all been very disheartening, sir."

"Yes?"

"Except for two domestics who don't live in, everyone under my roof would like to see me dead."

"That's nothing to be downcast about, Mr. Arlington."

"No?"

"If you realize how much you're not wanted on earth, you won't have the slightest regret about coming back up here."

"Hm. That's so, isn't it?"

"Anything else troubling you, Mr. Arlington?"

"As a matter of fact, sir, there is. I haven't found any clues."

"Look for some."

"That's just it. You see, in my books—and in real life, too—there are never any clues until *after* the murder. A murderer usually leaves clues at the time he commits the murder. What am I going to do about that?"

"My dear Mr. Arlington, I'm sure I don't know. You should have considered that difficulty before you left."

"I wish I had!"

"I'm afraid you'll have to sit tight and wait until midnight. See you then."

Alexander mixed himself a drink. It was four o'clock. One-third of his allotted time had already elapsed. He took his drink glumly to the window. Clouds had appeared in the sky, promising rain.

A good night for a murder.

It was thus by the merest accident, as he stood sipping his cocktail, that he saw his wife and Armbruster. The athletic young man was kissing her.

At that instant there was born in Alexander Arlington's heart a new determination.

He didn't smash his glass on the floor or crush it in his fist, as a more emotional man might have done. Instead, he stood there and slowly finished his drink while Armbruster slowly finished kissing his wife. For now, at last, Alexander had concocted a plan.

After he had drained his glass, he went to the kitchen. "Annie," he announced, "Mr. Armbruster will be staying to dinner, and so will Talbert and my nephew. And you may tell Harry to serve."

Up in Talbert's room he found his secretary packing. "You can put away that suitcase, Talbert."

"You told me I was fired," the secretary answered sulkily.

"You still are. But I'd like you to stay around until tomorrow. You may find it to your advantage, my boy."

Andrew was enjoying his afternoon nap when Alexander shook him awake. "If you have any plans for going out tonight, cancel them. I want to have a long talk with you. You may find it profitable."

Then Alexander went out to the garden.

"Sorry I couldn't have lunch with you, Armbruster," he told the man he had seen kissing his wife, "but I'd like you to stay for dinner."

Armbruster's handsome face registered surprise, but he mumbled that he would be delighted. Ariel was stricken dumb. Alexander smiled upon them with secret excitement. If his plan worked . . . !

Dinner was at seven-thirty. It was already dark and it had started to rain when Annie and her daughter left the house. Harry served in grim silence.

Alexander was the only one who ate heartily. The others went through the motions, but they were preoccupied. Ariel looked at Armbruster frequently, and Armbruster looked back at her. Talbert's thin face was a mask through which only a glint of his sullenness showed. Andrew usually possessed an excellent appetite, but it was not evident tonight. All of them watched Alexander stealthily.

It was nine o'clock before the meal ended. Alexander rose, smiling down at them. "I'll see you all in my study in an hour. Having a little celebration—a sort of farewell party."

This cryptic remark left them staring blankly. Alexander went complacently upstairs to his bedroom and began to pack a suitcase. He had hardly stowed two pairs of socks in the bag when the telephone rang.

"This is Michael."

"I was rather expecting your call."

"Your mood has changed considerably in the last several hours."

"Yes, it has . . . yes."

"Where do you think you're going with that suitcase?"

"I'm shortly to go on a long journey, am I not?"

"You don't need extra socks up here, Mr. Arlington. Everything is furnished."

"You've been spying on me."

"I don't have to spy on you."

"Sir, you're not worried about my double-crossing you—are you?"

There was no answer. The line was dead. But that in itself was answer enough. The archangel was worried. And if he was worried about a double-cross, a double-cross must be within the realm of possibility! Alexander went on packing and chuckling.

He put into the suitcase all he might need in the way of clothes for a few days. He packed his toothbrush and his razor. He went to the wall-safe and took from it the several hundred dollars he always kept there. From his dresser he took his automatic, checked to make certain it was loaded. It was. The automatic, he had decided, was a little extra insurance.

But he did not return downstairs in an hour as he had promised. He wanted to keep his suspects on edge. He knew they would wait. Especially the murderer—he *had* to wait. Alexander spent some time in his easy chair, smoking his pipe and planning the future.

Not until a quarter to eleven did he carry his suitcase downstairs and rejoin his wife and guests. He found them satisfactorily upset. Talbert's face was flushed; he had evidently been at the liquor cabinet. Andrew was sulking in a dark corner, like a surly hog. Ariel and Armbruster sat together on the couch, defiantly close to each other. Old Harry was lurking in the hallway, and Alexander ushered him inside. Then Alexander locked the door from within and sat down behind his desk to face them.

"Has any of you," he began, "noticed anything queer about this day, which will end in exactly one hour and ten minutes?"

They obviously did not understand. For a few moments his only answer was the steady tattoo of the rain against the house and an occasional clap of increasingly loud thunder.

"I don't know what you're talking about, Alexander." That was from his wife. She had risen from the sofa and advanced a step toward him.

He surveyed her coldly. She wore an evening gown which began very low on her torso and clung like skin the rest of the way. For Armbruster's benefit, no doubt.

"Sit down, my dear, and don't get excited." Something in his voice made her retreat. "I rather expected you to notice it, even if no one else did. You with your woman's intuition."

"Notice what, Alexander?"

"Haven't you sensed something strange about today? Haven't you had the feeling that all the things you've been doing and saying are somehow familiar? That you did and said those very same things once before?"

It was clear they all thought he was drunk or playing a joke on them.

"Last night," Alexander continued with a smile, "I was . . . well, perhaps it really wasn't last night. In Eternity one can't be sure about the passage of Time. But I wasn't Up There very long, so I believe it must have been last night. Last night I was murdered."

Ariel stifled a scream.

"Ah, that jogs your memory, my dear?"

"My memory?"

Her ignorance of what he was talking about seemed genuine. Alexander looked around at the other faces, all staring at him, without comprehension. So he told them. He told them about Michael, and he told them about why he was back. They listened, and occasionally they looked around at one another.

At the end of the recital, Andrew said, "Uncle Alex, you are completely out of your mind. You should see a doctor!"

"Fenton said you were slipping," Talbert said vindictively. "He didn't know how right he was."

"This is a madhouse!" said Armbruster, rising from the sofa. "I'm getting out of here."

"Sit down, all of you," said Alexander, producing the automatic.

They sat down. Just as the phone rang.

Alexander picked it up, and a voice began immediately, "What are you up to, Arlington?"

"It's an old gimmick, sir," Alexander answered glibly. "Used in lots of mystery novels. In the last chapter the detective herds all the suspects into one room. There he explains his deductions, and the murderer usually confesses or gives himself away. Just some small erasures on your Books, sir."

"Very well, I'll take your word for it, Arlington. But let me remind you that you have only half an hour left."

"That, I suppose," remarked Armbruster when Alexander had hung up, "was probably the archangel."

"Yes," said Alexander.

Armbruster subsided.

"I have been reminded," Alexander went on, "that my time is growing short. Consequently, I will proceed from my story, which none of you seems to believe, to the facts, which are indisputable. In this room there are five of you. All five have good reason to want to see me dead. One of you wants it so much that he—or she—will risk murder.

"There is my dear nephew Andrew, who is up to his ears in debt. Andrew's only hope for enough money to make him solvent lies in my willing it to him, which, unfortunately, I have done. Andrew's needs are immediate, but if I were dead and the will being probated, his creditors would undoubtedly become patient.

"Then there is Talbert, my former secretary. Talbert thinks that if I were out of the picture, he might take over the career of Slade Saunders. My publisher arrives tomorrow, and that will be Talbert's big chance—if I happen to be dead.

"And there is Harry. Harry is afraid I'll give him away to the police when I've quit writing and have no more use for his inexhaustible past.

"Lastly, there are my dear wife and her dear friend, Mr. Armbruster. Ariel would have left me before this if Mr. Armbruster had any money. If she gets her half of my estate, they can afford to live in the style to which I have accustomed her. So either of them might find it worth while to murder me."

"What a morbid mood you're in, Uncle Alex," said Andrew placatingly.

"Morbid but accurate, my dear nephew. Now here is my letter-opener. I am scheduled to go to sleep, sitting at this desk. At precisely twelve midnight the murderer—one of you five—will take this letter-opener and stab me in the back."

Talbert had grown very attentive. Despite himself, he had become fascinated with the problem. "Just supposing, Alexander," the secretary began, "that all you have told us is true. Are you going to go to sleep there at the desk in time for the murderer to commit his crime?"

"Of course not, Talbert. Now that I know I'm going to be murdered it would be pretty difficult, if not impossible, for me to go to sleep, don't you think?"

"Then that ruins the whole idea of the murder happening exactly as it did the first time."

"Precisely, Talbert. You've hit upon the very crux of the problem. It can't happen the same way. There will have to be some differences. But if you will recall, the archangel said he was prepared to make some few small erasures on the records."

All of them were now listening with the greatest interest, caught up by the spirit of the occasion.

"Alexander," Talbert continued, "I don't quite see how you're going to accomplish this feat of detection. Now in our books—rather, your books—the murder was committed, clues were left behind, and only then could the detective begin. But what clues are there in this case to begin on? To cite a crude example—that letter-opener would take fingerprints nicely, but the murderer wouldn't leave his prints until the moment of the murder, and by that time it would be too late for *you* to find them."

"A fascinating phase of the problem, Talbert. I have trained you well, I see. But that's exactly the difficulty which I confess

I didn't foresee when I undertook this venture. How am I to solve the crime *before* it is committed?"

"And you've only fifteen minutes left, Uncle Alex," said Andrew with rising excitement.

"Are you expecting somebody to confess even before he pulls the job?" The question came from old Harry.

"It could happen," said Alexander equably, "but I certainly am not counting on it."

"Perhaps you're going to sit there and wait for the murderer to start for you. You'll see who it is and that will satisfy your curiosity."

This suggestion was Armbruster's.

"Hardly that," Alexander retorted in a spirit of friendly debate. "That, I think, Mr. Armbruster, would take the kind of courage I don't possess—to sit calmly at my desk, watch the murderer over my shoulder, and offer my back to be stabbed."

"Then I can't see how it's going to happen," Ariel said peevishly.

"Of course you don't, my dear, so I will explain. You see, I have a plan. I'll keep my bargain with Michael—because he was so decent about the whole thing—to the extent of being right here at my desk at midnight. *But the murder will not occur!*"

They could not conceal their disappointment. Alexander smiled again.

"After twelve o'clock," he continued, "I shall be free of my obligation to the archangel. The murderer will have missed his date with destiny, and I shall live on—for years and years. But now that my eyes have been opened in respect to all of you, I shall of course not continue to live here. I have my suitcase packed, as you see. I am going away. Then I shall take steps to disinherit you, Ariel, and you, Andrew. As for my career, I have a new book in mind, dealing with this very case. I'm sure such an extraordinary plot will rescue Slade Saunders from the oblivion that threatens him. You'll be on your own, Talbert. As for you, Harry, you yourself have reminded me of my clear duty as a law-abiding citizen."

And Alexander smiled once more.

The five suspects were silent. The clock above the fireplace fixed the time at seven minutes to twelve. It was old Harry who spoke first.

"So you're going to keep us all here at the point of a gun, Mr. Arlington. Of course nobody can stab you with that letter-opener if you've got a gun on us. Is that what you call keeping your agreement with the archangel?"

"It is not my intention," replied Alexander serenely, "to hold you at bay with a gun." And to prove his point he returned the automatic to his pocket. "My plan is really much simpler and far less violent."

"Are you going to tell us?" Talbert demanded.

"Why not? Here I am, at the appointed hour and in the appointed place, per agreement. And I have seen to it that all the suspects are here. What can be fairer than that?"

"There's a catch to it," his nephew said.

"Naturally, Andrew. One of you five is the murderer. Now, murderer, you have two choices. At twelve o'clock you can do the deed if you wish, here in the light before four witnesses, excluding myself. In that case you'll surely be apprehended by the police, for I can guarantee that these other scurvy characters will be most anxious to give evidence against you. But you have another choice: you can pass up your chance of murdering me. Since it will be your doing, not mine, that will put me square with Michael, and at one minute past twelve I will walk out of this house and out of your lives."

The phone rang violently. Alexander picked up the receiver and said cordially, "Hello, sir."

"Arlington, you're cheating!" said the archangel.

"But I'm not, sir. This is the only way I can find the murderer. There are simply no clues beforehand and I won't be alive after. If the murderer decides not to go through with it, you certainly can't blame me."

"That's very clever, Arlington!"

"Thank you, sir."

"But not clever enough. You forget that the murderer has a date with midnight, just as you have. So the murderer may have a counter-plan, too."

Alexander returned the phone to its cradle, no longer smiling.

He *had* forgotten that. His shaken confidence did not go unnoticed by his attentive audience.

"What time is it?" asked Andrew, whose vision was imperfect.

"Three minutes to twelve." Old Harry was nearest to the clock.

A heavy silence settled over the room. Ariel and Armbruster changed brief glances. The rest kept their eyes on Alexander Arlington. There were no unbelievers now. And somewhere among them, the murderer was making a decision.

Quite suddenly, Armbruster rose and walked across the room to the door. He walked with the grace of a cat, and his tread was silent on the carpet. Alexander watched cautiously, feeling for his automatic. At the door Armbruster stopped and turned swiftly.

"Arlington is right in one thing," he said. "If the murderer kills in full view of the others, they'll be able to give evidence. It would insure their own safety. But suppose the murder could be done without the others witnessing it? Then none of us could be sure which one was the killer. It's true that each of us has a motive and we'd all be suspected—the police might even construe it as a conspiracy and we'd be tried for murder en masse. But suppose the police don't learn about this meeting? Then the rest of us are in the clear, the murderer does the job, and takes the same chances of getting away with it that he took before. It all depends on the murderer's being able to kill Arlington without being seen doing it."

It was one minute to twelve.

"And how is the murderer going to accomplish that?" Alexander Arlington inquired tartly, although he heard his voice quavering. "How am I to be killed without witnesses in a room full of people?"

Armbruster smiled. The smile of an enemy. "Why, that's simple," he answered. "How could you have overlooked it, Mr. Slade Saunders, famous writer of detective stories? *All I have to do is to turn out the lights!*"

Before Alexander could move, Armbruster's hand found the switch. Darkness came, and darkness remained. The lightning, which had been flashing almost continuously, perversely stopped flashing altogether. The rain slashed against the house, loud enough to muffle any footsteps.

The murderer was free to move with perfect anonymity!

If he had not been immobilized by surprise, Alexander might have done something. But he remained frozen in his chair.

There was somebody beside him. A hand pushed his head down upon the desk. Just as if he had fallen asleep. The other hand, Alexander knew, was seeking, finding, grasping the letter-opener.

The blow really didn't hurt very much.

Alexander dimly felt the hand which had pushed his head down exploring the left side-pocket of his jacket, removing his handkerchief. . . . The murderer was wiping fingerprints off the knife. . . .

There was a ringing in Alexander's head. . . .

Or perhaps it was the telephone. . . .

"Welcome back, Mr. Arlington! Right on schedule, too."

Alexander collapsed in the golden chair in front of Michael's desk.

"Have a nice time, Mr. Arlington?"

"I was murdered again."

"Of course."

"Who did it?"

The archangel laughed, a laugh that rang and echoed through the high-vaulted marble room. "Why, that's what you went back to Earth to find out. And here you are, Mr. Arlington, asking the same old question. You're not proposing to go through all that a *third* time, are you?"

"No, thanks," said Alexander wearily. "But I still won't be happy here—"

"Now let's not start that again," the archangel said hastily. "Let's think this problem over for a moment, shall we? Put yourself in the murderer's shoes, Mr. Arlington. When Armbruster turned the lights off, would *you* have gone over to the desk and committed the murder?"

Alexander thought with his head in his hands. "I might have suspected a double-cross. Somebody could have turned the lights back on while I was doing the stabbing, and I'd have been caught red-handed."

"Precisely, Mr. Arlington. Risky business. Now, another little problem. If you were the murderer, what reason could you possibly have for reaching into the *victim's* pocket and using the *victim's* handkerchief to wipe off your fingerprints?"

"I'd do that," answered Alexander, "only if I didn't have a handkerchief of my own."

"Right," nodded the archangel. "And which of your five suspects would be most likely to know that you carried your handkerchief *in the left side-pocket* of your jacket?"

"I see what you mean, sir!" Alexander perked up.

The archangel beamed. "Then maybe you'll be happy here after all, Mr. Arlington."

"Ariel's accomplice was at the light-switch," muttered Alexander. "She could trust Armbruster not to turn the lights back on till she was finished with the murder. For confirmation— Ariel couldn't have been carrying a handkerchief, because there was just no place for one in that low-cut dress she was wearing. And my wife, I presume, would be the most likely to know where I'm accustomed to carrying my handkerchief!"

"Exactly the way I had it figured out, Mr. Arlington."

"Say, you're a pretty good detective yourself, sir."

The archangel looked modest. "I've picked up a few tricks here and there," he admitted. "It's the company I've been keeping."

"Company?"

"Didn't I mention that, Mr. Arlington? Dear, dear. If I had, you might never have been dissatisfied in the first place. Well, well, we won't delay any longer. You come in and meet the boys, Mr. Arlington. There's Edgar and Sir Arthur and G.K.C.—"

"Edgar and Sir Arthur and G.K.C.!"

"Certainly, Mr. Arlington. Didn't you know that all mystery writers go to Heaven?"

THE
FINGER
OF
STONE

BY G. K. CHESTERTON

THREE YOUNG MEN ON A WALKING TOUR CAME TO A HALT OUTSIDE the little town of Carillon, in the south of France; which is doubtless described in the guide books as famous for its fine old Byzantine monastery, now the seat of a university; and for having been the scene of the labours of Boyg. At that name, at least, the reader will be reasonably thrilled; for he must have seen it in any number of newspapers and novels. Boyg and the Bible are periodically reconciled at religious conferences; Boyg broadens and slightly bewilders the minds of numberless heroes of long psychological stories, which begin in the nursery and nearly end in the madhouse. The journalist, writing rapidly his recurrent reference to the treatment meted out to pioneers like Galileo, pauses in the effort to think of another example, and always rounds off the sentence either with Bruno or with Boyg. But the mildly orthodox are equally fascinated, and feel a glow of agnosticism while they continue to say that, since the discoveries of Boyg, the doctrine of the Homoousian or of the human conscience does not stand where it did; wherever that was. It is needless to say that Boyg was a great discoverer, for the public has long regarded him with the warmest reverence and gratitude on that ground. It is also unnecessary to say what he discovered; for the public will never display the faintest curiosity about that. It is vaguely understood that it was something about fossils, or the long period required for petrifaction; and that it generally implied those anarchic or anonymous forces of evolution supposed to be hostile to religion. But certainly none of the discoveries he made while he was alive was so sensational, in the newspaper sense, as the discovery that was made about him when he was dead. And this, the more private and personal matter, is what concerns us here.

The three tourists had just agreed to separate for an hour, and meet again for luncheon at the little café opposite; and the different ways in which they occupied their time and indulged their tastes will serve for a sufficient working summary of their personalities. Arthur Armitage was a dark and grave young man, with a great deal of money, which he spent on a conscientious and continuous course of self-culture, especially in the matter of art and architecture; and his earnest aquiline profile was already set towards the Byzantine monastery, for the exhaustive examination of which he had already prepared himself, as if he were going to pass an examination rather than to make one. The man next him, though himself an artist, betrayed no such artistic ardour. He was a painter who wasted most of his time as a poet; but Armitage, who was always picking up geniuses, had become in some sense his patron in both departments. His name was Gabriel Gale; a long, loose, rather listless man with yellow hair; but a man not easy for any patron to patronize.

He generally did as he liked in an abstracted fashion; and what he very often liked to do was nothing. On this occasion he showed a lamentable disposition to drift towards the café first, and having drunk a glass or two of wine, he drifted not into the town but out of it, roaming about the steep bare slope above, with a rolling eye on the rolling clouds; and talking to himself until he found somebody else to talk to, which happened when he put his foot through the glass roof of a studio just below him on the steep incline. As it was an artist's studio, however, their quarrel fortunately ended in an argument about the future of realistic art; and when he turned up to lunch, that was the extent of his acquaintance with the quaint and historic town of Carillon.

The name of the third man was Garth; he was shorter and uglier and somewhat older than the others, but with a much livelier eye in his hatchet face; he stepped much more briskly, and in the matter of a knowledge of the world, the other two were babies under his charge. He was a very able medical practitioner, with a hobby of more fundamental scientific inquiry; and for him the whole town, university and studio, monastery and café, was only the temple of the presiding genius of Boyg. But in this case the practical instinct of Dr. Garth would seem to have guided him rightly; for he discovered things considerably more startling than anything the antiquarian found in the Romanesque arches or the poet in the rolling clouds. And it is his adventures, in that single hour before lunch, upon which this tale must turn.

The café tables stood on the pavement under a row of trees opposite the old round gate in the wall, through which could be seen the white gleam of the road up which they had just been walking. But the steep hills were so high round the town that they rose clear above the wall, in a more enormous wall of smooth and slanting rock, bare except for occasional clumps of cactus. There was no crack in that sloping wilderness of stone except the rather shallow and stony bed of a little stream. Lower down, where the stream reached the level of the valley, rose the dark domes of the basilica of the old monastery; and from this a curious stairway of rude stones ran some way up the hill beside the water-course, and stopped at a small and solitary building looking little more than a shed made of stones. Some little way higher the gleam of the glass roof of the studio, with which Gale had collided in his unconscious wanderings, marked the last spot of human habitation in all those rocky wastes that rose about the little town.

Armitage and Gale were already seated at the table when Dr. Garth walked up briskly and sat down somewhat abruptly.

"Have you fellows heard the news?" he asked.

He spoke somewhat sharply, for he was faintly annoyed by the attitudes of the antiquarian and the artist, who were deep in their own dreamier and less practical tastes and topics. Armitage was saying at the moment:

"Yes, I suppose I've seen to-day some of the very oldest sculpture of the veritable Dark Ages. And it's not stiff like some Byzantine work; there's a touch of the true grotesque you generally get in Gothic."

"Well, I've seen to-day some of the newest sculpture of the Modern Ages," replied Gale, "and I fancy they are the veritable

Dark Ages. Quite enough of the true grotesque up in that studio, I can tell you."

"Have you heard the news, I say?" rapped out the doctor. "Boyg is dead."

Gale stopped in a sentence about Gothic architecture, and said seriously, with a sort of hazy reverence:

"Requiescat in pace. Who was Boyg?"

"Well, really," replied the doctor, "I did think every baby had heard of Boyg."

"Well, I dare say you've never heard of Paradou," answered Gale. "Each of us lives in his little cosmos with its classes and degrees. Probably you haven't heard of the most advanced sculptor, or perhaps of the latest lacrosse expert or champion chess player."

It was characteristic of the two men, that while Gale went on talking in the air about an abstract subject, till he had finished his own train of thought, Armitage had a sufficient proper sense of the presence of something more urgent to relapse into silence. Nevertheless, he unconsciously looked down at his notes; at the name of the advanced sculptor he looked up.

"Who is Paradou?" he asked.

"Why, the man I've been talking to this morning," replied Gale. "His sculpture's advanced enough for anybody. He's no end of a chap; talks more than I do, and talks very well. Thinks too; I should think he could do everything except sculpt. There his theories get in his way. As I told him, this notion of the new realism—"

"Perhaps we might drop realism and attend to reality," said Dr. Garth grimly. "I tell you Boyg is dead. And that's not the worst either."

Armitage looked up from his notes with something of the vagueness of his friend the poet. "If I remember right," he said, "Professor Boyg's discovery was concerned with fossils."

"Professor Boyg's discovery involved the extension of the period required for petrifaction as distinct from fossilization," replied the doctor stiffly, "and thereby relegated biological origins to a period which permits the chronology necessary to the hypothesis of natural selection. It may affect you as humorous to

123

interject the observation 'loud cheers,' but I assure you the scientific world, which happens to be competent to judge, was really moved with amazement as well as admiration."

"In fact it was petrified to hear it couldn't be petrified," suggested the poet.

"I have really no time for your flippancy," said Garth. "I am up against a great ugly fact."

Armitage interposed in the benevolent manner of a chairman. "We must really let Garth speak; come, Doctor, what is it all about? Begin at the beginning."

"Very well," said the doctor, in his staccato way. "I'll begin at the beginning. I came to this town with a letter of introduction to Boyg himself; and as I particularly wanted to visit the geological museum, which his own munificence provided for this town, I went there first. I found all the windows of the Boyg Museum were broken; and the stones thrown by the rioters were actually lying about the room within a foot or two of the glass cases, one of which was smashed."

"Donations to the geological museum, no doubt," remarked Gale. "A munificent patron happens to pass by, and just heaves in a valuable exhibit through the window, I don't see why that shouldn't be done in what you call the world of science; I'm sure it's done all right in the world of art. Old Paradou's busts and bas-reliefs are just great rocks chucked at the public and—"

"Paradou may go to—Paradise, shall we say?" said Garth, with pardonable impatience. "Will nothing make you understand that something has really happened that isn't any of your ideas and isms? It wasn't only the geological museum; it was the same everywhere. I passed by the house Boyg first lived in, where they properly put up a medallion; and the medallion was all splashed with mud. I crossed the market-place, where they put up a statue to him just recently. It was still hung with wreaths of laurel by his pupils and the party that appreciates him; but they were half torn away, as if there had been a struggle, and stones had evidently been thrown, for a piece of the hand was chipped off."

"Paradou's statue, no doubt," observed Gale. "No wonder they threw things at it."

"I think not," replied the doctor, in the same hard voice. "It wasn't because it was Paradou's statue, but because it was Boyg's statue. It was the same business as the museum and the medallion. No, there's been something like a French Revolution here on the subject; the French are like that. You remember the riot in the Breton village where Renan was born, against having a statue of him. You know, I suppose, that Boyg was a Norwegian by birth, and only settled here because the geological formation, and the supposed mineral properties of that stream there, offered the best field for his investigations. Well, besides the fits the parsons were in at his theories in general, it seems he bumped into some barbarous local superstition as well; about it being a sacred stream that froze snakes into ammonites at a wink; a common myth, of course, for the same was told about St. Hilda at Whitby. But there are peculiar conditions that made it pretty hot in this place. The theological students fight with the medical students, one for Rome and the other for Reason; and they say there's a sort of raving lunatic of a Peter the Hermit, who lives in that hermitage on the hill over there, and every now and then comes out waving his arms and setting the place on fire."

"I heard something about that," remarked Armitage. "The priest who showed me over the monastery; I think he was the head man there—anyhow, he was a most learned and eloquent gentleman—told me about a holy man on the hill who was almost canonized already."

"One is tempted to wish he were martyred already; but the martyrdom, if any, was not his," said Garth darkly. "Allow me to continue my story in order. I had crossed the market-place to find Professor Boyg's private house, which stood at the corner of it. I found the shutters up and the house apparently empty, except for one old servant, who refused at first to tell me anything; indeed, I found a good deal of rustic reluctance on both sides to tell a foreigner anything. But when I had managed to make the nature of my introduction quite plain to him, he finally broke down; and told me his master was dead."

There was a pause, and then Gale, who seemed for the first time somewhat impressed, asked abstractedly:

"Where is his tomb? Your tale is really rather strange and

dramatic, and obviously it must go on to his tomb. Your pilgrimage ought to end in finding a magnificent monument of marble and gold, like the tomb of Napoleon, and then finding that even the grave had been desecrated."

"He had no tomb," replied Garth sternly, "though he will have many monuments. I hope to see the day when he will have a statue in every town, he whose statue is now insulted in his own town. But he will have no tomb."

"And why not?" asked the staring Armitage.

"His body cannot be found," answered the doctor; "no trace of him can be found anywhere."

"Then how do you know he is dead?" asked the other.

There was an instant of silence, and then the doctor spoke out in a voice fuller and stronger than before:

"Why, as to that," he said, "I think he is dead because I am sure he is murdered."

Armitage shut his note book, but continued to look down steadily at the table. "Go on with your story," he said.

"Boyg's old servant," resumed the doctor, "who is a queer, silent, yellow-faced old card, was at last induced to tell me of the existence of Boyg's assistant, of whom I think he was rather jealous. The professor's scientific helper and right-hand man is a man of the name of Bertrand, and a very able man, too, eminently worthy of the great man's confidence, and intensely devoted to his cause. He is carrying on Boyg's work so far as it can be carried on; and about Boyg's death or disappearance he knows the little that can be known. It was when I finally ran him to earth in a little house full of Boyg's books and instruments, at the bottom of the hill just beyond the town, that I first began to realize the nature of this sinister and mysterious business. Bertrand is a quiet man, though he had a little of the pardonable vanity which is not uncommon in assistants. One would sometimes fancy the great discovery was almost as much his as his master's; but that does no harm, since it only makes him fight for his master's fame almost as if it were his. But in fact he is not only concerned about the discovery; or rather, he is not only concerned about that discovery. I had not looked for long at the dark bright eyes and keen face of that quiet young man before

I realized that there was something else that he is trying to discover. As a matter of fact, he is no longer merely a scientific assistant, or even a scientific student. Unless I am much mistaken, he is playing the part of an amateur detective.

"Your artistic training, my friends, may be an excellent thing for discovering a poet, or even a sculptor; but you will forgive me for thinking a scientific training rather better for discovering a murderer. Bertrand has gone to work in a very workmanlike way, I consider, and I can tell you in outline what he had discovered so far. Boyg was last seen by Bertrand descending the hillside by the water-course, having just come away from the studio of Gale's friend the sculptor, where he was sitting for an hour every morning. I may say here, rather for the sake of logical method than because it is needed by the logical argument, that the sculptor at any rate had no quarrel with Boyg, but was, on the contrary, an ardent admirer of him as an advanced and revolutionary character."

"I know," said Gale, seeming to take his head suddenly out of the clouds. "Paradou says realistic art must be founded on the modern energy of science; but the fallacy of that—"

"Let me finish with the facts first before you retire into your theories," said the doctor firmly. "Bertrand saw Boyg sit down on the bare hillside for a smoke; and you can see from here how bare a hillside it is; a man walking for hours on it would still be as visible as a fly crawling on a ceiling. Bertrand says he was called away to the crisis of an experiment in the laboratory; when he looked again he could not see his master, and he has never seen him from that day to this.

"At the foot of the hill, and at the bottom of the flight of steps which runs up to the hermitage, is the entrance to the great monastic buildings on the very edge of the town. The very first thing you come to on that side is the great quadrangle, which is enclosed by cloisters, and by the rooms or cells of the clerical or semi-clerical students. I need not trouble you with the tale of the political compromise by which this part of the institution has remained clerical, while the scientific and other schools beyond it are now entirely secular. But it is important to fix in your mind the fact itself: that the monastic part is on the very edge of the town, and the other part bars its way, so to speak, to the inside of the town. Boyg could not possibly have gone past that secular barrier, dead or alive, without being under the eyes of crowds who were more excited about him than about anything else in the world. For the whole place was in a fuss, and even a riot for him as well as against him. Something happened to him on the hillside, or anyhow before he came to the internal barrier. My friend the amateur detective set to work to examine the hillside, or all of it that could seriously count; an enormous undertaking, but he did it as if with a miscroscope. Well, he found that rocky field, when examined closely, very much what it looks even from here. There are no caves or even holes, there are no chasms or even cracks in that surface or blank stone for miles and miles. A rat could not be hidden in those few tufts of prickly pear. He could not find a hiding-place; but for all that, he found a hint. The hint was nothing more than a faded scrap of paper, damp and draggled from the shallow bed of the brook, but faintly decipherable on it were words in the writing of the Master. They were but part of a sentence, but they included the words, 'will call on you tomorrow to tell you something you ought to know.'

"My friend Bertrand sat down and thought it out. The letter had been in the water, so it had not been thrown away in the town, for the highly scientific reason that the river does not flow uphill. There only remained on the higher ground the sculptor's studio and the hermitage. But Boyg would not write to the sculptor to warn him that he was going to call, since he went to his studio every morning. Presumably the person he was going to call on was the hermit; and a guess might well be made about the nature of what he had to say. Bertrand knew better than anybody that Boyg had just brought his great discovery to a crushing completeness, with fresh facts and ratifications; and it seems likely enough that he went to announce it to his most fanatical opponent, to warn him to give up the struggle."

Gale, who was gazing up into the sky with his eye on a bird, again abruptly intervened.

"In these attacks on Boyg," he said, "were there any attacks on his private character?"

"Even these madmen couldn't attack that," replied Garth with some heat. "He was the best sort of Scandinavian, as simple as a child, and I really believe as innocent. But they hated him for all that; and you can see for yourself that their hatred begins to appear on the horizon of our inquiry. He went to tell the truth in the hour of triumph; and he never reappeared to the light of the sun."

Armitage's far-away gaze was fixed on the solitary cell half-way up the hill. "You don't mean seriously," he said, "that the man they talk about as a saint, the friend of my friend the abbot, or whatever he is, is neither more nor less than an assassin?"

"You talked to your friend the abbot about Romanesque sculpture," replied Garth. "If you had talked to him about fossils, you might have seen another side of his character. These Latin priests are often polished enough, but you bet they're pointed as well. As for the other man on the hill, he's allowed by his superiors to live what they call the eremitical life; but he's jolly well allowed to do other things, too. On great occasions he's allowed to come down here and preach, and I can tell you there is Bedlam let loose when he does. I might be ready to excuse the man as a sort of a maniac; but I haven't the slightest difficulty in believing that he is a homicidal maniac."

"Did your friend Bertrand take any legal steps on his suspicions?" asked Armitage, after a pause.

"Ah, that's where the mystery begins," replied the doctor.

After a moment of frowning silence, he resumed. "Yes, he did make a formal charge to the police, and the Juge d'Instruction examined a good many people and so on, and said the charge had broken down. It broke down over the difficulty in most murders. Now the hermit, who is called Hyacinth, I believe, was summoned in due course; but he had no difficulty in showing that his hermitage was as bare and as hard as the hill-side. It seemed as if nobody could possibly have concealed a corpse in those stone walls, or dug a grave in that rocky floor. Then it was the turn of the abbot, as you call him, Father Bernard of the Catholic College. And he managed to convince the magistrate that the same was true of the cells surrounding the college quadrangle, and all the other rooms under his control. They were all like empty boxes, with barely a stick or two of furniture; less than usual, in fact, for some of the sticks had been broken up for the bonfire demonstration I told you of. Anyhow, that was the line of defence, and I dare say it was well conducted, for Bernard is a very able man, and knows about many other things besides Romanesque architecture; and Hyacinth, fanatic as he is, is famous as a persuasive orator. Anyhow, it was successful, the case broke down; but I am sure my friend Bertrand is only biding his time, and means to bring it up again. These difficulties about the concealment of a corpse—Hullo! Why here he is in person."

He broke off in surprise as a young man walking rapidly down the street paused a moment, and then approached the café table at which they sat. He was dressed with all the funereal French respectability: his black stove-pipe hat, his high and stiff black neckcloth resembling a stock, and the curious corners of dark beard at the edges of his chin, gave him an antiquated air like a character out of Gaboriau. But if he was out of Gaboriau, he was nobody less than Lecocq; the dark eyes in his pale face might indeed be called the eyes of a born detective. At this moment, the pale face was paler than usual with excitement, and as he stopped a moment behind the doctor's chair, he said to him in a low voice:

"I have found out."

Dr. Garth sprang to his feet, his eyes brilliant with curiosity; then, recovering his conventional manner, he presented M. Bertrand to his friends, saying to the former, "You may speak freely with us, I think; we have no interest except an interest in the truth."

"I have found the truth," said the Frenchman, with compressed lips. "I know now what these murderous monks have done with the body of Boyg."

"Are we to be allowed to hear it?" asked Armitage gravely.

"Everyone will hear it in three days' time," replied the pale Frenchman. "As the authorities refuse to reopen the question, we are holding a public meeting in the market-place to demand that they do so. The assassins will be there, doubtless, and I shall not only denounce but convict them to their faces. Be there yourself, monsieur, on Thursday at half-past two, and you will learn how one of the world's greatest men was done to death by his enemies. For the moment I will only say one word. As the great Edgar Poe said in your own language, 'Truth is not always in a well.' I believe it is sometimes too obvious to be seen."

Gabriel Gale, who had rather the appearance of having gone to sleep, seemed to rouse himself with an unusual animation.

"That's true," he said, "and that's the truth about the whole business."

Armitage turned to him with an expression of quiet amusement.

"Surely you're not playing the detective, Gale," he said. "I never pictured such a thing as your coming out of fairyland to assist Scotland Yard."

"Perhaps Gale thinks he can find the body," suggested Dr. Garth, laughing.

"Why, yes, in a way," he said; "in fact, I'm pretty sure I can find the body. In fact, in a manner of speaking, I've found it."

Those with any intimations of the personality of Mr. Arthur Armitage will not need to be told that he kept a diary; and endeavoured to note down his impressions of foreign travel with atmospheric sympathy and the *mot juste*. But the pen dropped from his hand, so to speak, or at least wandered over the page in a mazy desperation, in the attempt to describe the great mob meeting, or rather the meeting of two mobs, which took place in the picturesque market-place in which he had wandered alone a few days before, criticising the style of the statue, or admiring the sky-line of the basilica. He had read and written about democracy all his life; and when first he met it, it swallowed him like an earthquake. One actual and appalling difference divided this French mob in a provincial market from all the English mobs he had ever seen in Hyde Park or Trafalgar Square. These Frenchmen had not come there to get rid of their feelings, but to get rid of their enemies. Something would be done as a result of this sort of public meeting; it might be murder, but it would be something.

And although, or rather because, it had this militant ferocity, it had also a sort of military discipline. The clusters of men voluntarily deployed into cordons, and in some rough fashion followed the command of leaders. Father Bernard was there, with a face of bronze, like the mast of a Roman emperor, eagerly obeyed by his crowd of crusading devotees, and beside him the wild preacher, Hyacinth, who looked himself like a dead man brought out of the grave, with a face built out of bones, and cavernous eye-sockets deep and dark enough to hide the eyes. On the other side were the grim pallor of Bertrand and the rat-like activity of the red-haired Dr. Garth; their own anti-clerical mob was roaring behind them, and their eyes were alight with triumph. Before Armitage could collect himself sufficiently to make proper notes of any of these things, Bertrand had sprung upon a chair placed near the pedestal of the statue, and announced almost without words, by one dramatic gesture, that he had come to avenge the dead.

Then the words came, and they came thick and fast, telling and terrible; but Armitage heard them as in a dream till they reached the point for which he was waiting; the point that would awaken any dreamer. He heard the prose poems of laudation, the hymn to Boyg the hero, the tale of his tragedy so far as he knew it already. He heard the official decision about the impossibility of the clerics concealing the corpse, as he had heard it already. And then he and the whole crowd leapt together at something they did not know before; or rather, as in all such riddles, something they did know and did not understand.

"They plead that their cells are bare and their lives simple," Bertrand was saying, "and it is true that these slaves of super-stition are cut off from the natural joys of men. But they have their joys; oh, believe me, they have their festivities. If they cannot rejoice in love, they can rejoice in hatred. And everybody seems to have forgotten that on the very day the Master van-ished, the theological students in their own quadrangle burnt him in effigy. In effigy."

A thrill that was hardly a whisper, but was wilder than a cry, went through the whole crowd; and men had taken in the whole meaning before they could keep pace with the words that fol-lowed.

"Did they burn Bruno in effigy? Did they burn Dolet in effigy?"

Bertrand was saying, with a white fanatical face. "Those martyrs of the truth were burned alive for the good of their Church and for the glory of their God. Oh, yes, progress has improved them; and they did not burn Boyg alive. But they burned him dead; and that is how they obliterated the traces of the way they had done him to death. I have said that truth is not always hidden in a well, but rather high on a tower. And while I have searched every crevice and cactus bush for the bones of my master, it was in truth in public, under the open sky, before a roaring crowd in the quadrangle, that his body vanished from the sight of men."

When the last cheer and howl of a whole hell of such noises had died away, Father Bernard succeeded in making his voice heard.

"It is enough to say in answer to this maniac charge that the atheists who bring it against us cannot induce their own atheistic government to support them. But as the charge is against Father Hyacinth rather than against me, I will ask him to reply to it."

There was another tornado of conflicting noises when the eremitical preacher opened his mouth; but his very tones had a certain power of piercing, and quelling it. There was something strange in such a voice coming out of such a skull-and-crossbones of a countenance; for it was unmistakably the musical and moving voice that had stirred so many congregations and pilgrimages. Only in this crisis it had an awful accent of reality, which was beyond any arts of oratory. But before the tumult had yet died away Armitage, moved by some odd nervous instinct, had turned abruptly to Garth and said, "What's become of Gale? He said he was going to be here. Didn't he talk some nonsense about bringing the body himself?"

Dr. Garth shrugged his shoulders. "I imagine he's talking some other nonsense at the top of the hill somewhere else. You mustn't ask poets to remember all the nonsense they talk."

"My friends," Father Hyacinth was saying, in quiet but penetrating tones. "I have no answer to give to this charge. I have no proofs with which to refute it. If a man can be sent to the guillotine on such evidence, to the guillotine I will go. Do you fancy I do not know that innocent men have been guillotined? M Bertrand spoke of the burning of Bruno, as if it is only the enemies of the Church that have been burned. Does any Frenchman forget that Joan of Arc was burned; and was she guilty? The first Christians were tortured for being cannibals, a charge as probable as the charge against me. Do you imagine because you kill men now by modern machinery and modern law, that we do not know that you are as likely to kill unjustly as Herod or Heliogabalus? Do you think we do not know that the powers of the world are what they always were, that your lawyers who oppress the poor for hire will shed innocent blood for gold? If I were here to bandy such lawyer's talk, I could use it against you more reasonably than you against me. For what reason am I supposed to have imperilled my soul by such a monstrous crime? For a theory about a theory; for a hypothesis, for some thin fantastic notion that a discovery about fossils threatened the everlasting truth. I could point to others who had better reasons for murder than that. I could point to a man who by the death of Boyg has inherited the whole power and position of Boyg. I could point to one who is truly the heir and the man whom the crime benefits; who is known to claim much of the discovery as his own; who has been not so much the assistant as the rival of the dead. He alone has given evidence that Boyg was seen on the hill at all on that fatal day. He alone inherits by the death anything solid, from the largest ambitions in the scientific world, to the smallest magnifying glass in his collection. The man lives, and I could stretch out my hand and touch him."

Hundreds of faces were turned upon Bertrand with a frightful expression of inhuman eagerness; the turn of the debate had been too dramatic to raise a cry. Bertrand's very lips were pale, but they smiled as they formed the words:

"And what did I do with the body?"

"God grant that you did nothing with it, dead or alive," answered the other. "I do not charge you; but if ever you are charged as I am unjustly, you may need a God on that day. Though I were ten times guillotined, God would testify to my innocence; if it were by bidding me walk these streets, like St. Denis, with my head in my hand. I have no other proof. I can call no other witness. He can deliver me if He will."

There was a sudden silence, which was somehow stronger than a pause; and in it Armitage could be heard saying sharply, and almost querulously:

"Why, here's Gale again, after all. Have you dropped from the sky?"

Gale was indeed sauntering in a clear space round the corner of the statue with all the appearance of having just arrived at a crowded At Home; and Bertrand was quick to seize the chance of an anti-climax to the hermit's oratory.

"This," he cried, "is a gentleman who thinks he can find the body himself. Have you brought it with you, monsieur?"

The joke about the poet as detective had already been passed round among many people, and the suggestion received a new kind of applause. Somebody called out in a high, piping voice, "He's got it in his pocket"; and another, in deep sepulchral tones, "His waistcoat pocket."

Mr. Gale certainly had his hands in his pockets, whether or no he had anything else in them; and it was with great non-chalance that he replied:

"Well, in that sense, I suppose I haven't got it. But you have."

The next moment he had astonished his friends, who were not used to seeing him so alert, by leaping on the chair, and himself addressing the crowd in clear tones, and in excellent French:

"Well, my friends," he said, "the first thing I have to do is to associate myself with everything said by my honourable friend, if he will allow me to call him so, but the merits and high moral qualities of the late Professor Boyg. Boyg, at any rate, is in every way worthy of all the honour you can pay to him. Whatever else is doubtful, whatever else we differ about, we can all salute in him that search for truth which is the most disinterested of all our duties to God. I agree with my friend Dr. Garth that he deserves to have a statue, not only in his own town, but in every town in the world."

The anti-clericals began to cheer warmly, while their opponents watched in silence, wondering where this last eccentric development might lead. The poet seemed to realize their mystification, and smiled as he continued:

"Perhaps you wonder why I should say that so emphatically. Well, I suppose you all to have your own reasons for recognizing this genuine love of truth in the late professor. But I say it because I happen to know something that perhaps you don't know, which makes me specially certain about his honesty."

"And what is that?" asked Father Bernard, in the pause that followed.

"Because," said Gale, "he was going to see Father Hyacinth to own himself wrong."

Bertrand made a swift movement forward that seemed almost to threaten an assault: but Garth arrested it, and Gale went on, without noticing it.

"Professor Boyg had discovered that his theory was wrong after all. That was the sensational discovery he had made in those last days and with those last experiments. I suspected it when I compared the current tale with his reputation as a simple and kindly man. I did not believe he would have gone merely to triumph over his worst enemy; it was far more probable that he thought it a point of honour to acknowledge his mistake. For, without professing to know much about these things, I am sure that it was a mistake. Things do not, after all, need all those thousand years to petrify in that particular fashion. Under certain conditions, which chemists could explain better than I, they do not need more than one year, or even one day. Something in the properties of the local water, applied or intensified by special methods, can really in a few hours turn an animal organism into a fossil. The scientific experiment has been made; and the proof is before you."

He made a gesture with his hand, and went on, with something more like excitement:

"M. Bertrand is right in saying that truth is not in a well, but on a tower. It is on a pedestal. You have looked at it every day. There is the body of Boyg!"

And he pointed to the statue in the middle of the market-place, wreathed with laurel and defaced with stones, as it had stood so long in that quiet square, and looked down at so many casual passers-by.

"Somebody suggested just now," he went on, glancing over a

sea of gaping faces, "that I carried the statue in my waistcoat pocket. Well, I don't carry all of it, of course, but this is a part of it," and he took out a small object like a stick of grey chalk; "this is a finger of it knocked off by a stone. I picked it up by the pedestal. If anybody who understands these things likes to look at it, he will agree that the consistency is precisely the same as the admitted fossils in the geological museums."

He held it out to them, but the whole mob stood still as if it also was a mob of men turned to stone.

"Perhaps you think I'm mad," he said pleasantly. "Well, I'm not exactly mad, but I have an odd sort of sympathy with madmen. I can manage them better than most people can, because I can fancy somehow the wild way their minds will work. I understand the man who did this. I know he did, because I talked to him for half the morning; and it's exactly the sort of thing he would do. And when first I heard talk of fossil shells and petrified insects and so on, I did the same thing that such men always do. I exaggerated it into a sort of extravagant vision, a vision of fossil forests, and fossil cattle, and fossil elephants and camels; and so, naturally, to another thought: a coincidence that somehow turned me cold. A Fossil Man.

"It was then that I looked up at the statue; and knew it was not a statue. It was a corpse petrified by the curious chemistry of your strange mountain stream. I call it a fossil as a loose popular term; of course I know enough geology to know it is not the correct term. But I was not concerned with a problem of geology. I was concerned with what some prefer to call criminology and I prefer to call crime. If that extraordinary erection was the corpse, who and where was the criminal? Who was the assassin who had set up the dead man to be at once obvious and invisible; and had, so to speak, hidden him in the broad daylight; Well, you have all heard the arguments about the stream and the scrap of paper, and up to a point I have entirely followed them. Everyone agreed that the secret was somewhere hidden on that bare hill where there was nothing but the grass-roofed studio and the lonely hermitage; and suspicion centered entirely upon the hermitage. For the man in the studio was a fervent friend of the man who was murdered, and one of those rejoicing most heartily at what he had discovered. But perhaps you have rather forgotten what he really had discovered. His real discovery was of the sort that infuriates friends and not foes. The man who has the courage to say he is wrong has to face the worst hatred; the hatred of those who think he is right. Boyg's final discovery, like our final discovery, rather reverses the relations of those two little houses on the hill. Even if Father Hyacinth had been a fiend instead of a saint, he had no possible motive to prevent his enemy from offering him a public apology. It was a believer in Boygism who struck down Boyg. It was his follower who became his pursuer and persecutor; who at last turned in unreasonable fury upon him. It was Paradou the sculptor who snatched up a chisel and struck his philosophical teacher, at the end of some furious argument about the theory which the artist had valued only as a wild inspiration, being quite indifferent to the tame question of its truth. I don't think he meant to kill Boyg; I doubt whether anybody could possibly prove he did; and even if he did, I rather doubt whether he can be held responsible for that or for anything else. But though Paradou may be a lunatic, he is also a logician; and there is one more interesting logical step in this story.

"I met Paradou myself this morning; owing to my good luck in putting my leg through his skylight. He also has his theories and controversies; and this morning he was very controversial. As I say, I had a long argument with him, all about realism in sculpture. I know many people will tell you that nothing has ever come out of arguments; and anyhow, if you want to know what has come out of this, you've got to understand this argument. Everybody was always jeering at poor old Paradou as a sculptor and saying he turned men into monsters; that his figures had flat heads like snakes, or sagging knees like elephants, or humps like human camels. And he was always shouting back at them, 'Yes, and eyes like blindworms when it comes to seeing your own hideous selves! This is what you *do* look like, you ugly brutes! These are the crooked, clownish, lumpish attitudes in which you really do stand; only a lot of lying fashionable portrait-painters have persuaded you that you look like Graces and Greek gods.' He was at it hammer and tongs with me this morning; and I dare say I was lucky he didn't finish that argument with a chisel. But anyhow the argument wasn't started then. It all came upon him with a rush, when he had committed his real though probably unintentional killing. As he stood staring at the corpse, there arose out of the very abyss of his disappointment the vision of a strange vengeance or reparation. He began to see the vast outlines of a joke as gigantic as the Great Pyramid. He would set up that grim granite jest in the market-place, to grin for ever at his critics and detractors. The dead man himself had just been explaining to him the process by which the water of that place would rapidly petrify organic substances. The notes and documents of his proof lay scattered about the studio where he had fallen. His own proof should be applied to his own body, for a purpose of which he had never dreamed. If the sculptor simply lifted the body in the ungainly attitude in which it had actually fallen, if he froze or fixed it in the stream and set it upon the public pedestal, it would be the very thing about which he had so bitterly debated; a real man, in a real posture, held up to the scorn of men.

"That insane genius promised himself a lonely laughter, and a secret superiority to all his enemies, in hearing the critics discuss it as the crazy creation of a crank sculptor. He looked forward to the groups that would stand before the statue, and prove the anatomy to be wrong, and clearly demonstrate the posture to be impossible. And he would listen, and laugh inwardly like a true lunatic, knowing that they were proving the utter unreality of a real man. That being his dream, he had no difficulty in carrying it out. He had no need to hide the body; he had it brought down from his studio, not secretly but publicly and even pompously, the finished work of a great sculptor escorted by the devotees of a great discoverer. But indeed, Boyg was something more than a man who made a discovery; and there is, in comparison, a sort of cant even in the talk of a man having the courage to discover it. What other man would have had the courage to undiscover it? That monument that hides a strange sin, hides a much stranger and much rarer virtue. Yes, you do well to hail it as a true scientific trophy. That is the statue of Boyg the Undiscoverer. That cold chimera of the rock is not only the abortion born of some horrible chemical change; it is the outcome of a nobler experiment, which attests for ever the honour and probity of science. You may well praise him as a man of science; for he, at least, in an affair of science, acted like a man. You may well set up statues to him as a hero of science; for he was more of a hero in being wrong than he could ever have been in being right. And though the stars have seen rise, from the soils and substance of our native star, no such monstrosity as that man of stone, heaven may look down with more wonder at the man than at the monster. And we of all schools and of all philosophies can pass it like a funeral procession taking leave of an illustrious grave and, like soldiers, salute it as we pass."

THE
PATRON
SAINT
OF
THE
IMPOSSIBLE

BY RUFUS KING

THE MURDER BACKDROP WAS THE FLORIDA ROOM OF THE HOFFMANN home in Halcyon, which is a small Florida town composed of the modestly retired, seasonal tourists, native crackers, horse-happy railbirds, amiable bookies, and glazed divorcées. It rests, this gentle haven, on the Atlantic seaboard between the gilt splendors of Miami Beach and the ormolu patina of Fort Lauderdale.

The Hoffmann house is one of the older and more pretentious of Halcyon's estates, being surrounded with lush masses of semi-tropical shrubbery and flowering trees that afford a screening of privacy from neighbors.

The hour when Monsignor Lavigny became involved in the crime (he lived directly to the east of the Hoffmanns) was eight o'clock on a Tuesday morning in April, during a tranquil moment in which the Monsignor was annoying several aphids on his Bella Romana camellias with a nicotine spray. Sunshine slanted gently onto his silver-crested head and distinguished appearance, which bore a nostalgic resemblance to the late Walter Hampden in his portrayal of Cardinal Richelieu.

The people involved in the tragedy he knew very well. They were Candice Hoffmann, the murdered man's teen-age niece-and-ward, and a black-browed athletic young ox with the romantic name of Raul Eusebio Fuentes, who was the Hoffmanns' neighbor to the west.

The youngsters were, of course, in love. It was the first and therefore the fiercest sort of blind emotion on Candice's part, but hardly the first on Raul's, whose reservoir of sentiment had begun operations in his birthplace in the Oriente province of Cuba at the tender age of twelve. This in no fashion diluted the young man's intensity, nor the passionate resentment he held toward Hoffmann (now a corpse) over Hoffmann's refusal to consent to his ward's marriage while she remained a minor and legally under his skeletal thumb.

Perhaps skeletal was a touch extreme, as Monsignor Lavigny believed that Hoffmann's air of fleshlessness, both physically and in the amenities, was basically due to the man's several ailments, among which was a rickety heart, and all of which combined to make him a decidedly acid character.

It was a character to be deplored even for its lesser sins of pride, conceit, and a miserly grip on possessions both human and material. So convinced was Hoffmann of his control over his body that he even refused to acknowledge the existence of physical pain. As for the parading of any bodily deficiency, that was out of the question. And yet, in spite of it all, Monsignor Lavigny had always looked upon Hoffmann as a soul to be enticed into the fold. Difficult, and now (thanks to a bashed skull) beyond further attempt.

The fourth member of the blood-tinged masque was Hoffmann's wife, Elise. She seemed a brave and handsome asset, much younger than her husband, and a woman whom Monsignor Lavigny considered to have been a bride of circumstance. Just what the circumstances were that induced her into a marriage with Hoffmann he did not know, but he imagined they had lain within the periphery of economics, perhaps of loneliness, perhaps of some fortuitous avenue of escape. Gratitude also was a possible explanation—but never love.

The curtain rose at eight in the morning on the tooting of an automobile horn.

Monsignor Lavigny left the outraged aphids in a state of suspended peace, and responded with a wave to the gloved hand of Elise Hoffmann as she drove by in her foreign convertible, heading for home. The glimpse of her cotton-crisp freshness and gaily insolent excuse-for-a-hat blended pleasingly with the tone of the morning.

As he later told his young friend Stuff Driscoll, chief criminal investigator for the sheriff's department, not many minutes seemed to have passed before the Monsignor heard the scream.

Even across the distance that separated the two houses, the scream came clearly through the dulling flora as one of shock mingled with horror.

The prelate cast dignity to the winds and broke into a lope that halted at the open jalousies of the Hoffmann Florida room, where the scene was appallingly similar to the final curtain of a Greek tragedy.

Elise Hoffmann, still hatted and gloved, stood stage center and had been turned, apparently, into a pillar of stone. At her feet, with his acid face flecked with blood, lay Hoffmann, flat as only the dead can lie flat. Then to complete the ghastly tableau, under an archway leading into a central hall, young Candice was stretched out on terrazzo tiling in a state of collapse.

The pillar of stone swayed as shock began to recede from Elise. Her clouded eyes seemed to clear as she focused them upon Monsignor Lavigny.

"He ran out," she said. "He struck Candice brutally—senselessly—"

"Who did, Elise?"

There was a flicker of irritation in her voice, as though the answer should be obvious.

"Why, Raul, of course."

"The thought is beyond belief," Monsignor Lavigny said to Stuff Driscoll as they sat in the Lavigny patio eating cashew nuts and drinking cooled Chablis.

"The evidence proves otherwise, Father." (The prelate preferred the usage of that title by his friends rather than Monsignor, with the latter's stiltedness and variety of mispronunciations.) "I am sorry about it, too, because I know you like the bum."

"Bum? No, never that. Patriot, if you wish. Raul is a youngster who is deeply, devoutedly in love and hence unpredictable, but he is neither a killer nor a bum."

Stuff, whose mind and experience inclined him to the dogma that a fact was ruler-straight, could never accustom himself to Monsignor Lavigny's ability to throw a few curves across the plate. There had been that child-kidnaping case last year, the beach robbery of the Terressi diamonds the year before . . .

"What has patriotism got to do with it?" he asked skeptically, even while filing the thought for further consideration. "Raul Fuentes has been naturalized and living here for years."

"Perhaps it has everything to do with it. Or nothing. There is a parable—"

Stuff interrupted with a certain firmness, but still within the limits of respect. Monsignor Lavigny's parables were notoriously of interminable length. "Father, let me give you the picture as we are turning it over to the county prosecutor. I think you'll agree that the job was one of passion? Balked love, then murderous hate?"

"Yes, with some reservations."

"But what's left? Money? Profit? Neither motive figures. Whatever else he is, Fuentes is a rich kid, and Candice is a wealthy girl. Just happens she is under age. They could elope and get hitched by some J.P. up in Georgia but they're both sincerely religious, and surely such a marriage would not be acceptable in the eyes of the Church. Especially with her guardian forbidding it."

Monsignor Lavigny absently inclined his head.

"Actually," Stuff went on, "they had no alternative but to persuade Hoffmann to change his decision. Do you know his reasons for objecting to the match?"

"I did talk with him, and it is possible to understand his point of view."

"It makes good sense to me, too. Elise Hoffmann discussed it while you were staying over at the Sacred Heart with Candice." (This was the hospital where the young girl had been taken.) "Consider Raul's actions. He's in his early twenties and rich, but where does the money come from?"

"Why, from his paternal estate in Cuba, as I understand it."

"So he says. Then why within the past year did he set up a phony ranch in the boondocks west of Davie? Why does he keep a plane there which he pilots himself, and a camouflage stable of mixed-up plugs strictly out of old milk routes?"

Monsignor smiled blandly. "Hope springs eternal, especially on the race track."

"Now that's nonsense, Father, and you know it. If one of those antique platers even caught sight of a starting gate he'd collapse from fright. And what about Raul's habit of disappearing for a day, or a week, and then side-stepping questions as to where he was or why? According to Mrs. Hoffmann, even Candice can't dig it out of him."

"There are certain things that cannot be discussed except," Monsignor Lavigny murmured, "in the confessional. If I may refer to certain of the martyrs—"

"Fuentes? A martyr? In my book the guy's up to his neck in some sort of a racket."

"My reference was oblique."

"Well, there was nothing oblique about the three-cornered row Elise Hoffmann overheard yesterday morning before she drove over to Pompano. She got a load of it while she was packing her bag in her bedroom. Hoffmann, Candice, and Fuentes were in the patio just outside her windows. Fuentes gave them *both* the works, the gist being that Hoffmann either change his mind, or Candice agree to forego the Church and elope, and then he tacked on the threadbare old cliché 'or else.'"

"The boy was overwrought. In his heart he did not mean it."

"Father, Father!" Stuff's tone was kindly with pity. "The evidence proves that Raul was sitting right at the table this morning while Hoffmann ate breakfast, and where he was killed."

"Did any of the servants—but they couldn't have. I remember that they are gone."

"Yes, the staff left yesterday to open up the Hoffmann summer place on Sea Island. The family were to drive up there today, which is why Elise Hoffmann made her early start back from Pompano." Stuff studied Monsignor Lavigny with a slight frown. "You have something on your mind, Father?"

"There is a definite contradiction. Please explain your conviction that Raul was seated at the breakfast table with Hoffmann."

"For one thing, you yourself were told by Mrs. Hoffmann that the man she saw escaping was Fuentes."

"The poor woman was in a state of shock."

"We'll have further confirmation when Candice recovers consciousness. But even if Candice didn't see who struck her, there is the circumstantial evidence of the drinking glass, and you can't get around it."

"What glass?"

"First, let's follow Elise Hoffmann's story. She waves hello to you as she drives by and you wave back. She puts her car in the garage, then carries her overnight bag into the house. She passes Candice's room and knows the girl is in it because through the closed door she hears Candice's portable TV set turned on. She leaves her bag in Hoffmann's and her suite, figures he's breakfasting in the Florida room, and goes there. You know what she found."

"A shocking, hideous thing!"

"She is stunned into senselessness. I will admit—in fact, she admits it herself—that her vision may have become blurred by the shock. She sees this figure who she thinks is Fuentes, and the drinking glass proves he *was* Fuentes, doing a quicksilver exit toward the archway where he bumps into Candice, bashes her with some sort of metal bar, and beats it as Mrs. Hoffmann gets back her vocal powers and starts to screech."

Monsignor Lavigny said patiently, "The glass?"

"Yes, the all-important glass. Now get this, Father. The breakfast table was laid for one, or Hoffmann. Candice had her own tray in her bedroom. Apart from other things like coffee and toast, there were a pitcher of orange juice and two glasses on the table. Both glasses had been used and each still contained some juice. One glass was beside Hoffmann's plate. The other was across the table where someone else had been sitting."

"Surely it was Candice, joining her uncle in a glass of orange juice after having prepared his breakfast?"

"No, Father—no on a couple of counts. Apart from the fact that she was probably in a huff over yesterday's row and therefore steering clear of Hoffmann, Elise Hoffmann tells me that Candice dislikes any citrus fruit or juice. All of which is purely academic, due to the fingerprints."

"On the second glass?"

"Yes. There are those of Fuentes where he held it while drinking. They have been identified by comparison with ones found on objects in his bathroom and on silver toilet articles on his dresser. Now this is the clincher, Father. There are *also*—on that second glass, mind you—prints of the thumb and three fingers of Hoffmann's left hand, put there when he poured the orange juice into the glass and handed it to Fuentes."

Monsignor Lavigny's eyes were clouded. He said softly, "The contradictions increase."

"We think," Stuff continued, "that Fuentes stepped over to renew his demands of yesterday, or possibly to apologize and make peace with Candice. We think that somehow Hoffmann had discovered the nature of Fuentes's racket, the reason in back of his unexplained disappearances, and threatened exposure if the kid didn't agree to give Candice up. Well, you know Fuentes. You can imagine how his hot Spanish blood took over." Stuff felt sudden contrition at the expression on Monsignor Lavigny's kindly face. "Do not take it so hard, Father. Isn't it possible even for you to be mistaken in a man's character?"

"I am not mistaken, but I am a bewildered and a deeply disturbed old man."

"There's nothing to be bewildered about, Father."

Monsignor Lavigny disagreed, speaking with difficulty, as though he were trying to establish for himself a sounder belief in what he was saying. "At the Sacred Heart after several hours that I spent at Candice's bedside there was one moment, brief but perfectly sane and clear, when consciousness returned."

"She spoke? She recognized you?"

"She did. She said she had heard a crash as if someone had fallen—obviously her uncle when he was killed. It took a moment or two for the sound to register, then she ran out of her bedroom and got as far as the archway to the Florida room when she was struck on the head and knew nothing further."

"She didn't see who it was?"

Monsignor Lavigny spoke more hesitantly, as though reluctant to go on. "I must tell you that at this point her voice weakened in answer to my question as to whether her attacker might have been Raul. She said that that was impossible, that Raul was in New York City this morning, that—*she had seen him there*. Then her voice faltered and she relapsed into coma. She has been so every since."

"Obviously it was delirium speaking, just a hallucination."

"Perhaps, and yet you have not found Raul out at his house, nor out at his ranch. And," Monsignor Lavigny added succinctly, "his plane is gone."

"Of course it is. When he fled from the Hoffmann's he would have driven directly out to the ranch and used the plane for escape."

Monsignor said with what, for him, held a quality of fierceness, "If it were only not for Elise Hoffmann's cloudy identification and the two sets of fingerprints on the glass!"

"An unsurmountable if, Father."

"Yes, perhaps. I can conceive that under certain provocation Raul might kill—but as for striking Candice, never!"

"He may not have known who it was—just heard a person running toward the archway and struck blindly. You're not exactly icy calm after you've just killed a man."

"I still cannot bring myself to accept it. I have had a sudden thought—it may be fantasy, and yet might lead us to the truth. Yes—I shall test it out. I shall be gone from here until tomorrow evening. And you, you will not be offended? Not think me officious if I make a few suggestions?"

"Why do you suppose I'm here? What are they, Father?"

"I would continue the search for the murder weapon or—what may even be of more importance—try to establish its absence from the place where it might normally be."

"I take it you have an idea what it was?"

"Forgive me if I seem evasive, but to be more specific at this moment might bring grievous injustice upon the innocent. I would suggest that you look for a glove that is perhaps stained with dark grease. Also, it might be advisable to consider the *types* of glasses that contained the orange juice."

"You are confusing me badly, Father."

"Have patience, and a reliance on your own excellent deductive powers. Your department has a plane at its disposal, has it not?"

"Yes."

"Then a flight to Sea Island might also be indicated, and a questioning of the Hoffmann staff."

Stuff looked at the prelate sharply. "Along any particular line?"

"Perhaps as to any unusual visitor who may have called at the Hoffmanns' during the past few weeks."

"Unusual in what way?"

"Let us say in the sense of being a stranger to the servants." Monsignor Lavigny grew deadly serious. "And this is the most important suggestion of all."

"Yes?"

"You might arrange with Mother Superior at the Sacred Heart to permit two women from your department, dressed in nursing habits, to alternate watches in keeping a constant guard over Candice. Never should she be left unattended in the company of *anyone*."

"There is a man posted there now, but we'll do as you say. Both Candice and Mrs. Hoffmann are under protection. And will be until Fuentes is caught."

"Until," Monsignor Lavigny murmured in polite correction, "the murderer is trapped."

"And you, Father? Where will you be while we're doing all this?"

Monsignor Lavigny's smile was both enigmatic and affectionate. His eyes held what Stuff later described as a beyond-the-horizon look.

"I am considering a pilgrimage accompanied by Saint Jude. He has helped me in the past, and I shall ask him to help me now. Saint Jude, as you know, is the patron saint of the impossible, of the seeming impasse. He is of inestimable assistance at a time when there seems no hope left."

The following evening, again in the patio with its velvet chiaroscuro of moonlight and the night-released scent of jasmine, Monsignor Lavigny sat in troubled contemplation absently sipping his after-dinner brandy and awaiting the arrival of Stuff Driscoll.

The prelate had paused at the Sacred Heart on his way home from the airport and had satisfied himself that Candice was under watchful observation by women from the sheriff's department in their borrowed nursing habits.

He had learned that the girl's condition remained unchanged, that the coma continued unbroken. Elise Hoffmann had been at the hospital and had also telephoned anxious inquiries a number of times, as had many of Candice's young friends. There had been (perhaps understandably) no message or inquiry from Raul Fuentes—this, even though the Hoffmann case continued to be front-page news.

Stuff came. He slumped into a chair, accepted brandy, and went directly to the point.

"Father, your suggestions have opened up a new slant. We believe now that Elise Hoffmann did the job, but the evidence is slim, entirely circumstantial, and a topflight trial counsel might easily get her off."

"My thoughts lay that way, too. I suspected, and I still suspect, a frame-up. The nature of it is almost clear, but not quite. We will find it exceedingly clever, the work of a truly devious mind. Is Mrs. Hoffmann under arrest?"

"No. She is under surveillance. We won't haul her in until we've got Fuentes. The case against that young buzzard is still too strong. Unless," Stuff added with a friendly grin, "your pilgrimage with Saint Jude cleared his slate?"

"To a certain extent it did—at least to my own satisfaction. I am infinitely grateful. When I flew to New York I carried with me a good photograph of Raul. Now then, I shall ask for your strict attention. You will remember Elise Hoffmann saying that when she passed the closed door of Candice's bedroom she heard a TV program going on inside?"

"Yes?"

"Well, it occurred to me that the broadcast might have offered a solution to Candice's apparent hallucination—when she told me that she, with herself being here in Halcyon, had *seen* Raul in New York City yesterday morning."

A light broke across Stuff's face. "You've hit it, Father—it was the right hour for the Dave Garroway program 'Today'—people in the street before the exhibition-hall window." (It should be noted that this occurred before the program had been moved to its new, its present quarters.) "Haven't I read, or seen—"

"Yes, there was nothing especially original in my thought, nor in the fact itself. I, too, have read of similar incidents—one in which

151

a spectator in a ringside seat at a televised prizefight was recognized by his wife, who was watching the program at home. She later divorced him, I believe, naming his rather notorious lady companion at the bout as corespondent. No, the thought was nothing new, but it served as a possible lead to casting doubt on Elise Hoffmann's eyewitness identification of Raul."

"What was the result?"

"Mr. Garroway was most courteous, most kind—as were Mr. Lescoulie and Mr. Blair. They studied Raul's picture, and *did remember a man who might have been he.* They had noticed the man because of his gestures."

"But why on earth would Fuentes risk showing himself on a nationwide hookup if he wanted to keep his 'mysterious' absences secret? It doesn't make sense."

"A man in love often makes no sense. He was asking forgiveness."

"Of Candice?"

"Yes, forgiveness for his tantrum with its hotheaded 'or else.' He knew Candice's habit of watching that broadcast, and took a chance on her doing so yesterday morning. Raul's gestures were quite compelling in, Mr. Garroway informed me, an operatic fashion. A Latinesque pantomiming of forgive-me-and-I-love-you, done with bravura."

"Would they make the identification under oath in court, or by sworn affidavit?"

"No. I asked. They would hesitate to do so. There would be in their minds too strong an element of uncertainty. In my own mind there is none."

"At least the kid's got one strike in his favor. Then there's the hotel he must have stayed at, or his friends. He should be able to prove an alibi."

"He might not be willing to."

"Why on earth not, Father?"

"He may flatly refuse to talk about his business in New York or his contacts there."

"He'd better. Because if he doesn't, the two sets of fingerprints on that second glass will knock our case against Elise Hoffmann into the nearest ashcan."

"Just what have you got on her so far?"

Stuff gave the prelate a concise account. The murder weapon had been found. Its place of concealment was in a large clump of star jasmine. It was a jack bar, and had been searched for specifically because of its absence from where it should have been (as Father had suggested), along with the jack in the trunk compartment of Elise Hoffmann's car.

There was more. The two glasses were of different types. No gloves were found, but they could have been disposed of later and at greater leisure than the jack bar.

The Sea Island questioning of the Hoffmann staff revealed that there *had* been a stranger. Ten days ago. He had been closeted with Hoffmann for over half an hour. No name, but the Hoffmann maid who had let him in had given a general description which included a noticeable cast in the man's left eye. Identification had proved simple. The man was a local private investigator, well known to the department and to Stuff personally. Up to the time of Hoffmann's death the man had been in Hoffmann's employ, his assignment to obtain evidence for a divorce. A Miami Beach character, a young muscle-operator of the Hercules type, came into the picture as the "other man." This handsome hulk and a legal separation from the Hoffmann assets by divorce offered plenty of motive for the elimination of Hoffmann . . .

A houseboy interrupted. Mister Stuff was urgently wanted on the telephone.

Monsignor Lavigny, while Stuff went into the house, mused on all human frailty, deploring, yet understanding it very well. It was not for him to judge, certainly not for him to punish. That was within the province of the law, while the ultimate appeal lay in the discretion of God. What malignant germ was it that festered in the brain of murder? Never had it been isolated since the days of Cain. What flaw . . .

"Word from the office," Stuff said, rejoining him. "They caught Fuentes. His plane just landed at the ranch. He clammed up. A 'no comment' to end all 'no comments.' They put him in a car, started for headquarters, and he jumped. Now the boondocks have him, not us." Stuff smashed an angry fist into the palm of his hand. "One other report. The guard we've kept on Elise Hoffmann called in that she left the house and drove off in her convertible. It caught him without warning, too late to check on where she's heading. Father, we're doing just fine!"

Monsignor Lavigny stood up. "It would be wise for us to go to the Sacred Heart. On the way we can discuss the advisability of certain arrangements. I believe I can persuade Mother Superior to give her consent to them. Mrs. Hoffmann will take time to drive about while solidifying her next move. Before," he added softly, "she strikes again."

Owing to a regional wave of the Asian flu with its subsequent complications, and that vague bête noire labeled virus, even some of the corridors of the Sacred Heart held beds, and a suppressed air of tension pervaded the hospital. With it existed a certain laxity of the less imperative regulations, while a greater than usual ebb and flow of traffic—nurses, sisters, interns, orderlies, visiting relatives, an occasional doctor—gave the place a semblance of Grand Central Station during what would have been a normally quiet evening hour.

Candice Hoffmann had been fortunate in having been placed in a private room, one vacated by a fatal case of pneumonia. It was a pleasant, impersonal room, its main furnishings being a hospital bed, a dresser, a locker, and some chairs. There were two doors, one to the corridor, the other to a private bathroom. There was about the room an aseptic openness that made concealment impossible.

Two windows, open to the trade wind with its odors of the flowering night, were frames for pale moonlight, while a shaded night lamp washed faint amber across the bed's white pillow and the white-bandaged head with its contusion-marked face resting motionlessly upon it.

Stuff and Monsignor Lavigny stood in the bathroom, in a state of tense expectancy. The bathroom door was opened a crack, sufficiently for them to have a view that included the bed and the corridor door. The two men were continuing an argument in whispers.

"Father, it is still a crime against the federal government."

"Technically, yes. But isn't it the *intention* that truly constitutes a crime? More so, even, than the crime itself? Remember that Raul has been running guns and ammunition to the rebels at his own expense, paying for them out of his own pocket. There has never been any question of illicit gain. Granted, he is a naturalized citizen, but his roots go back to Cuba. He feels that his family and many of his friends have suffered intolerable injustices from the present regime."

"A case of patriotism once-removed."

"Precisely. And precisely why he would rather suffer death than betray his rebel contacts by revealing the truth about his 'mysterious' disappearances. So far there exists no proof of his activities and he will never speak. Just as I, except for your trusted and confidential ear, shall never speak."

A sudden pressure of Stuff's fingers on Monsignor Lavigny's arm brought immobility and silence.

Elise Hoffmann looked in, satisfying herself that the room, with the exception of the patient, was empty. She had been keeping the door under observation for the past five minutes from an inconspicuous post in the traffic-filled corridor, after having noted the departure from the room of a nurse who presumably had arranged her patient for the night.

She came inside and closed the door. A few hurried footsteps carried her to the bed where in fumbling haste her hands pulled the pillow from under the bandage-swathed head, while her dark, abandoned eyes flickered in apprehensive observation between pale windows and the closed corridor door.

She pressed the pillow firmly down on the bruise-marked face.

There was no movement, no struggle. A noise made Mrs. Hoffmann look toward the bathroom door which, remarkably, now stood open with, more remarkably still, that sheriff's man, Mr. Driscoll, framed there with a Leica camera leveled against one eye. Then he was saying, almost casually, "All right, Miss Brown. I have it. You can get up now."

The strong arms of Miss Brown (sheriff's dept., physical ed. grad., adept at judo) gave a practiced shove, knocking Elise Hoffmann backward and into a fortuitously located chair.

Extraordinary, the mind, the nerves of a murderer, with what fierce egomaniac clinging to avoid punishment, to save his neck until the last ditch failed! Those were Monsignor Lavigny's thoughts as he watched Elise Hoffmann stiffen into an icy rage on the chair while, assisted by Stuff, Miss Brown was unswathed from bandages and cleaned of the grease-paint bruise marks that had camouflaged her face.

"I was rearranging the pillow more comfortably," Elise Hoffmann said in a clear frigid tone. "Seeing you quite naturally gave me a shock. Unconsciously I put the pillow down. That photograph you have just taken, Mr. Driscoll, shall be the basis of a suit I shall bring against your office."

No, there was not even a quiver, much less a break. Elise Hoffmann's control was superb and it was perfectly obvious that she intended to fight right on to the well-known last ditch.

Stuff took over.

Dispassionately, courteously, he outlined the case against her, tracing the probable moves, both physical and mental, that she had gone through.

Her years of oppression under Hoffmann's domination, with a fretful hatred inevitably building up. The threat of imminent divorce proceedings, ruining her share under the community property laws between man and wife.

(*Elise Hoffmann did not even start to break. She sat as a figure of chiseled stone, waiting for an idiot to finish with his maunderings. And Monsignor Lavigny again had that over-the-horizon look.*)

Stuff continued. Opportunity presented itself with the morning of the servant-free house, when the staff would be gone to Sea Island, when Candice would, as was her habit, be breakfasting while watching TV in her bedroom, when Hoffmann would be breakfasting alone in the Florida room.

Opportunity aligned itself with the fortuitous fight overheard among Fuentes and Candice and Hoffmann. Fuentes stepped immediately into the role of being groomed as Suspect Number One for the proposed crime.

Then the actual, and this time the true steps. After passing Monsignor Lavigny with a toot of her horn and a good-morning hand wave, the car was garaged. The jack bar was removed from the trunk compartment.

(*Elise Hoffmann's face remained a superciliously interested mask. Monsignor Lavigny had begun to mutter quietly in his Richelieu beard.*)

Candice was, as expected, in her bedroom. Hoffmann was, as expected, breakfasting alone in the Florida room. Not much of a blow on the head was required to cause death—his rickety heart contributed to the result. He toppled sideways off the chair and crashed down to the floor. Then the sound of running footsteps—Candice. A hasty flattening against the wall beside the archway and a blow with the jack bar as Candice ran through —a blow to silence her as an eyewitness to the immediate picture of the crime.

(*Elise Hoffmann smiled. Monsignor Lavigny's muttering grew faintly feverish.*)

Stuff resolutely went on. Not yet the screams. First, the run outdoors to conceal the jack bar among the jasmines. Then the hurried return to the Florida room with the assuming of a horror-stricken pose. Then the screams.

Stuff's recapitulation was a dud.

In the hush of the room, as Stuff's voice died out, Elise Hoffmann laughed. A cold, amused, diamond-hard laugh.

"Isn't there a rather important piece of evidence omitted, Mr. Driscoll? Even the newspaper accounts have played it up quite strongly. I refer, of course, to the second glass."

Yes, Stuff realized, her bastions of defense still held. She would never yield while the contradiction offered by the fingerprints remained unresolved. Disheartedly he noticed that Monsignor Lavigny's mutterings were approaching the decipherable. They seemed to be a murmured supplication to Saint Jude. Then the prelate's voice exploded with the effect of a minor bomb.

"I have it! The solution to the second glass. The glass was," he said, "a different type from the one beside your husband's plate, because it came from no set of glassware in your house."

"Merely an odd one, Monsignor," Elise Hoffmann said indifferently. "A leftover from a former set."

Monsignor Lavigny wrapped himself in the full dignity of his high office. His voice might remotely be said to have thundered.

"Madame, we are through with lies! You had determined to make Raul Fuentes the scapegoat. You could not place him physically upon the scene, so you placed an object he had handled upon the scene. I am convinced that you stopped at Raul's house as you started off for Pompano with the direct intention of picking up just such an object. You had the excuse of mediating the quarrel that had shortly occurred. But you did not need the excuse. You found him gone. You were able unobserved to find and take a glass, probably from his bathroom shelf. It is conceivable that its pattern will match a set in use in his house.

"You were wearing driving gloves of chamois, the ones you wore when you waved to me, the ones you have since destroyed. You carried that glass with you to Pompano, guarding and preserving Raul's fingerprints with some protective such as a scarf.

"After you had killed your husband and struck Candice down, you concealed the jack bar, got the glass, poured orange juice into it and set it on the table—*after*, I am convinced, you pressed your dead husband's fingerprints upon it to indicate that he had filled and handed the glass to Raul."

"You are convinced," Elise Hoffmann said. "But will a jury be?"

"They will be because you made one fatal error. When you pressed your husband's fingerprints upon the glass *two of those prints were superimposed upon those of Raul*. Proving that Raul's were on the glass first, and that your husband's were put upon it after his death. You look ill, madame—and well you may!"

She broke completely.

The moon continued its coursing through the scented night.

Raul had been intercepted, and released, in the hospital grounds while on his way to Candice. He was with her now in the room to which she had been transferred when the sheriff's Miss Brown had masqueraded in her place.

Scotch and soda rested on the patio table.

"Father, was it Saint Jude?"

Monsignor Lavigny's voice mellowed with a modest note. "I

am gratefully certain that it was. My own poor wits could never have achieved it of themselves."

"And I suppose," said Stuff, "that it was Saint Jude who cracked Elise Hoffmann's nerve? That it was not you, Father, who made the miraculous statement that two of Hoffmann's prints were superimposed upon those of Fuentes?"

Monsignor Lavigny's eyes were the essence of pious innocence as he said, "Well, weren't they?"

"They were not, Father—as you very well know."

TOO
MANY
COINCIDENCES

BY PAUL EIDEN

THE FUNERAL SERVICE WAS IN AN ANCIENT, DARK LITTLE CATHOLIC church on Washington Street in the Village. Starbuck watched Kathy carefully throughout the unfamiliar requiem, following her up and down from the kneeler in the back pew, although he was certain she knew little more about the service than he did. Starbuck's religion was mathematics.

He sensed the Mass was nearing its end when the priests and servers in their black vestments were down at the far end of the aisle opposite them, bearing a heavy book and a crucifix-tipped staff. It was then Starbuck took his first good look at the short, blond man on his left.

He had become aware of him when the man first slid into the pew, his hat in his hand, bowing hesitantly, a tentatively introductory smile on his lips. Starbuck knew at once that he had seen him somewhere before. Perhaps, he hazarded, at one of the wakes for Kathy's old room-mates. He darted looks at him throughout the Mass, now and then catching a half-smile on his thick, mobile lips, wishing he could tap Kathy on the arm and nod at her for her quick, remembering smile and the artful reintroduction.

Starbuck hated unresolved problems of any sort. Now, sensing imminent escape from the church, he tried to concentrate on the man. A faint odor clung to him. It reminded Starbuck of hospitals. A doctor perhaps? A friend of the dead nurse, or one of the others?

It was hopeless. Starbuck was used to doing his thinking in a nearly soundless air-conditioned office. The priest just beyond Kathy was chanting in Latin and an altar boy swung a censer filled with burning incense that overcame and banished the smell that seemed to cling to the blond man's clothes. Starbuck was left wondering if he had imagined it, as the priests and servers went up the nave and into the chancel.

The pallbearers—six solemn, hulking Irish youths—brought the casket down to the foot of the aisle then. He could feel Kathy begin to sob beside him, as it was borne out into the sudden sunlight of the opened doors and the undertaker began calling out the carloads for the procession to the cemetery. Starbuck took his young wife's arm and led her out through a side door. The blond man followed them out.

Kathy had not seen the dead girl in more than a year. Even last night at the wake, the coffin had been sealed. *I don't blame them,* Starbuck had thought. *Four days in the water.* He had felt nothing at all at the wake or the funeral. He never did. Now, vaguely embarrassed, he wondered how Kathy could be so emotional.

He saw with irritation that the blond man had not left them. Starbuck watched, as, still smiling faintly, the man touched his wife's forearm.

Kathy withdrew the tiny handkerchief with which she had been dabbing under her veil. Her eyes still wet, she smiled promptly at him. "Why, Mr. Carlson!"

Carlson ducked his head. "Very sad, very sad," he said.

Not a doctor, Starbuck's mind registered. "You've met my husband," Kathy was saying. "John Carlson, Alfred. Mr. Carlson was Pat Phelan's fiancé."

Starbuck shook his hand. Pat Phelan, one of the two that had been killed by the hit-and-run driver. "I wondered," Carlson was asking in a voice with a faint linguistic accent, "are you going out to the cemetery . . . ?"

"Yes," Starbuck told him. "But we have our own car."

"That's what I wanted to ask," Carlson said, speaking to Kathy. "Could you drive me out?"

"Why, of course," Kathy said with her quick friendliness, taking his arm.

The last of the rented limousines was pulling away from the church. Starbuck led them down Sixth Avenue to where he had parked the car, repressing a frown of annoyance. After the burial, he had a long drive back across Brooklyn to the Battery Tunnel. He couldn't be in the office much before one as it was, and he was sure Kathy would quickly volunteer a side trip to drop this stranger off anywhere he asked.

He had wanted Kathy, for her outgoing friendliness and fresh red-haired beauty, the first moment he saw her in the hospital; after eight years of marriage, her emotionalism and sentimentality were a constant reproof and minor annoyance to Starbuck's own closely-reasoned sense of order and convenience. She could have been satisfied with the church service this morning, he thought; but she had insisted on the trip out to the graveside, and, even after he got her back downtown, she would have another hour's cab ride back up to Riverdale.

She was chatting volubly with Carlson in the back seat as Starbuck swung the Lincoln into the line of the cortege. The blond man leaned forward to offer them cigarettes from his pack. In the rear vision mirror, Starbuck saw his faint smile become pronounced as Kathy accepted one from him. He decided he didn't like Carlson much.

Kathy chattered effortlessly with Carlson as Starbuck followed the limousines out over the Williamsburg Bridge and down Meeker to New Calvary. No, Carlson hadn't married since they saw him last. Yes, he was still working for the pharmaceutical firm as a detail man, contacting physicians. *Unsuccessful*, Starbuck catalogued him, and all but forgot him. Kathy touched the blond man's hand sympathetically. "You have to forget Pat, you know. You'll meet someone else, just as nice. Wait and see."

No one had ever had to reassure him he would marry someone as desirable as Kathy, Starbuck reflected. He had known it all through his long bachelorhood, just as he had known he would make himself a wealthy man. The matter of a wife could wait until he had the money. Long ago, he had read Voltaire's words: "A woman is never more sincere than when she is telling a millionaire: 'I love you.'" That had been the only reassurance Starbuck needed.

It was a cynical bit of wisdom which served Starbuck as a minor article of faith. The major article was that hard work and a cold faith in the logic of arithmetic would give him everything else that he wanted out of life. He had been right. Kathy was his wife. And for six years, he had been president of the fourth largest insurance company in America.

Mathematics was Starbuck's religion and logic its dogma; a sturdy staff, it supported him through all the storms and doubts of his career. It was to numbers and probabilities that Starbuck turned for strength. Take the question of Kathy's faithfulness to him. Or take the matter of her dead room-mates, for instance . . .

Take the poor bloated corpse in the hearse up ahead (Eileen. Eileen Something, wasn't it?) was the fourth one of Kathy's old nursing school room-mates to die in a little over two years. All young girls, under thirty. Five, if you counted back to the first one, years ago. The one whose death Kathy always referred to as "that horrible accident."

Starbuck remembered the consternation last summer when Kathy had mentioned the rate at which her old room-mates were dying off. They had a group of their friends out to their place on the Cape for a week-end—mostly Starbuck's fellow executives from the company, with their wives and young Quinlan from the legal department.

Smiling inwardly, Starbuck remembered his amusement. Really, it was amazing, but most people couldn't grasp the simplest equations in mathematical probabilities. Quinlan had become as excited as the women.

"My God!" he demanded accusingly, "aren't you worried at all? Four of her room-mates have died! Suppose something happens to her!"

Starbuck grinned at him tolerantly. "Isn't that silly, coming from an insurance man, Ed? Even one in the law office? Suppose all four had died of cancer. Would that increase Kathy's chances of dying of cancer?"

"But they've all died violently!" Quinlan exploded. "This first girl burned to death. Then the other was strangled to death in bed. And now two more run over by a hit-and-run driver!"

"Well?" Starbuck asked. "It's just a string of coincidences. Unlikely, of course, but the unlikely thing often happens in life." He looked around the group, an apostle expounding his gospel. "Their deaths don't alter Kathy's chances of living to a ripe old age. That would be like saying the chances of a roulette wheel stopping on red are increased because it has stopped on red four times in a row. Actually red's chances of turning up on the next spin are exactly the same as they ever were."

Starbuck smiled, warming at this chance to lecture. "In that example you are running into the principle of statistical independence—"

Behind their guests, Kathy smiled fondly and shook her head at him, the perfect hostess. Starbuck played to the older men for his laugh. "You draw dangerous—fatal—conclusions when you reason from too small a sample."

He got his laugh from the men, and even the wives seemed to relax, but young Quinlan was still in a flap. *"You're not worried? Suppose— Suppose . . . ?"*

"Suppose there's a curse on them?" Starbuck suggested urbanely enjoying himself. Really, Quinlan must read mystery novels. "Like the one on the men who opened King Tut's tomb?"

Quinlan had subsided then, but not without a fretful look at Kathy. Starbuck grinned reminiscently, turning the car onto Laurel Hill in the procession. It had been ridiculous, just another example of the way undisciplined thinkers jumped to conclusions from insufficient facts. Starbuck never let his judgment or his emotions run away from him like that. He kept them firmly in check.

Take this marital fidelity thing, for instance. After all, he was fifty-three and Kathy was only twenty-nine. What was more natural than that she should one day choose a lover? It was right there in Kinsey—although he had some reservations about Kinsey's data-gathering and his disdain of the probability sample. Starbuck ran the IBM machine of his mind for the card bearing the statistic he wanted. Accumulative Incidence: Extra-Marital Coital Experience, By Decade of Birth. Twelve per cent of the married women born between 1920 and 1929 had betrayed their husbands by the age of twenty-five.

Of course, the book had been compiled in 1953 and the findings did not extend beyond the age of twenty-five, but it seemed reasonable to extrapolate a percentage twice as large by age twenty-nine. The chances that Kathy would remain faithful to even a younger husband were, at best, no better than three out of four. There was a fact, and Starbuck liked to think that he had never grown emotional about a fact in his life.

He watched Kathy as the casket was lowered into the grave. Her face went white and she bit her lips, but no tears came. She was generally beyond the crying stage when they reached the cemetery.

All you could ask of a wife was that she be discreet about it when the time came. Starbuck rather suspected that Kathy had begun to cheat on him already. In his secret heart, he was proud of her for giving him not even the shadow of proof.

He had the Lincoln back on the highway, already thinking ahead to the work at the office, before Starbuck remembered Carlson. "Mr. uhh—uhh— Where can we drop you?"

The thick, flexible lips formed a deferential smile and Carlson ducked his head and said in his polite, faintly accented voice: "Anywhere at all. I am taking the rest of the day off."

The fool couldn't even make up his mind where he was going. "Well, I'm taking the car back down to Wall Street," Starbuck said curtly, conscious of Kathy's still white, troubled face. "I'm leaving it there, and then Mrs. Starbuck will be going back uptown by cab. Any place that's convenient for you."

Carlson raised his eyebrows. "Oh? You don't drive?" he asked Kathy. She shook her head absently. "Then, perhaps—a suggestion—I could drive you home in this fine car? It would save your husband trouble, too."

Kathy smiled broadly, instantly cheerful again. "Oh, wonderful! That's wonderful!"

Even Starbuck felt something like gratitude. He never brought the car to the office when it was avoidable. He hated the drive up or down in rush hour traffic. "Nice of you," he murmured.

He kissed Kathy and turned the keys over to Carlson at the corner of Wall and Broadway.

A thick sheaf of real estate reports on the company's properties across the nation waited on his desk. Starbuck turned from them in an oddly dilatory mood. He stood at the window for a long time, treasuring its panoramic view of the harbor, watching a rusty tramp plow toward the Narrows.

This had been his office since 1952; he had worked toward it for twenty-five years before that. Nearly two-thirds of Starbuck's life had been spent in this building. In the beginning there had been the long subway rides uptown to Columbia for that all-important first degree, then years more of nights afterwards at NYU, City College, mastering law, investment banking, real estate.

There was no ulcer. And he was eight years into the coronary bracket, Starbuck reminded himself smugly, without a first attack. Seven more years and he was past even that hurdle. In twelve he would be retired, moved up to chair the board. Kathy would be forty-one then, a dutiful, artfully unfaithful wife. He had everything he wanted.

Starbuck took an irritable turn around the office on the thick Persian rug, unable to attack the work on his desk. Something about today nagged at his mind, some danger signal. Angrily, hating it for the distraction, he assaulted it, free-associating.

The girl just buried, her swollen body crammed into her coffin? Supposedly, she had slipped off the ferry returning her from the night shift at the Staten Island Hospital. Starbuck snorted. If the company holding her policy paid off on that without the suicide clause first becoming effective they were criminal fools.

Nobody fell off the Staten Island ferry, unless they were pushed, and the girl had been alone. If he were the emotional, excitable type like Ed Quinlan, Starbuck knew, he could blame his disquiet on these successive deaths of Kathy's old friends. But there was nothing there, but a simple chain of coincidences.

Six girls, strangers, randomly assigned an apartment by a hospital personnel director. One commits suicide. Two others, the closest friends in the group, are smashed down by a hit-and-run driver, who is never apprehended. One slain in bed by a strangler, also never found. But the husband had been held a long time, hadn't he? Starbuck's mind challenged the coincidences. The police knew their business. The husband must have been guilty, even if they never found enough evidence to go into court.

And the first girl—that was nothing but a tragic, unforseeable accident. Some of the girls sharing the apartment—it was never made quite clear just which ones—had doused her with ether.

Starbuck remembered the joke from his high-school science days. A drop of ether on the bare flesh, or even on the clothes, gave the body a freezing chill, far more intense than the one you experienced when a masseur spills rubbing alcohol on your back.

The girls had failed to notice though, that their victim held a lit cigarette. The ether had caught instantly. The girl burned to death in the kitchen. A tragic, horrible accident.

Starbuck caught himself in midstride. Ether? That faint smell that had hung about Carlson when he first came into the church this morning, that had been overcome by the burning incense. It had reminded him somehow of hospitals. It could have been . . . It *was* ether! Starbuck felt the heavy stroke of his heart.

Now, wait a minute. This was the kind of lurid imagining that Ed Quinlan would supply. For this hypothesis to fit, Carlson would have to be some mad avenger out of a paper-back thriller, bent on executing Kathy in an ether immolation the same way the first girl had died.

There must be some other explanation. Too many implausibilities had to be explained. Carlson would have to be the murderer of four other girls. He would have to have known the first girl, loved her. Starbuck clawed his cheeks in an agony of recall. What did he remember of her?

Kathy had said she was shy, stand-offish, the butt of the group's teasing. There had been no family. But a fiancé, yes! Someone the other girls had never met, just a portrait on her dresser.

Starbuck sank into his chair, his disciplined, card-index memory racing. The fiancé? He had been a refugee. The last surviving member of a gypsy family that had disappeared into Hitler's concentration camp ovens. That could unhinge a mind. And, then, to have his girl die in the same way. It could start him on a mad search for vengeance against her killers—the whole group, whether guilty or innocent. Was it possible?

Starbuck remembered Carlson's accent, and panicked. He reached for the phone on his desk. But a gypsy. Carlson was blond. *A blond gypsy?* Starbuck sighed and settled back in the chair, shamefaced. Well, possible, of course, but just barely possible.

And what about the girl who was murdered? The husband had done that. Of course, the police couldn't prove it, and they released him, but that was no proof of innocence.

There was an implausibility for you: A *blond* gypsy, who *had to be driven insane* by an accidental murder to give him a motive, strangles a girl who was *probably murdered* by her husband.

But how do you explain the ether smell on him? Starbuck looked longingly at the phone. He could reach Kathy at home now. He wanted to call her.

To warn her? Of what? That a mad man with a bottle of ether in his pocket was about to murder her?

He knew Kathy. She would have chatted gaily with Carlson, all the way up the West Side Drive, glad of his company, as she was always glad of anyone's company. She wouldn't let him escape. He would have to come upstairs for coffee, tea, a drink. *And if he did have that ether . . .*

Suddenly, chillingly, Starbuck remembered the enigmatic smile on Carlson's face when Kathy accepted the cigarette from him. He had been so weirdly, unexplainably happy that she smoked!

"Are you all right, Mr. Starbuck?"

Mrs. Enlow, his secretary, was standing in the door, a soft, motherly frown on her face.

Starbuck's mind raced like a rat in a maze. This was insane. He had to convince himself that this wild speculation could not be true, that Kathy was safe at home, mixing a cocktail for Carlson.

"Would you like your coffee now?" Mrs. Enlow prodded him.

"Uh, yes." He had to talk to someone. Mrs. Enlow? No. "Would you ask young Quinlan, in Law, if he's not— Would you just tell him I'd like a word with him right away?"

There had to be some flaw in this mad hypothesis, Starbuck told himself. It broke every law of mathematical probability.

Carlson. Carlson. But, of course! Carlson had been the fiancé of one of those two girl friends who were run down by the hit-and-run driver. That was where Kathy knew him from. Surely, if he had been the first girl's fiancé, the fact would never have been hidden. They all would have certainly known him.

Starbuck smiled and leaned back in his chair. For a moment there, he had been on the point of calling the police, sending them rushing with sirens to his apartment. Wouldn't that have been a gorgeous mess!

This wild theory was certainly collapsing under a dead-weight of implausibilities. A *blond* gypsy, who *had to be driven insane,* who strangled a girl *murdered by another man,* and then ran down his own fiancée!

That exploded the Mad Avenger hypothesis, of course, but it didn't explain why Carlson should be so pleased to see Kathy take a cigarette, or why he should smell of ether.

Raggedly, Starbuck's mind went back to the problem. This fool theory had to crumble before a scientific, dialectical approach. None of the room-mates had ever *seen* the first girl's boy friend, Kathy said. Just a picture in her room. They could have forgotten his face. His appearance could have changed in a few years. He could have arranged to meet the other girl, make love to her, run her and the other down in a car.

But what about the last girl? The one buried today. She was a suicide. How could that fit in? But was she a suicide? There were no witnesses. *She could have fallen.*

But nobody falls off the Staten Island ferry.

She could have been pushed. Starbuck's hand snatched up the phone.

At his barked command, Mrs. Enlow, in the outer office, got his home number. He counted twelve rings before he dropped it back on the hand-set. Thursday, the maid's day off. There was no one there to answer until Kathy arrived. Unless she already was there, dead. Sweating, Starbuck glanced at his watch. She'd had time to get up to Riverdale. Barely.

"Good afternoon, sir." Quinlan stood in the door, blond and handsome and youthful in beautifully cut flannels.

"Of course," Starbuck said, and almost giggled. "Oh, of course."

Carlson had said he was a contact man for a drug outfit, calling on doctors. That accounted for the smell of ether about him. And the pleasure when Kathy accepted his cigarette? Well, just put it down to nervous relief. After all, Carlson was a man without much social poise, an unsuccessful foreigner riding in the car of a man like Starbuck.

"I beg your pardon?" Quinlan said.

Starbuck regretted the impulse that had caused him to send for this young fool. He felt shaken. He was aware of sweat on his palms and upper lip, a nervous trembling in his thighs and biceps. Were his nerves going? Was he losing his grip on a mind he had trained to function like a precision machine? Never, since he was a child, had Starbuck spent such a half-hour of fearful fantasying as this one just past.

At least he hadn't done anything foolish about summoning the police. It was a blessing he hadn't been able to reach Kathy on the phone. He had betrayed his lapse to no one. He set himself to chatting politely with Quinlan while they drank the coffee, already thinking of the work on his desk. Actually, Quinlan wasn't a bad young fellow. Pretty good lawyer.

Starbuck reached avidly for the stack of real estate reports when Quinlan left, and Mrs. Enlow had cleared off the cups. He should phone Kathy now. Husbandly check-up to see that she was home safe.

He listened to twenty unanswered rings before he disconnected.

"Mrs. Enlow," Starbuck said into the phone when her voice came back, "there's a Mrs. Kyle in my building. They have the other apartment on the floor. Would you ring her up for me, please? Mrs. Charles Kyle, I believe it is. And hurry, please."

Unreasonably, the fear was creeping back, but he was proud of the steadiness of his voice.

It took a long time for the woman's phone to be answered. Then Starbuck found himself talking to a soft, Negro maid's voice, tense and hard to understand because of a volume of unidentifiable background noise. It took a long time for Starbuck to make her understand who he was, and to whom he wanted to talk.

When Mrs. Kyle finally came to the phone, her voice was almost comically tearful. "Oh, Mr. Starbuck! That I should have to be the one to tell you!"

"What? Tell me what, for God's sake!"

"Can't you hear the sirens? There's a terrible fire in your apartment, Mr. Starbuck!"

Starbuck set the phone down. The expression on his face was that of a saint whose God had denied him.

THE
GREEN
SCARF

BY A. M. BURRAGE

WHEN THE WELLINGFORD FAMILY BECAME EXTINCT THE DAYS OF Wellingford Hall as one of the great country houses of England were already numbered. The estate passed into the hands of commercial-minded people who had no reverence for the history of a great house. The acres surrounding the hall became too valuable as building-sites to be allowed to remain as a park surrounding a country mansion. So the fat Wellingford sheep were driven elsewhere to pasture, and surveyors and architects heralded the coming of navvies and builders.

All this happened many years ago. The old park became crossed and crisscrossed by new roads, and perky little villas with names like "Ivyleigh" and "Dulce Domum" sprang up like monstrous red fungi. Even these have since mellowed, and grown their own ivy and Virginia creeper, and put on airs of respectable maturity. The Hall itself, forlorn and abandoned, like some poor human wretch deserted in his old age, began slowly to crumble into decay.

Wellingford Hall was no more than an embarrassment to the new owners of the estate, who were willing to let it or sell it at the prospective tenant's or purchaser's own price; but to dispose of a great house with no land attached to it and surrounded by a garden city is no easy matter. It was too big for its environment. After some vicissitudes as a private school and the home of a small community of nuns, it was abandoned to its natural fate: "for," said one of the directors of the Wellington Estate, Limited, a gentleman not above mixing his metaphors, "what was the sense of keeping a white elephant in a state of repair?"

Three years before this present time of writing came Aubrey

Vair, the painter, as poor as most other painters, a lover of old buildings and all the cobwebby branches of archaeology, and took Wellingford Hall at a weekly rental of fewer shillings than might be demanded for the use of a gardener's cottage. He knew one of the directors, and he had discovered that a few rooms in the middle of the block of buildings were still inhabitable. The directors, I suppose, wondered why anyone should wish to live in the damp-ridden, rat-riddled old hole, but they did not despise shillings, and they let him come.

Vair wrote me several letters, begging me to come down and rough it with him. It was just the place for a writer, he assured me; it would give me ideas. He had been searching after priests'-holes and had discovered no less than five. One of the great rooms made the finest studio he had yet painted in. And really, as regards comfort, he avowed, it wasn't so bad, so long as one came there already warned to expect only the amenities of a poor bachelor establishment. And then, he added temptingly, there were the historical associations.

I already knew something about the latter, having discovered my facts in a book dealing with old English country houses. Charles the First had spent a night there during the Great Civil War. Charles the Second was supposed to have hidden there after the battle of Worcester. But best of all was the romantic tale of the capture and execution of Sir Peter Wellingford in 1649.

Briefly, Sir Peter was a proscribed Royalist who lived hunted and in hiding after the failure of the royal arms. A wiser man would have crossed the Channel, but Sir Peter had a young wife at Wellingford Hall. He had often visited her in safety, and might have continued to do so, but for a traitor in his own household. This fellow, so the story went, betrayed his master by waving a green scarf from one of the windows, this being a prearranged signal to inform a detachment of Parliamentary troops that the head of the house was secretly in residence. The soldiers burst in at night, and ransacked the house before Sir Peter Wellingford was discovered in a hiding-hole—or "privacie" as the old chronicle described it. The cavalier was dragged outside and shot in his own courtyard.

Here was a story romantic enough to inveigle the fancy of most men with a grain of imagination. I fully intended to visit Wellingford Hall, but circumstances caused me to defer my intention for the first summer and it was not until the following May, when Vair had been in residence for a full year, that I paid him my deferred visit. I journeyed by road, driving myself in my small two-seater, so that Vair had no opportunity to meet me, and I had my first view of Wellingford Hall before I could be biased by his enthusiasm.

Holy Writ speaks of the abomination of desolation standing where it ought not; and here was this grim, forbidding, crumbling old ruin still surrounded by its moat and standing in the midst of jerry-built "Chumleighs" and "Rosemounts." It was like finding the House of Usher in the middle of a new garden city. In spite of its moat the Hall had never been intended for a fortress and the bridge I crossed must have been nearly as old as the house itself.

Vair heard me coming and pushed open the great nail-studded door under the archway of the main entrance to come and greet me with a grin and a handshake. He climbed up beside me and directed me round into the yard, where there was plenty of accomodation for a dozen cars. Strangely enough, the stables and coach-houses were in better repair than the old house itself.

The hall had once been magnificent, but most of the ceiling was gone, and the oak balustrade of the staircase, having a commercial value, had been long since removed. A trail of sacking across broken paving stones pointed the way to Vair's apartments beyond. He ushered me into a fine room, in quite a reasonable state of repair, furnished with products of his speculations at country auctions. Although the month was May the weather was none too warm, and I was glad of the sight of the log fire which lent the room an additional air of comfort. Vair laughed to hear me exclaim, and asked if I were ready for tea.

He lived there, he explained, entirely alone, except that a charwoman came each morning to do the rough work and cook his one hot meal of the day.

"You won't mind putting up with cold stuff and tinned things of an evening?" he asked anxiously.

I hate tinned foods, but, of course, I could not say so.

After tea Vair showed me the rest of the rooms which he had made habitable, and, really, he had managed to make himself much more comfortable than I had expected. He had contrived —Heaven knows how—to learn a lot of intimate history of the old place, and knew the name by which every room had been called in the house's palmy days of dignity and prosperity. My bedroom, for instance, was known as "Lady Ursula's Nursery," although history had long since forgotten who Lady Ursula was.

It was easy to see that Vair had a boyish enthusiasm for the place. He was a queer chap, with more than the average artist's share of eccentricities, and he believed in all manner of superstitions and pseudo sciences. He was one of those ageless men who might have been anything in the twenties, thirties, or forties. I happened to know that he was nearly fifty, but his thin wiriness of figure and boyish zest for life kept him youthful. Obviously his pleasure at having me down was not so much for my own sake as his. I was somebody to whom he could "show off" the house. He was clearly as proud of it as if it had been restored to its former dignity and he were the actual owner.

"For Heaven's sake, don't go about the place by yourself," he said, "or you'll break your neck. I've nearly broken mine a dozen times, and I'm beginning to know where it isn't safe to walk. It must be rather rare to find damp-rot and dry-rot in the same house, but we've got both here."

I promised faithfully that I wouldn't move without him. Even the main staircase did not appear too safe to me, but Vair assured me that it was all right.

After tea he took me over such parts of the house as it was safe to visit, but I shall make no attempt to describe most of this pilgrimage. My memory carries dreary pictures of damp and decay, of dust and dirt, and cobwebs, mouldering walls and crumbling floors. The old place must have been a warren of secret rooms and passages, and he showed me those he had discovered. All I can say is that the refugees of the bad old days must have been very uncomfortable, and those who escaped deserved to.

One large room under the roof, which we visited, had once been a secret chamber. It was called the Chapel, and here Mass had been said in defiance of the law throughout part of the sixteenth and seventeenth centuries.

"There must be a lot more secret rooms," Vair remarked. "Little Owen, who was a master at constructing such places, is known to have spent months here during the reign of Elizabeth. The house was always being raided, and the raiders had little satisfaction."

"They got the poor old cavalier," I laughed.

"Oh, yes. But he was given away, or sold, by a servant. I've shown you the place where I'm almost sure he hid—behind where the bed-head used to be in the room called the King's Chamber. We'll see if we can find some more while you're here, if you like."

It suddenly occurred to me that Vair had always called himself "sensitive," or psychic, and it was perhaps natural of me to put on the noncommittal smile of the polite sceptic and inquire if he had seen any ghosts. Rather to my surprise, he shook his head.

"No," he answered; "it isn't at all that kind of place. The house is quite friendly. I should have felt it at once if it had been otherwise."

"But I should have thought with its history—"

"Ah, it's seen troubled days, but they were always nice people who lived here. There are no dreadful legends of bloodshed and cruelty."

"There is the story of the cavalier," I objected. "Surely his ghost ought to haunt the place."

"Why? He was a good man from all accounts and he died a man's death. Only troubled or wicked people linger about the scenes of their earth-life. When he was taken out and slaughtered all the hatred and blood-lust came from *outside*. If any impressions of those spent passions remain, they're not inside the house, and I don't want them inside."

I smiled to myself, knowing that, from Vair's point of view, the house *ought* to be haunted, and his excuses for the non-appearance of a ghost or two struck me as ingenious but far-fetched.

"That's a pity," I said, tongue in cheek. "I quite hoped to be introduced to a Grey Lady or a Spectre Cavalier."

He frowned, knowing that I was laughing at him.

"Well, you won't be," he said, "unless—"

"Unless what?"

"Well, unless something happens to alter present conditions. If, for instance, we were to find something which someone long forgotten desired should remain hidden."

"I see."

"I doubt if you do. And I doubt if anything could be done now to disturb any of the Wellingfords in their long sleep. They seem to have been an ideal family; I haven't been able to find a word of scandal on any page of their history. Where there has once been bitterness and hatred, there you may look for ghosts. There was none here. All that came from outside. That frenzied desire, for instance, to trap and kill a man because he had fought for his king, long after his cause was well lost; that bitter bigotry which sought to prevent folk from worshipping according to their consciences. It all came from outside, I tell you!"

Vair's voice had risen. Like most men with no particular faith, he respected all creeds, and religious intolerance always moved him to violent anger. Respect for his deadly seriousness kept my face grave.

"Do you mean just outside?" I asked.

"How do I know? And so long as they remain outside what does it matter? I assure you, I don't want them brought in."

To my relief, he then veered away from a subject which was hardly within my scope of conversation. There was little of the mystic in me. All the same, when at last I retired to bed in Lady Ursula's nursery, I was glad to remember that Vair had given the house a clean bill of health in the psychic sense. By the time I had been Vair's guest for twenty-four hours I had begun to feel with him that the old ruin had a kindly and friendly atmosphere, in spite of its apparent gloom, and that this might have been the legacy of good people who had lived and died within its walls.

At the risk of giving this narrative an air of being disconnected, I must pass hurriedly over the next two or three days of my visit, for they brought forth little that is worth recording.

Sometimes Vair did a little painting, and then his preoccupation drove me to my own work. We did a little fishing and sometimes walked three-quarters of a mile to the Wellingford Arms where, according to Vair, who accounted himself an expert, the bitter beer was better than the average. Sometimes we risked our necks on rickety stairs and crumbling floors, looking for more secret hiding-places, an occupation in which I soon became infected with some of Vair's schoolboy zest.

The place was quiet enough during the day, but the villas and bungalows which had marched almost to the edge of the moat made themselves audible at night. Every Lyndhurst and Balmoral seemed able to boast of a musical daughter or a powerful gramophone. The effect of sitting in one of those dignified old rooms with the windows open and hearing echoes from the musical comedies was grotesque in the extreme. Vair had evidently grown used to it, for he made no comment.

I had arrived on a Saturday, and it was on the afternoon of the Tuesday following that, between us, we made a discovery of historical interest; a discovery which we came afterwards bitterly to regret having made. We were on the first floor landing, where long windows, deep in a recess, looked out over the Wellingford Park estate, when Vair mentioned that he had never examined the window-seats.

"Sliding panels," he said, "certainly have existed, but they belong mostly to fiction. They were too hard to construct and too easily discovered. Take the five hiding-places you've seen in this house. Three of them are behind fireplaces, one under the stairs, and the other must have been masked at one time by the head of a bedstead. Window-seats were very often used, and this one looks likely. Let's try it."

We rapped it with our knuckles, and although it did not sound hollow, there was obviously an empty space beneath it. We pushed and tugged and teased the surface of the wood with our fingers. And suddenly I saw a crack widen, and part of the seat which had fitted into the rest of the woodwork as neatly as a drawer came away in my hands, and we stared at each other with laughter and curiosity in our eyes.

"Hallo, what's this!" Vair exclaimed.

The cavity disclosed was very small. It was obviously not the entrance to any place of concealment capable of holding a human being. I lit a match and thrust it down into the darkness. Then cheek by jowl we peered together into a cavity no more than three feet deep.

"Nothing here," I said, breaking cobwebs as I moved my wrist to and fro.

"Isn't there!" exclaimed Vair.

He brushed me aside and his arm disappeared up to the shoulder. His hand was black when he drew it forth, and an end of something like a black rag was between his fingers. It was an old piece of silk, so rotten with age that it almost crumbled under our touch; but when we had blown on it and brushed it with our fingers we saw that it owed its present color to the dirt of ages, and that it had once been green. On the instant the old tale leaped into the minds of both of us, and we exclaimed together:

"The Green Scarf!"

I forget what we said for the first minute or two. We were both excited and elated. There is some peculiar pleasure, difficult to analyze or explain, in discovering a relic which serves to corroborate some old tale or passage of ancient history. We neither of us doubted that we had discovered the green scarf by which Sir Peter Wellingford had been betrayed nearly three hundred years before.

"The traitor must have kept it here in readiness," said Vair, his eyes dancing. "And when he'd signalled he dropped it back again, and there it has lain from that day to this."

"And most likely," I added, taking the relic from his hands, "this is the very window he waved from."

The window was open and I leaned out and let the dingy rag flutter from my hand in the warm afternoon breeze.

"Don't!" said Vair sharply, and pulled me back.

The silk was so rotten with age that even the weak breeze tore it slightly, and I thought at the time that Vair's sharp "Don't!" was uttered because of the damage I had unwittingly done. It was a relic of treachery and bloodshed, but we both regarded it with a queer sort of reverence, as if it were associated with something sacred.

I should think an hour must have passed before we mentioned anything else. We were both agreed that one of us should write to a newspaper announcing our discovery and that the scarf should be cleaned by an expert and offered to a museum. One remark of Vair's struck me at the time as a little strange, but the full force of it did not come to me until some hours later.

"I wish you hadn't waved it out of the window," he said. "It's what that damned traitor did. That's what made you do it, of course—trying to re-enact part of an old tragedy."

"I don't see that it matters," I returned lightly. "Nobody saw." He turned on me at once.

"*How do you know?*" he demanded sharply.

I could not help laughing then.

"My dear fellow," I exclaimed, "are you afraid that the wife or daughter of one of your neighbors will think—"

"I wasn't thinking of *them*," he returned curtly. "When that rag was waved out of that window nearly three hundred years ago, you know what happened, you know what it brought into the house."

I thought I had caught the drift of his meaning. Vair had always declined to walk under ladders or make the thirteenth of a party, and he was unhappy for days after he had spilled the contents of a salt-cellar.

"Oh, don't be an ass, Vair," I begged. "If there's any ill-luck about I give it leave to attack me and leave you alone."

He did not answer, and in a few minutes the incident had passed temporarily from my mind.

I have tried to tell this story so many times by word of mouth, and been compelled at this point to pause and hesitate, as now I am compelled to pause and think. It is not that my memory fails me; memory, indeed, serves me all too well. But hereabouts I am brought to realize the failure of my small command of words. A bad speaker can at least convey something otherwise unexpressed by look, gesture, hesitation, tone of voice. But with nothing but pen, ink, paper, and a limited vocabulary, I see little chance of giving an adequate account of what happened to us that night; of how with the twilight depression was laid upon us, straw by straw, and how with the coming of darkness horror was laid upon us, load by load.

Even before supper I found myself restless and ill at ease. Something began to weigh upon my spirit as if my mind carried the knowledge of some ordeal which I had presently to face. Of course, I put it down to an attack of "liver" and made up my mind to forget it. The intention was good, but it was unjustified by the desired result.

My discovery that Vair was suffering from a similar *malaise* did not help my own case. His spirits were far below normal, and I think our mutual discovery that the other was "below form" added weight to that which was already dragging at our hearts. To make matters worse we each began to act for the other's benefit, to force laughter, to crack heavy jokes, and make cumbersome epigrams. But when at twilight we lit the lamp and sat down to supper we tacitly agreed to give up pretending.

"Do you feel that there's a weight crushing you whenever there's thunder about?" Vair asked suddenly.

I was glad to think of some excuse to account for my mood, and answered quickly:

"Yes, very often. And I wouldn't mind betting there's some thunder about to-night."

Vair looked at me and seemed suddenly to change his mind over what he had been about to say. He shook his head.

"The glass hasn't gone down."

I rose from the table without apology, went to the window, pulled aside the curtains, and looked out. It was just after sunset on a very perfect May evening. There was a red glow in the west, and around this glow there was an area of sky which was almost apple-green. This merged into a very deep blue in which one or two pale stars were already beginning to play hide-and-seek.

"No," I agreed grudgingly, "there isn't a cloud in the sky. Still, storms come up very quickly."

"Yes," said Vair, "and so do other things."

My lips moved to ask him what he meant, but I thought better of it. Whatever morbid imaginings he might be entertaining, they were scarcely likely to help my own mood. We ate in silence, continuing thus for a long time before I forced a laugh and exclaimed:

"Well, we're a jolly pair, aren't we? What the devil's the matter with us this evening? I only wish I knew."

"I only wish I didn't think I knew," he answered strangely.

"Well, what do you think—"

"I think we ought to go out somewhere to-night and stay out."

"Why? You haven't felt like this before—"

"No. And it's because I haven't felt like this before—"

He came to another sudden pause, and we looked into each other's faces for a moment before he lowered his gaze.

"Now, look here," I said, trying to keep my voice steady, "let's be as honest as we can and try to analyse this thing. I'll say it first. We're both afraid of something."

He went a step further.

"We're both afraid of the same thing," he said.

"Well, what is it, then? Let's find it out and confront it. When a horse shies at a tree you lead him up to it and show him that it's only a tree."

"If it happens to be a tree or something like a tree. But if it isn't . . . Look here, let's go out. Straight away now, while there's time. They've got bed-rooms at the Wellingford Arms. Let's go and spend the night there."

With all my heart I wanted to. But Pride borrowed the voice of Reason and spoke for me.

"Oh, don't let's make fools of ourselves," I urged. "I for one don't want to truckle to my nerves. If we give way like this once we shall always be doing it."

He shrugged his shoulders.

"Let's have a drink."

He brought out the whiskey. I am a temperate man with a weak head for spirits, and I admit that I exceeded my usual allowance, but it made no more difference to me than if it were water. We sat facing each other gloomily in a silence which became increasingly difficult to break.

The unusual quality of this silence had already begun to impress me when Vair mentioned it, as if my thought had communicated itself to him.

"Don't you notice how extraordinarily still everything seems?" he asked presently.

"Yes," I agreed, and snatched suddenly at a straw. "The silence before the storm. There *is* a storm about, you see."

He shook his head.

"No," he said. "It isn't that kind of stillness."

And then, with a little leap of the heart and a tingling of the nostrils I suddenly realized a fact which seemed to me inexpressibly ugly. This stillness was not the hush of Nature before some electrical disturbance. For some time past we had heard no sound at all from the outer world. The gramophones and pianos in the little houses around us were all silent. It was the hour when at many houses on the estate hosts and guests were parting for the night, yet there was not the faint echo of a voice, nor the comfortable workaday sound of a car droning along a road. It may seem ludicrous, but I would have given a hundred pounds just then to hear the distant shunting of a train.

Vair rose suddenly, went to the window and looked out. I followed him. For some while now it had been completely dark. Overhead in a very clear sky the stars looked peacefully into our troubled eyes.

"No storm about," said Vair shortly.

He heard me catch my breath, and a moment later he was aware of what I had already perceived.

"Look! There aren't any lights! There isn't a light anywhere!"

It was true. The hour was not late, and yet from the rows of houses which began not so many yards distant, not a light was visible, nor was it possible to discern an outline of roof or chimney against the sky. We had been cut off from the lights and sounds of the outside world as completely as if we were in a cavern miles under the ground, save that our isolation—I can think of no other word—was lateral.

Vair's voice had risen high and thin. He made no effort to disguise the terror in it.

"There must be some fog about," I said; and I was so anxious lest my voice should sound like Vair's that I spoke out of the base of my chest.

"Fog! Look, man!"

I looked. Truly there was not the least sign of fog or mist. Until we raised our eyes to the sky we stared into impenetrable, featureless darkness.

Vair let the window curtains fall from his hand. He turned to me in the oppressive stillness, and his face worked until by an effort he controlled the muscles.

"Try and tell me," he said hoarsely, "*what* you've been feeling all evening."

"How can I? The same as you, I suppose!" A reminiscence of soldiering came back to me. "It's been like waiting to go over the top. A horrible aching anxiety. No, something more than that. A sense of being trapped, of being surrounded—"

"Surrounded!" He caught up the word with a cry. "That's just what you are! That's just what we both are!"

I drew him away from the curtained window.

"Surrounded? By what?" I made myself ask.

He spread out his hands and shook them helplessly.

"The Powers of Darkness, Hatred, Blood-lust, Intolerance—they were all waiting, waiting for the signal. Do you think these things die like spent matches? Do you think the black act of treachery, which brought them into this house, left nothing behind it. *They* were waiting—all these years—I tell you!" Suddenly he bared his teeth at me. "You fool, to have waved that rag at them!"

Just for a moment I felt my brain turning like a wheel, but I made a fight for my sanity and won it back.

"Look here," I said, "for God's sake don't let's behave like madmen. Let's get out of it if the house is going to affect us like this."

He stared back at me, giving me a look which I could not read.

"No," he muttered; "you wanted to stay."

"Let's go down to the Wellingford Arms."

"They're closed now."

"It doesn't matter. They know you. They'll open for you."

I found myself lusting for the world beyond that unnatural girdle of darkness. The Wellingford Arms with its vulgar tin advertisements of Somebody's Beer, and Somebody Else's Whiskey, and its framed Christmas Number plates—at least there was sanity there.

But Vair suddenly turned on me the eyes of a hunted animal.

"You fool!" he burst out. "It's too late! We can't pass through *them!*"

"What do you mean?" I faltered.

"They're all around us. You know it, too. They'll break in—in their own good time—as they did before. We're trapped, I tell you!"

Against my will, and Heaven knows how hard I fought for disbelief, Vair had captured my powers of reason. In theory, if not in action, I was now prepared to follow him like a child.

"What do they want?" I stammered.

"Us! One of us or both! What did Murder and Hatred and Blood-lust ever want but sacrifice?"

He fairly spat the worlds at me and I seized his arm.

"Come on," I said, "we're going to get out of this. We're going to run the gauntlet."

"Ah," said Vair thickly. "If we can."

We must have crossed the hall, although I do not remember it. My next recollection is of helping Vair in his fumbling with the bolts and lock of the great door. We wrenched it open and stood looking out at an opaque wall of darkness.

I tried to force myself across the threshold, only to find myself standing rigid. As in a nightmare, my legs were shackled so that I could not move a step forward, but although terror clawed at me like a wild beast, my senses were keenly and even painfully alert.

I knew that this belt of darkness around the house was alive with whisperings and movements, with all manner of stealthiness, which lurked only just beyond the horizon of vision and the limits of hearing. And as I stood straining eyes and ears I knew that the barriers must soon break and that I should see and hear.

We stood thus a long while on the edge of the threshold we

could not pass, but whether it were seconds or minutes I could not say. To us it seemed hours ere the darkness passed, melting into the living forms of men. We could *see*, and there was movement everywhere; we could *hear*, and voices were shouting orders, although the actual words eluded us. They were human voices with strange nasal intonations, snarling and shouting. Even in my extremity I remembered having heard the soldiery of Cromwell had affected a hideous nasal accent. And now the darkness was sundered and shivered by a score of lights, the lights of naked torches which nodded to the rhythm of men marching. I saw the glint of them on the metal heads of pikes, and on the long barrels of muskets outlined clearly now against a naked sky of stars.

Terror may bind a man to the spot, but another turn of the rack may torture him back into motion. So it was with us. Blind instinct alone made me slam the great door and shoot the nearest heavy bolt. I saw Vair groping for me like a tear-blinded child and I took his arm. We ran futilely back into the room we had vacated and crouched in the corner farthest from the door, while great noises like thunder began to reverberate through the house, as pike handles and musket-butts crashed sickeningly on the great outer door.

We must have taken leave of reason then, for neither Vair nor I can remember anything more until the great nail-studded door, smashed off its hinges, fell onto the broken flags of the hall with the loudest crash of all. The tramp of feet mingled with the sound of arms carelessly handled, thudding against floor and wall, and with the sharp nasal snarling of voices. In a moment it seemed they were everywhere—in the hall, on the main staircase, in the room over our heads.

Vair had all this time the grip of a madman on my wrist, and suddenly he leaned to me and screamed into my ear:

"*The Chapel . . . under the roof . . . it's consecrated . . . there's a chance . . . there's a chance, I tell you. . . .*"

"They're on the stairs!" I cried back in despair.

"The back stairs! Come on!"

A second door in the old room gave access to a passage leading to the back stairs. Those stairs we knew to be unsafe, but ordinary human peril was something far beyond and beneath our consideration. I remember the rumble and murmur of sounds about the house as we rushed out into the passage. Footfalls and voices sounded everywhere, and musket-butts were smiting heavily against walls and stairs. As we stumbled and ran I expected at every step to be seized and overwhelmed by some horrible and nameless Power.

How we reached the attic I cannot say. The narrow, crumbling staircase creaked and swayed under us, and once I went down thigh-deep through the rotten stairs, with splinters of hard wood tearing clothes and flesh. But we were near the top ere the hunt had scented their game and sounds of pursuit began to clamor behind us.

Vair forced open the door of the little room which had once been a chapel. I blundered in over his body, which lay prone just across the threshold. He had fallen unconscious, and I had to force his legs aside before I could close the door. I slammed it to in the faces of vague forms which filled the passage to the stair-head, and drove home the wooden bolt inside. And then it seemed to me that our pursuers recoiled from that closed door like a great wave from the base of a cliff, and ugly cries outside died down to uneasy whisperings—and instinctively I knew that we were safe.

I must have fainted then, for I remember nothing more until I woke in the bright sunshine. Vair was sitting beside me, watching me, with a chalk-like face. We hardly spoke, but sought each other's hands like frightened children.

Eventually we nerved ourselves to go downstairs into the ruin and disorder of the old house, through which, one might have thought, a whirlwind had passed during the night.

ROGUES' GALLERY

BY MACKINLAY KANTOR

NOW ONCE AGAIN MEYER CRUCIFIED THE CHRIST. HE ESTABLISHED the Crucifixion in moist sand on the banks of the Red Fox Creek, thirty-one miles from Chicago.

If he had been aware that this was to be his final work of art, the pathetic culmination of a long life in which dreams and sculpture and whiskey were inextricably confused, he could not have brought more tenderness and skill to the creation than he did bring.

He wrought well, did Meyer—with a rusty bucket and a sack of salt to harden the mixture, and makeshift sticks and paddles for delivering anguish and beauty out of a sand bank. He worked from dawn on into the late afternoon.

Meyer was building the attendant cherubs—life-size visages complete with wings and wonder—when the blue car stopped by the deserted sand-pit road, and the four young men got out with their golf bags.

There may have been blood on their hands, but Meyer could not see it. He saw only that they were hard-faced and nervous, that they wore open shirts and sweaters and flannel slacks like those worn by golfers on the near-by course. The zippers whistled in their bright leather bags, and out came ugly short-barreled guns, and out came money.

Money did not interest Meyer. He worked on, silently as an earthworm.

"It was Borelli cleaned that first cage," said Augie Shertz.

"Like hell," whined Borelli. "It was Pete."

Pete nodded. "I got it in this bag. A good twenty grand."

They lifted out the masses of fluttering banknotes: some were

194

wrapped, some were crumpled, some were twenties and some were hundreds. "You're the top!" Shertz snarled at Borelli. "Damn you, why'd you squirt at that old dame?"

"She started to run out the door."

"Never make a chair date when you don't have to. Some day you're gonna fry!"

"Come on, come on," Pete implored; "ain't it the same rap for everybody? Casey had already pushed over the teller and that old bank cop."

Shertz was estimating with a shrewd, opaque gaze. "Looks like sixty or seventy grand. But we shouldn't have left the silver in that first car—"

"The heat'll be on," Borelli prophesied. "On us, too. Even changing cars three times, and changing to golf clothes."

"We'll bust apart, at the golf links," Shertz told them. "Go back to town, each guy by himself. What are you squawking about, Borelli? Nobody dropped a handkerchief off of his face. We wore gloves; it's airtight."

Then it was that Casey Wilchinski, who was lookout at the entrance of the old sand pit, drew his automatic and said things out of the corner of his mouth. The other men turned with ready guns, and they discovered Da Vinci's Crucifixion—modeled life-size in the sunlit sand, with half-shaped cherubs lifting up their faces under the skillful turn of skillful fingers.

The men put their blue-steel muzzles to Meyer's head.

"Gonna lay quiet and then turn us in to the cops, wasn't you? Keep digging in the sand and then sing."

"You haff tramped mein statue," cried Meyer.

"Let him have it, then sling him in the weeds," Casey suggested.

Borelli said, "Wait! We got a split to make. It'll take time. Wait till we go. . . ."

"In Rome I studied," Meyer informed them. "In Paris, in Milan, in many places—"

"Yeh," Shertz kicked a foot from the recumbent statue, and the sand flew. "Maybe you never studied in Asbury Park, you old heel! If you'd had sense to make this sand statue somewhere else than off here in the weeds, you would have lived longer."

Meyer explained: "The sand, it vas so clean, so bright. . . . I make my great statue of Crucifixion! But nobody comes to see. I do not care." His thin shoulders quivered beneath the frayed, stained shirt.

"He's nuts," said Pete. "Look at that sign he's got stuck up: 'On this coat put nickel for a poor artist.' And there ain't nobody around here to put nickels on it, except snakes and things—"

Augie Shertz slid his gun back inside his waistband. "Sure, he's nuts. But just the same, he ain't gonna sing. We'll split the dough, and then—"

They split. It took a long while, but they watched with care, and not a car turned off the humming highway a half-mile beyond. Meyer crouched in his beloved sand, and watched, and worked. He was afraid of these men, but, more than that, he was angry because they had broken the foot of his statue, and had talked with no respect. He touched up the foot, and remodeled his choir of heavenly admirers. He hoped that these cruel young men would be punished for trampling the thing over which he had toiled, and which he knew to be beautiful.

After the money had been counted and divided (for none would trust the others to carry it to Chicago), the four young men abandoned their stolen car, tramped through the lonely weeds and woodland to mingle with the hordes of city-bound golfers who had spent a pleasant afternoon at the Red Fox Public Golf Course.

They killed Meyer before they left. They did it quickly, but he had been able to complete his task.

It was about one o'clock the next morning when three squads of detectives swooped down on the celebrants at the Chez Vienna restaurant, and gathered in Casey Wilchinski, Augie Shertz and Pete Skolnit. They would have gathered in Nick Borelli as well, but Borelli went haywire and reached for his gun, when somebody shoved a glistening badge under his nose. He had three slugs in him before he hit the floor.

The survivors howled and stammered as they were hauled into the squad cars. "Not a thing," they chanted. "You ain't got a thing on us! We'll be out in an hour."

"There was a bank stick-up on Milwaukee Avenue yesterday noon," said grey-haired old Sergeant Kahn. "Three people killed."

They screamed amid the sirens, "You can't hang that on us! You won't get a dime's worth on us. We're alibied!"

"There was an old tramp killed, yesterday afternoon," said Sergeant Kahn. "Some hikers found him, knocked on the head, away out by Red Fox Creek in the country. He was a queer old devil, kind of crazy. His name was Winky Meyer. And under the bridge by where Meyer was killed, there was paper ribbons and currency wrappers from the Milwaukee Avenue Householders' Savings Bank."

He told them, quietly, "Listen to this, rats! Old Winky Meyer made Crucifixions for a good many years. He was pretty good at it—even artists used to say so. And he made cherubs, always—four of them. . . . And this time, when the detectives saw his cherubs, they didn't look like any angels in heaven. They looked like you, Augie—and you, Casey and Pete—and like Borelli. They were your faces, and the old man had sculptured them in the sand before he died."

THE
APPLES
OF
THE
HESPERIDES

BY AGATHA CHRISTIE

HERCULE POIROT LOOKED THOUGHTFULLY INTO THE FACE OF THE man behind the big mahogany desk. He noted the generous brow, the mean mouth, the rapacious line of the jaw, and the piercing visionary eyes. He understood from looking at the man why Emery Power had become the great financial force that he was.

And his eyes falling to the long delicate hands, exquisitely shaped, that lay on the desk, he understood, too, why Emery Power had attained renown as a great collector. He was known on both sides of the Atlantic as a connoisseur of works of art. His passion for the artistic went hand in hand with an equal passion for the historic. It was not enough for him that a thing should be beautiful—he demanded also that it should have a tradition behind it.

Emery Power was speaking. His voice was quiet—a small, distinct voice that was more effective than any mere volume of sound could have been.

"You do not, I know, take many cases nowadays. But I think you will take this one."

"It is, then, an affair of great moment?"

Emery Power said, "It is of moment to me."

Poirot remained in an inquiring attitude, his head slightly on one side. He looked like a meditative robin.

The other went on.

"It concerns the recovery of a work of art. To be exact, a gold chased goblet, dating from the Renaissance. It is said to be the goblet used by Pope Alexander VI—Roderigo Borgia. He sometimes presented it to a favored guest to drink from. That guest, M. Poirot, usually died."

"A pretty history," Poirot murmured.

"Its career has always been associated with violence. It has been stolen more than once. Murder has been done to gain possession of it. A trail of bloodshed has followed it through the ages."

"On account of its intrinsic value or for other reasons?"

"Its intrinsic value is certainly considerable. The workmanship is exquisite (it is said to have been made by Benvenuto Cellini). The design represents a tree round which a jeweled serpent is coiled and the apples on the tree are formed of very beautiful emeralds."

Poirot murmured with an apparent quickening of interest, "Apples?"

"The emeralds are particularly fine, so are the rubies in the serpent, but of course the real value of the cup is its historical associations. It was put up for sale by the Marchese di San Veratrino ten years ago. Collectors bid against each other and I secured it finally for a sum equaling (at the then rate of exchange) thirty thousand pounds."

Poirot raised his eyebrows.

He murmured, "Indeed a princely sum! The Marchese di San Veratrino was fortunate."

Emery Power said, "When I really want a thing, I am willing to pay for it, M. Poirot."

Hercule Poirot said softly, "You have no doubt heard the Spanish proverb: *Take what you want—and pay for it, says God.*"

For a moment the financier frowned—a swift light of anger showed in his eyes.

He said coldly, "You are by way of being a philosopher, M. Poirot."

"I have arrived at the age of reflection, monsieur."

"Doubtless. But it is not reflection that will restore my goblet to me."

"You think not?"

"I fancy action will be necessary."

Hercule Poirot nodded placidly. "A lot of people make the

same mistake. But I demand your pardon, Mr. Power, we have digressed from the matter in hand. You were saying that you had bought the cup from the Marchese di San Veratrino?"

"Exactly. What I have now to tell you is that it was stolen before it actually came into my possession."

"How did that happen?"

"The Marchese's Palace was broken into on the night of the sale and eight or ten pieces of considerable value were stolen, including the goblet."

"What was done in the matter?"

Power shrugged his shoulders. "The police, of course, took the matter in hand. The robbery was recognized to be the work of a well-known international gang of thieves. Two of their number, a Frenchman called Dublay and an Italian called Riccovetti, were caught and tried—some of the stolen goods were found in their possession."

"But not the Borgia goblet?"

"But not the Borgia goblet. There were, as far as the police could ascertain, three men actually engaged in the robbery—the two I have just mentioned and a third, an Irishman named Patrick Casey. This last was an expert cat burglar. It was he who is said to have actually stolen the things. Dublay was the brains of the group and planned their coups; Riccovetti drove the car and waited below for the goods to be lowered down to him."

"And the stolen goods? Were they split up into three parts?"

"Possibly. On the other hand, the articles that were recovered were those of least value. It seems possible that the more noteworthy and spectacular pieces had been hastily smuggled out of the country."

"What about the third man, Casey? Was he never brought to justice?"

"Not in the sense you mean. He was not a very young man. His muscles were stiffer than formerly. Two weeks later he fell from the fifth floor of a building and was killed instantly."

"Where was this?"

"In Paris. He was attempting to rob the house of the millionaire banker, Duvauglier."

"And the goblet has never been seen since?"

"Exactly."

"It has never been offered for sale?"

"I am quite sure it has not. I may say that not only the police, but also private inquiry agents, have been on the lookout for it."

"What about the money you had paid over?"

"The Marchese, a very punctilious person, offered to refund it to me, as the cup had been stolen from his house."

"But you did not accept?"

"No."

"Why was that?"

"Shall we say because I preferred to keep the matter in my own hands?"

"You mean that if you had accepted the Marchese's offer, the goblet, if recovered, would be his property, whereas now it is legally yours?"

"Exactly."

Poirot asked, "What was there behind that attitude of yours?"

Emery Power said with a smile, "You appreciate that point, I see. Well, M. Poirot, it is quite simple. I thought I knew who was actually in possession of the goblet."

"Very interesting. And who was it?"

"Sir Reuben Rosenthal. He was not only a fellow collector but he was at the time a personal enemy. We had been rivals in several business deals—and on the whole I had come out the better. Our animosity culminated in this rivalry over the Borgia goblet. Each of us was determined to possess it. It was more or less a point of honor. Our appointed representatives bid against each other at the sale."

"And your representative's final bid secured the treasure?"

"Not precisely. I took the precaution of having a second agent—ostensibly the representative of a Paris dealer. Neither of us, you understand, would have been willing to yield to the other, but to allow a third party to acquire the cup, with the possibility of approaching that third party quietly afterward—that was a very different matter."

"In fact, *une petite deception.*"

"Exactly."

"Which was successful—and immediately afterward Sir Reuben discovered how he had been tricked?"

Power smiled.

It was a revealing smile.

Poirot said, "I see the position now. You believed that Sir Reuben, determined not to be beaten, deliberately commissioned the theft?"

Emery Power raised a hand.

"Oh, no, no! It would not be so crude as that. It amounted to this—shortly afterward Sir Reuben would have purchased a Renaissance goblet, provenance unspecified."

"The description of which would have been circulated by the police?"

"The goblet would not have been placed openly on view."

"You think it would have been sufficient for Sir Reuben to *know* that he possessed it?"

"Yes. Moreover, if I had accepted the Marchese's offer—it would have been possible for Sir Reuben to conclude a private arrangement with him later, thus allowing the goblet to pass legally into his possession."

He paused a minute and then said:

"But by retaining the legal ownership, there were still possibilities left open to me of recovering my property."

"You mean," said Poirot bluntly, "that you could arrange for it to be stolen from Sir Reuben."

"Not stolen, M. Poirot. I should have been merely recovering my own property."

"But I gather that you were not successful?"

"For a very good reason. Rosenthal has never had the goblet in his possession."

"How do you know?"

"Recently there has been a merger of oil interests. Rosenthal's interests and mine now coincide. We are allies and not enemies. I spoke to him frankly on the subject and he at once assured me that the cup had never been in his possession."

"And you believe him?"

"Yes."

Poirot said thoughtfully, "Then for ten years you have been, as you say in this country, barking up the mistaken tree?"

The financier said bitterly, "Yes, that is exactly what I have been doing!"

"And now—it is all to start again from the beginning?"

The other nodded.

"And that is where I come in? I am the dog that you set upon the cold scent—a very cold scent."

Emery Power said dryly, "If the affair were easy it would not have been necessary for me to send for you. Of course, if you think it impossible—"

He had found the right word.

Hercule Poirot drew himself up. He said coldly, "I do not recognize the word impossible, monsieur! I ask myself only—is this affair sufficiently interesting for me to undertake?"

Emery Power smiled again.

He said, "It has this interest—you may name your own fee."

The small man looked at the big man.

He said softly, "Do you then desire this work of art so much? Surely not!"

Emery Power said, "Put it that I, like yourself, do not accept defeat."

He said, "Yes—put that way—I understand."

Inspector Wagstaffe was interested.

"The Veratrino cup? Yes, I remember all about it. I was in charge of the business this end. I speak a bit of Italiano, you know, and I went over and had a powwow with the Macaronis. It's never turned up from that day to this. Funny thing, that."

"What is your explanation? A private sale?"

"I doubt it. Of course, it's remotely possible. . . . No, my explanation is a good deal simpler. The stuff was cached—and the only man who knew where it was is dead."

"You mean Casey?"

"Yes. He may have cached it somewhere in Italy, or he may have succeeded in smuggling it out of the country. But *he* hid it and wherever he hid it, there it still is."

Hercule Poirot sighed. "It is a romantic theory. Pearls stuffed into plaster casts—what is the story—the Bust of Napoleon, is it not? But in this case it is not jewels—it is a large solid-gold cup. Not so easy to hide that, one would think."

Wagstaffe said vaguely, "Oh, I don't know. It could be done, I suppose. Under the floor boards—something of that kind."

"Had Casey a house of his own?"

"Yes—in Liverpool." He grinned. "It wasn't under the floor boards there. We made sure of that."

"What about his family?"

"Wife was a decent sort of woman—tubercular. Worried to death by her husband's way of life. She was religious—a devout Catholic—but couldn't make up her mind to leave him. She died a couple of years ago. Daughter took after her—she became a nun. The son was different—a chip of the old block. Last I heard of him he was doing time in America."

Hercule Poirot wrote in his little notebook. *America.*

He said, "It is possible that Casey's son may have known the hiding-place?"

"Don't believe he did. It would have come into the fences' hands by now."

"The cup might have been melted down."

"It might. Quite possible, I should say. But I don't know—its supreme value is to collectors—and there's a lot of funny business goes on with collectors—you'd be surprised! Sometimes," said Wagstaffe virtuously, "I think collectors haven't any morals at all."

"Ah! Would you be surprised if Sir Reuben Rosenthal, for instance, were engaged in what you describe as 'funny business?'"

Wagstaffe grinned. "I wouldn't put it past him. He's not supposed to be very scrupulous where works of art are concerned."

"What about the other members of the gang?"

"Riccovetti and Dublay both got stiff sentences. I should imagine they'll be coming out about now."

"Dublay is a Frenchman, is he not?"

"Yes, he was the brains of the gang."

"Were there other members of it?"

"There was a girl—Red Kate she used to be called. Took a job as a lady's maid and found out all about a crib—where stuff was kept and so on. She went to Australia, I believe, after the gang broke up."

"Anyone else?"

"Chap called Yougouian was suspected of being in with them. He's a dealer. Headquarters in Stamboul but he has a shop in Paris. Nothing proved against him—but he's a slippery customer."

Poirot sighed. He looked at his little notebook. In it was written: *America, Australia, Italy, France, Turkey.*

He murmured, "I'll put a girdle round the earth—"

"Pardon?" said Inspector Wagstaffe.

"I was observing," said Hercule Poirot, "that a world tour seems indicated."

It was the habit of Hercule Poirot to discuss his cases with his capable valet, Georges. That is to say, Hercule Poirot would let drop certain observations to which Georges would reply with the worldly wisdom which he had acquired in the course of his career as a gentleman's gentleman.

"If you were faced, Georges," said Poirot, "with the necessity of conducting investigations in five different parts of the globe, how would you set about it?"

"Well, sir, air travel is very quick, though some say as it upsets the stomach. I couldn't say myself."

"One asks oneself," said Hercule Poirot, "what Hercules would have done?"

"You mean the bicycle chap, sir?"

"Or," pursued Hercule Poirot, "one simply asks, what did he do? And the answer, Georges, is that he traveled energetically. But he was forced in the end to obtain information—as some say—from Prometheus—others from Nereus."

"Indeed, sir?" said Georges. "I never heard of either of those gentlemen. Are they travel agencies, sir?"

Hercule Poirot, enjoying the sound of his own voice, went on:

"My client, Emery Power, understands only one thing—action! But it is useless to dispense energy by unnecessary action. There is a golden rule in life, Georges: never do anything yourself that others can do for you.

"Especially," added Hercule Poirot, rising and going to the bookshelf, "when expense is no object!"

He took from the shelf a file labled with the letter D. and opened it at the words *Detective Agencies—Reliable.*

"The modern Prometheus," he murmured. "Be so obliging, Georges, as to copy out for me certain names and addresses. Messrs. Hankerton, New York. Messrs. Laden & Bosher, Sydney. Messrs. Roget et Franconard, Paris."

He paused while Georges finished this. Then he said:

"And now be so kind as to look up the trains for Liverpool."

"Yes, sir, you are going to Liverpool, sir?"

"I am afraid so. It is possible, Georges, that I may have to go even farther. But not just yet."

It was three months later that Hercule Poirot stood on a rocky point and surveyed the Atlantic Ocean. Gulls rose and swooped down again with long melancholy cries. The air was soft and damp.

Hercule Poirot had the feeling, not uncommon in those who come to Inishgowlan for the first time, that he had reached the end of the world. He had never in his life imagined anything so remote, so desolate, so abandoned. It had beauty, a melancholy, haunted beauty, the beauty of a remote and incredible past. Here, in the west of Ireland, the Romans had never marched, tramp, tramp, tramp; had never fortified a camp; had never built a well-ordered, sensible, useful road. It was a land where common sense and an orderly way of life were unknown.

Hercule Poirot looked down at the tips of his patent leather shoes and sighed. He felt forlorn and very much alone. The standards by which he lived were here not appreciated.

His eyes swept slowly up and down the desolate coastline, then once more out to sea. Somewhere out there, so tradition had it, were the Isles of the Blest, the Land of Youth.

He murmured to himself, *The Apple Tree, the Singing and the Gold* . . .

And suddenly Hercule Poirot was himself again—the spell was broken, he was once more in harmony with his patent leather shoes and natty dark-gray gent's suiting.

Not very far away he had heard the toll of a bell. He understood that bell. It was a sound he had been familiar with from early youth.

He set out briskly along the cliff. In about ten minutes he came in sight of the building on the cliff. A high wall surrounded it and a great wooden door studded with nails was set in the wall. Hercule Poirot came to this door and knocked. There was a vast iron knocker. Then he cautiously pulled at a rusty chain and a shrill little bell tinkled briskly inside the door.

A small panel in the door was pushed aside and showed a face. It was a suspicious face, framed in starched white. There was a distinct mustache on the upper lip, but the voice was the voice of a woman; it was the voice of what Hercule Poirot called a *femme formidable*.

It demanded his business.

"Is this the Convent of St. Mary and All Angels?"

The formidable woman said with asperity, "And what else would it be?"

Hercule Poirot did not attempt to answer that. He said to the dragon:

"I would like to see the Mother Superior."

The dragon was unwilling, but in the end she yielded. Bars were drawn back, the door opened, and Hercule Poirot was conducted to a small bare room where visitors to the convent were received.

Presently a nun glided in, her rosary swinging at her waist.

Hercule Poirot was a Catholic by birth. He understood the atmosphere in which he found himself.

"I apologize for troubling you *ma mère*," he said, "but you have here, I think, a *religieuse* who was, in the world, Kate Casey."

The Mother Superior bowed her head.

She said, "That is so. Sister Mary Ursula in religion."

Hercule Poirot said, "There is a certain wrong that needs righting. I believe that Sister Mary Ursula could help me. She has information that might be invaluable."

The Mother Superior shook her head. Her face was placid, her voice calm and remote. She said:

"Sister Mary Ursula cannot help you."

"But I assure you—"

He broke off. The Mother Superior said:

"Sister Mary Ursula died two months ago."

In the saloon bar of Jimmy Donovan's Hotel, Hercule Poirot sat uncomfortably against the wall. The hotel did not come up to his ideas of what a hotel should be. His bed was broken—so were two of the window panes in his room—thereby admitting that night air which Hercule Poirot distrusted so much. The hot water brought him had been tepid and the meal he had eaten was producing curious and painful sensations in his inside.

There were five men in the bar and they were all talking politics. For the most part Hercule Poirot could not understand what they said. In any case, he did not much care.

Presently he found one of the men sitting beside him. This was a man of a slightly different class to the others. He had the stamp of the seedy townsman upon him.

He said with immense dignity, "I tell you, sir. I tell you— Pegeen's Pride hasn't got a chance, not a chance . . . bound to finish right down the course—right down the course. You take my tip . . . everybody ought to take my tip. Know who I am, shir, do you know, I shay? Atlas, thatsh who I am—Atlas of the Dublin *Sun*. . . . Been tipping winnersh all the season. . . . Didn't I give Larry's Girl? Twenty-five to one—twenty-five to one. Follow Atlas and you can't go wrong."

Hercule Poirot regarded him with a strange reverence. He said, and his voice trembled:

"*Mon Dieu*, it is an omen!"

It was some hours later. The moon showed from time to time, peeping out coquettishly from behind the clouds. Poirot and his new friend had walked some miles. The former was limping. The idea crossed his mind that there were, after all, other shoes— more suitable to country walking than patent leather. Actually Georges had respectfully conveyed as much. "A nice pair of brogues," was what Georges had said.

Hercule Poirot had not cared for the idea. He liked his feet to look neat and well shod. But now, tramping along this stony path, he realized that there were other shoes. . . .

His companion said suddenly, "Is it the way the priest would be after me for this? I'll not have a mortal sin upon my conscience."

Hercule Poirot said, "You are only restoring to Caesar the things which are Caesar's."

They had come to the wall of the convent. Atlas prepared to do his part.

A groan burst from him and he exclaimed in low, poignant tones that he was destroyed entirely!

Hercule Poirot spoke with authority.

"Be quiet. It is not the weight of the world that you have to support—only the weight of Hercule Poirot."

Atlas was turning over two new crisp five-pound notes.

He said hopefully, "Maybe I'll not remember in the morning the way I earned this. I'm after worrying that Father O'Reilly will be after me."

"Forget everything, my friend. Tomorrow the world is yours."

Atlas murmured, "And what'll I put it on? There's Working Lad, he's a grand horse, a lovely horse he is! And there's Sheila Boyne—seven to one I'd get on her."

He paused.

"Was it my fancy now or did I hear you mention the name of a heathen god? Hercules, you said, and glory be to God, there's a Hercules running in the three-thirty tomorrow."

"My friend," said Hercule Poirot, "put your money on that horse. I tell you this, Hercules cannot fail."

And it is certainly true that on the following day Mr. Rosslyn's Hercules very unexpectedly won the Boynan Stakes, starting price sixty to one.

Deftly Hercule Poirot unwrapped the neatly done up parcel. First the brown paper, then the wadding, lastly the tissue paper.

On the desk in front of Emery Power he placed a gleaming golden cup. Chased on it was a tree bearing apples of green emeralds.

The financier drew a deep breath. He said, "I congratulate you, M. Poirot."

Hercule Poirot bowed.

Emery Power stretched out a hand. He touched the rim of the goblet, drawing his finger round it.

He said in a deep voice, "Mine!"

Hercule Poirot agreed. "Yours!"

The other gave a sigh. He leaned back in his chair.

He said in a businesslike voice, "Where did you find it?"

Hercule Poirot said, "I found it on an altar."

Emery Power stared.

Poirot went on: "Casey's daughter was a nun. She was about to take her final vows at the time of her father's death. She was an ignorant but a devout girl. The cup was hidden in her father's house in Liverpool. She took it to the convent, wanting, I think, to atone for her father's sins. She gave it to be used to the glory of God. I do not think that the nuns themselves ever realized its value. They took it, probably, for a family heirloom. In their eyes it was a chalice and they used it as such."

Emery Power said, "An extraordinary story!" He added, "What made you think of going there?"

Poirot shrugged his shoulders.

"Perhaps—a process of elimination. And then there was the extraordinary fact that no one had ever tried to dispose of the cup. That looked, you see, as though it were in a place where ordinary material values did not apply. I remembered that Patrick Casey's daughter was a nun."

Power said heartily, "Well, as I said before, I congratulate you. Let me know your fee and I'll write you a check."

Hercule Poirot said, "There is no fee."

The other stared at him.

"What do you mean?"

"Did you ever read fairy stories when you were a child? The King in them would say, 'Ask of me what you will?'"

"So you are asking something?"

"Yes, but not money. Merely a simple request."

"Well, what is it? D'you want a tip for the markets?"

"That would be only money in another form. My request is much simpler than that."

"What is it?"

Hercule Poirot laid his hand on the cup.

"Send this back to the convent."

There was a pause. Then Emery Power said:

"Are you quite mad?"

Hercule Poirot shook his head.

"No, I am not mad. See, I will show you something."

He picked up the goblet. With his fingernail, he pressed hard into the open jaws of the snake that was coiled round the tree. Inside the cup a tiny portion of gold chased interior slid aside leaving an aperture into the hollow handle.

Poirot said, "You see? This was the drinking-cup of the Borgia Pope. Through this little hole the poison passed into the drink. You have said yourself that the history of this cup is evil. Violence and blood and evil passions have accompanied its possession. Evil will perhaps come to you in your turn."

"Superstition!"

"Possibly. But why were you so anxious to possess this thing? Not for its beauty. Not for its value. You have a hundred—a thousand, perhaps—beautiful and rare things. You wanted it to sustain your pride. You were determined not to be beaten. *Eh bien*, you are not beaten. You win! The goblet is in your possession. But now, why not make a great—a supreme gesture? Send it back to where it has dwelt in peace for nearly ten years. Let the evil of it be purified there. It belonged to the Church once—let it return to the Church. Let it stand once more on the altar, purified and absolved as we hope that the souls of men shall be also purified and absolved from their sins."

He leaned forward.

"Let me describe for you the place where I found it—the Garden of Peace, looking out over the Western Sea toward a forgotten Paradise of Youth and Eternal Beauty."

He spoke on, describing in simple words the remote charm of Inishgowlan.

Emery Power sat back, one hand over his eyes.

He said at last, "I was born on the west coat of Ireland. I left there as a boy to go to America."

Poirot said gently, "I heard that."

The financier sat up. His eyes were shrewd again. He said, and there was a faint smile on his lips:

"You are a strange man, M. Poirot. You shall have your way. Take the goblet to the convent as a gift in my name. A pretty costly gift. Thirty thousand pounds—and what shall I get in exchange?"

Poirot said gravely, "The nuns will have Masses said for your soul."

The rich man's smile widened—a rapacious hungry smile.

He said, "So, after all, it may be an investment! Perhaps, the best one I ever made."

In the little parlor of the convent, Hercule Poirot told his story and restored the chalice to the Mother Superior.

She murmured, "Tell him we thank him and we will pray for him."

Hercule Poirot said gently, "He needs your prayers."

"Is he then an unhappy man?"

Poirot said, "So unhappy that he has forgotten what happiness means. So unhappy that he does not know he is unhappy."

The nun said softly, "Ah, a rich man . . ."

Hercule Poirot said nothing—for he knew there was nothing to say.

THE
VIGIL
OF
BROTHER
FERNANDO

BY JOAN VATSEK

BROTHER FERNANDO STOOD NEAR THE CHURCH DOOR, IN THE SIDE chapel where Guido Reni's painting had hung for the last hundred and fifty years. Just now it was a little dusty, but the blue of St. George's tunic still held its original soft hue, hanging in Grecian Brevity below the breastplate which seemed made of gray velvet scales rather than hard metal. The dragon under his feet writhed with unfaded, greenish contortions, bright gore spumed from its wounds, and the flying draperies, that somehow managed to be there in the background, wind-blown and billowing, glowed with color.

The head of St. George was really the head of Lucrezia, who had gone to visit Guido in prison. Even if one did not know that she had been his model, it was evident that the head was out of proportion, reflected Brother Fernando. It perched, in small blonde glory, on a massive warrior's neck, over a gigantic masculine torso with one muscled, sandaled leg held straight, like a piece of bronze, and the other gouging into the dragon's side.

Yes, one would have surely known the head was the head of a woman. It was delicate and dreamy, with blue eyes that gazed out, blandly unaware of the dragon's twisting, and her own enormous hand that poised negligently, holding a slim, wand-like spear, in preparation to plunging it once more into the dragon's many-tinted flesh.

It was obvious that when Guido had come to the head of St. George, he forgot all the extravagant paraphernalia of dragon and spear and blood, and painted Lucrezia as he saw her, looking at him.

Brother Fernando was not primarily concerned with this curious effect, he had observed it before. Neither was he praying before this attractive and ineffectual tableau, to be delivered from evil. As a matter of fact, he was trying to get some joy out of the color. For the singular thing had happened to him, that all colors seemed the same.

Now in the years that had hurried him so imperceptibly and quietly toward forty, color had been one of his greatest pleasures. The mellow splendor of stained glass windows were a continual joy to him. He had spent hours toiling through difficult old Latin books, for the illumination—the tiny, miraculously clear figures, the gay, unstinted splattering of gold leaf and minute flowers—electrified his labors.

He was not given to moods. Occasionally some one of his pupils chafed at him for his lack of imagination, but this did not disturb him in the least. He had originally entered orders because a regulated, religious and scholarly life was the only one that appealed to him. This was the first time that anything had gone wrong, and Brother Fernando would far rather have lost his imperturbable capacity for sleep, or his equable temper, or his appetite, than his appreciation of color.

It was not that his eyes were growing weak. His eyes were clear, and fine. His eyes saw sharply everything that passed in the classroom.

But instead of being glad when he got up in the morning and looked out of his tight little window, and saw the clipped, gemlike green of the hedges, and the crowding fertility of the grass, it seemed to him that grass and trees and sky, all shared the same dreadful abnegation of color.

He greeted his companions at the refectory, and noted with an unfamiliar sourness, that their faces all looked the same, and that the dark carved woodwork of the panels, which had seemed to him always unobtrusively magnificent, was drab, uninspiring and dull.

He walked along the aisle among the congregation, and thought how heavy and cloddish they were. The rainbow of hats the women wore, in which he had always taken a half humorous interest, with the unpredictable conceits that varied from season to season—for it was a fashionable church, one of the richest little churches in Rome, in fact—the whole crowd looked to him a vague, dark gray.

And now, even Guido's picture, to which Brother Fernando had come as a last resort, for all its soft gaudiness, had failed him. The oil was certainly a little mottled, he admitted to himself reluctantly. Odd that he had never thought so before.

The tall, bronze-studded church door was heaved open just then, and a little group of tourists was ushered in by one of the innumerable cocky guides who lead strangers like sheep about Rome.

"And this great masterpiece," declared the guide at once, in spluttering English, "is by Guido Reni. By Guido Reni, ladies and gentlemen, the same who painted 'Aurora.'"

Brother Fernando moved off in solitary scorn, his brown robes lightly brushing his bare legs as he moved, his sandals making a little echo on the stone.

The guide suddenly left his charges and began to pursue him. Brother Fernando covered distance swiftly, and the rather stout guide had a hard time to catch him before he entered the sacristy.

"*Ecco!*" exclaimed the guide. "How fast you hurry, Father! Would the sacristan take us below? I have promised these people that they should see the place of skulls. They will put something in the box," he added placatingly.

"The sacristan is at dinner," replied Brother Fernando shortly. "Let them come back later, if they wish."

"But—but this tour is all arranged!" exclaimed the guide. "We cannot come back to the same place twice! There is no time! We are going to the Coliseum now and the baths, and the Vatican"—he checked them off on his pudgy fingers.

"What is that to me?" said Brother Fernando.

"But they will be angry! I promised them this, and they won't be satisfied if they don't have it! I beg of you, Father!"

Brother Fernando shrugged.

"Oh, very well. I will get the keys."

The guide, beaming, returned to his flock.

They were waiting when Brother Fernando returned. He could not help smiling a little, tourists had always struck him as so childish.

"Tell them to be careful about their heads," he said to the guide.

"Be careful!" cried the guide. *"Prenez garde!"*

They all obediently ducked, when they entered the winding passage which led to the vaults below.

"Now, I am telling you," said the guide, "you are about to see the most unique, the most extraordinary curiosity in Rome. I am telling you."

The place which was usually kept for the special tombs of prelates and for monuments was, instead, crowded with little chapels side by side, like booths. Brother Fernando led them to the first one and there was a gasp of astonishment from the group behind him. He turned and looked at their faces with ironical amusement. Horror, shock, disbelief, and the kind of unnatural smile that is struck from the face by strong and unexpected emotion, were all present, in varying degrees.

Then they all broke out in exclamations, and laughter burst from them. It was too grotesque to take seriously.

Skulls were placed, with meticulous exactitude, into the plaster of the wall. They formed a geometrical design, varied with a nice eye for the effect, by crossbones and hip bones and collarbones, and, in fact, by every bone in the human anatomy. During the Middle Ages a monk, with a penchant for the unusual, had begun the game and it was kept up by generation after generation of the order, with a scrupulous perseverance and ever growing rivalry.

The first chapel was quite modest in its basic pattern; the next was more ambitious, attempting a little flourish with ribs—the third had a rather terrifying pyramid effect; the fourth had managed two great rosettes of skulls, and a circular design, and so on, sixteen in all.

"Tell them these are the heads of my predecessors," said Brother Fernando.

219

The guide translated with gusto, into three languages.

There was a little flurry, and Brother Fernando could feel that they were looking at him for the first time as a living man, instead of an impersonal brown robe.

"Yes," said Brother Fernando, "these are all the bodies of monks. They are piled here in this offhand manner, to remind us that we must die also. Have your charges examined them to their satisfaction?"

The guide said, a little nonplussed, that they had.

And so, thanking Brother Fernando with nods and rather hesitant smiles, the visitors were herded up again, and whisked off by their competent manager, presumably to the Coliseum, the baths and the Vatican.

Brother Fernando followed them slowly, locked the door, and went to take a short rest before going to his class of eager and argumentative theological students.

But he had no spirit for argument that day, his research, his knowledge, his insight, seemed things of the past. He listened to the words falling drearily from his own lips, and longed to escape from the eyes that fastened on him first with expectation, then with puzzled disappointment. In the end he apologized, before leaving them.

"Brother Fernando is not well," said one to the other, in explanation.

Brother Fernando, indeed, felt like a ghost. Intensity had left him, there was nothing to be explored, or learned, or discovered. Vaguely he wandered up to his room, looked around, and wandered disconsolately down again, into the courtyard. There he stood for a moment in the sunshine, looking at the small fountain that had seemed so peaceful to him a short time ago. Now the continuous trickle of water made him irritable.

Across the courtyard, on a stone bench under the portico, he could see Brother Luigi sitting, reading. It seemed peculiarly fitting that he should be there, in just that position, with his delicate and noble head like a fine fresco against the wall. His tonsure had grown over again, and his head was a mass of brown curls. His body, young and supple, showed its elasticity beneath the graceful folds of his robe. As Brother Fernando's glance rested on him, he looked up and waved his hand cheerfully. He yawned and got up.

"I don't believe him for a moment," he said, coming to join Brother Fernando.

"Who?"

"This man. He is all mixed up. He doesn't know enough history to put in a teaspoon."

"Well," said Brother Fernando.

They began to walk up and down, under the eaves, and around the courtyard, getting the most out of the little square of space.

Suddenly Brother Luigi began to talk about the Last Judgment. It was evident that he had been reading heavily on the subject, for his phantasy caught fire as he spoke, and described the coming of the angels and the rising of the dead.

"Do you think it will be so?" he asked at last.

"I don't know," said Brother Fernando, and left him abruptly.

For many days after that, Brother Fernando looked for color, but could not find it. He became more and more morose. At last he decided to go to his superior, a man whom he did not care for, whom in fact he despised a little, for certainly his erudition was not equal to Brother Fernando's own, and he had a rough manner that was more becoming a butcher than a monk.

When Brother Fernando knocked and entered he did not alter his comfortable slump in an old easy chair.

"What is it, Brother?" he asked. Brother Fernando looked at his florid face over his large and well-fed paunch, and felt unable to begin.

He stood silent for a moment, his rather long and earnestly enquiring face unrelieved by any trace of his usual half ironical smile.

"Father," he said, "I am at the end of my usefulness."

"Indeed?" said Father Jerome. He did not move, only his eyes narrowed a little, shrewdly. "I would say that you were at the height of it: active, healthy—how old are you, forty, forty-two?— at any rate, you have always seemed to me one of our best men."

"Thank you. At this moment, I am no good to anybody, least of all to myself."

"Well, well," said Father Jerome, and he got up and began to stump about the room. "It is a pity that you had to disturb my siesta with this unpleasant news," he said with a grimace.

"I am sorry." Brother Fernando wished he could explain more fully. He could not state, bluntly, that he could not see color any more.

"Yes, now I shan't be able to sleep as well as usual. It is a great pity."

Brother Fernando smiled slightly, apologetically. His lips felt quite strange when he did so: he realized that he had not smiled for a long time.

"Now, if it were another man," said Father Jerome, talking to himself and gesticulating with his heavy, ham-like hands, "I would dismiss it as temperament, and humor him out of it. Or I would bully him a little," he added, reflectively. "But you now, that's a different case." He sighed. "What is the matter?" he asked.

Brother Fernando shook his head. "That's what I should like to know," he said. "I've never been depressed before—I don't know what to do about it."

Father Jerome sat down again, puffing a little in annoyance. But he was not unfriendly, in fact he had already rather lifted the weight from Brother Fernando.

"Sit down, sit down," he said, motioning. "Why can't you sit down by yourself? Are you a little boy?"

Brother Fernando sat down. This time he laughed a little. "Forgive my saying so, Father," he remarked, "but I have never appreciated you before."

"You did not need me before," retorted his superior. "Well, I shall tell you something at which you will laugh, but all the same, I suggest that you try it. Spend a night in the chapels below, as I did once. There is nothing like death to make you enjoy life. It is since then that I have taken on so much weight."

Brother Fernando stared, frankly astonished.

"I know, I know!" said Father Jerome, shaking one hand dismissively, "I know what you are thinking! An old fool if there ever was one! Well, well. But try it. Spend tonight down there, and let me know in the morning how you fare."

Brother Fernando shrugged. "I will fall asleep," he said, "and that is all." He got up. "But," he added, "I shall certainly do as you say. I am under your orders." And he made a rather questionable bow. It was a little too humble.

He was deeply annoyed with Father Jerome. What idiocy! he thought, as he took his leave.

But at nine o'clock he said good night gravely, took a blanket, a flashlight, and the keys, and locked himself in the underground chapels. He wrapped himself in the blanket, lay down on the cold stone floor, and fell promptly asleep, in spite of the dank chilliness.

At night he awoke with a start, and sat up. He was perfectly convinced that he was not alone. He groped for the flashlight, and turned it on, sweeping the bright arc into every one of the little chapels set with skeletons. There was nothing, nobody. He lay down and tried to go to sleep again, but his senses were keenly awake. He listened, and listening made him sweat a little, for it was so quiet.

He felt helpless, lying straight on his back, as though he were being kept down by a stone on his chest. So he sat up again, cross-legged, turned on his flashlight dimly, and waited. He wondered what he was waiting for. What were the dead waiting for? There was certainly something disconcertingly expectant in the way a skull faced your gaze, with sockets just as good as yours except that they were empty.

He was sitting up opposite the third chapel, with the heads placed in a rising pile. The one at the summit was of singularly fine structure. It looked familiar, and Brother Fernando could not imagine why. It reminded him of someone.

He got up, and went into the small enclosure, going quite close to the central skull. It had a high brow, narrow cheekbones, and gave the impression, even in that stark state, of having contained a highly intelligent brain. But when he was near it, the familiarity vanished. He went further away again, experimentally. Again it seemed as if he had known the man, as if he had seen him often. But bones look much alike, and perhaps it was only the dominant position, enjoyed by the central skull, that made it stand out so.

His thoughts slipped into the past, when the monks were, say, halfway through this very chapel. Did some artistic fingers itch for just one more bone to complete a design. He smiled at the thought. Were any of the monks disturbed at the idea that, when their bones were blanched enough, they would be dug up again and apportioned a place in the wall?

His mind began to play with words, conversationally, in his solitude. Entertaining custom, he thought—undress burial. Three or four centuries ago, they enjoyed such things.

Perhaps it is Brother Luigi, he thought suddenly, for his eyes were drawn again to the central skull, and he remembered Brother Luigi's fine contour against the shadowed wall that afternoon. But concentrating on the skull, he saw that it was much longer, and guessed, at a hazard, that it had belonged to an older man.

He had an impulse to examine some of the other chapels, but hesitated. He had become used to this one. There's nothing to look at anyway! he thought crossly.

But after a little while, since he felt no hint of sleepiness, he got up and looked at some length at each design, weighing their relative merits.

One could see the historic deterioration from the primal simple arrangement, no more than an array of heads, to a veritable orgy of Byzantine curlicues and complications. He preferred the third chapel, with his friend at the top of the pyramidal pattern. His friend was really a royal conclusion; the monk who unearthed him must have been very well pleased.

It struck Brother Fernando that even for as large an order as it had been, there were a few too many well-preserved remains. He laughed a little to himself, and his laughter was scattered softly in the silence. He was laughing at the creative eagerness of his colleagues that had made them rob graves.

"Weren't you afraid?" he asked out loud, in a mild bantering tone, "that a few murderers would slip into the company?"

"Imagine, my friends," he went on, finding it a relief to talk, "imagine if, as Brother Luigi believes, the dead will rise? What a scrambling for bones there will be! And what surprise to find, perhaps, a woman or two in your midst?" He laughed again.

He thought of Lucrezia's head, on the body of St. George. It was a pity that it, too, had not a niche somewhere. He looked at his watch. "Witching hour," he remarked.

Of course he did not expect anything to happen, but once he had spoken, it was more than ever as though he were waiting for something. He became annoyed. He began to stalk up and down, angrily. Tomorrow he would be exhausted, not having slept all night. What a fool Father Jerome was. It was really a pity that Brother Fernando was not in his shoes—he would be so much more dignified, and give so much better advice. He wondered what Father Jerome had thought about when he spent the night in the chapels. He had probably had lugubrious thoughts about death. Brother Fernando sneered. "This has no power over me," he said coldly, and as he spoke more loudly than before the words were thrown back at him, startlingly.

When, at that moment, a bit of bone, loosened from the plaster, crumbled away and fell, making a tiny noise, Brother Fernando was seized with a fit of shuddering. Even his teeth chattered. He sat down, and put the blanket around his shoulders.

For distraction, he decided to go over the theological lesson he was planning for the next day. He did not often do this, formally, but it was as good a way to spend the time as any.

"Now, class," he began, with jesting bravado, and choked. All the white skulls gleamed at him.

"There is heaven and earth," he whispered, and paused for a long time.

He could say nothing that the gathering before him did not question, though listening quietly enough.

He recalled his powerful sensation of not being alone when he woke up. This feeling had not been dispelled, but he had grown used to it. He realized now that it was not a single presence, but made up by the piles and piles of chalky remains, which appealed to him mutely, making his bones ache in sympathy.

He thought with a wistful longing, of the sunny garden in the afternoon, and the blades of pushing crowding grass.

"My poor friend," he said to the skull on top of the pyramid, "You won't know the sun's warmth again."

Suddenly, with a horror-stricken shriek, he leaped up. He knew who the skull reminded him of—it was himself.

His hands went to his head in a wild gesture, and he tried to press its warmth in, to catch it and hold it there forever. He fell on his knees.

Father Jerome always had his breakfast brought to him in his room. It began with pale purple smoked ham and fresh canta-loupe. He was just beginning on the sweet, flushed orange of the cantaloupe when Brother Fernando entered, looking haggard and woebegone.

Father Jerome put down his fork, regretfully, but firmly.

"Well, my son," he said, "what did you find in the chapels?"

"Nothing," replied Brother Fernando.

Because Father Jerome's eyes looked at him so piercingly, and he felt so weak, he turned and went to the window, which was as small as his own and latticed. But it was open, and the balmy air of Rome blew in lazily, bringing the smell of grass from the garden plot below. A few doves had settled by the fountain, and were ruffling their white feathers in the morning sun, and darting their pink bills into the clear water.

He saw that Brother Luigi was out early, walking up and down the narrow pebbled path—under the eaved porticos, and that he had pulled a little blue gentian, from the border of care-fully planted flowers, and was swinging it in one hand in an inconsequential manner and looking at the sky—which, as Brother Fernando noted with a start, was certainly blue. Every wisp of cloud had been melted against its deep dye, and it stretched in lazy and casual perfection before his unexpectedly delighted eyes.

He turned back to Father Jerome slowly, and looked at his red, round face worriedly gazing at him, and the smoked ham and juicy cantaloupe on his plate, untouched. It struck him as very funny.

"Eat, Father," he said. He sat down on the window ledge, and threw back his head in a long, refreshing laugh. The sun was very warm on his back. "It is certainly good to be alive," he remarked lightly.

Then he jumped up. "I must have a look at St. George's mantle," he said.

THE
SECRET
GARDEN

BY G. K. CHESTERTON

ARISTIDE VALENTIN, CHIEF OF THE PARIS POLICE, WAS LATE FOR HIS dinner, and some of his guests began to arrive before him. These were, however, reassured by his confidential servant, Ivan, the old man with a scar, and a face almost as grey as his moustaches, who always sat at a table in the entrance hall—a hall hung with weapons. Valentin's house was perhaps as peculiar and celebrated as its master. It was an old house, with high walls and tall poplars almost overhanging the Seine; but the oddity—and perhaps the police value—of its architecture was this: that there was no ultimate exit at all except through this front door, which was guarded by Ivan and the armoury. The garden was large and elaborate, and there were many exits from the house into the garden. But there was no exit from the garden into the world outside; all round it ran a tall, smooth, unscalable wall with special spikes at the top; no bad garden, perhaps, for a man to reflect in whom some hundred criminals had sworn to kill.

As Ivan explained to the guests, their host had telephoned that he was detained for ten minutes. He was, in truth, making some last arrangements about executions and such ugly things; and though these duties were rootedly repulsive to him, he always performed them with precision. Ruthless in the pursuit of criminals, he was very mild about their punishment. Since he had been supreme over French—and largely over European —policial methods, his great influence had been honourably used for the mitigation of sentences and the purification of prisons. He was one of the great humanitarian French free-thinkers; and the only thing wrong with them is that they make mercy even colder than justice.

When Valentin arrived he was already dressed in black clothes and the red rosette—an elegant figure, his dark beard already streaked with grey. He went straight through his house to his study, which opened on the grounds behind. The garden door of it was open, and after he had carefully locked his box in its official place, he stood for a few seconds at the open door looking out upon the garden. A sharp moon was fighting with the flying rags and tatters of a storm, and Valentin regarded it with a wistfulness unusual in such scientific natures as his. Perhaps such scientific natures have some psychic prevision of the most tremendous problem of their lives. From any such occult mood, at least, he quickly recovered, for he knew he was late, and that his guests had already begun to arrive. A glance at his drawing-room when he entered it was enough to make certain that his principal guest was not there, at any rate. He saw all the other pillars of the little party; he saw Lord Galloway, the English Ambassador—a choleric old man with a russet face like an apple, wearing the blue ribbon of the Garter. He saw Lady Galloway, slim and threadlike, with silver hair and a face sensitive and superior. He saw her daughter, Lady Margaret Graham, a pale and pretty girl with an elfish face and copper-coloured hair. He saw the Duchess of Mont St. Michel, black-eyed and opulent, and with her her two daughters, black-eyed and opulent also. He saw Dr. Simon, a typical French scientist, with glasses, a pointed brown beard, and a forehead barred with those parallel wrinkles which are the penalty of superciliousness, since they come through constantly elevating the eyebrows. He saw Father Brown, of Cobhole, in Essex, whom he had recently met in England. He saw—perhaps with more interest than any of these —a tall man in uniform, who had bowed to the Galloways without receiving any very hearty acknowledgment, and who now advanced alone to pay his respects to his host. This was Commandant O'Brien, of the French Foreign Legion. He was a slim yet somewhat swaggering figure, clean-shaven, dark-haired, and blue-eyed, and, as seemed natural in an officer of that famous regiment of victorious failures and successful suicides, he had an air at once dashing and melancholy. He was by birth an Irish gentleman, and in boyhood had known the Galloways—especially

Margaret Graham. He had left his country after some crash of debts, and now expressed his complete freedom from British etiquette by swinging about in uniform, sabre and spurs. When he bowed to the Ambassador's family, Lord and Lady Galloway bent stiffly, and Lady Margaret looked away.

But for whatever old causes such people might be interested in each other, their distinguished host was not specially interested in them. No one of them at least was in his eyes the guest of the evening. Valentin was expecting, for special reasons, a man of world-wide fame, whose friendship he had secured during some of his great detective tours and triumphs in the United States. He was expecting Julius K. Brayne, that multi-millionaire whose colossal and even crushing endowments of small religions have occasioned so much easy sport and easier solemnity for the American and English papers. Nobody could quite make out whether Mr. Brayne was an atheist or a Mormon or a Christian Scientist; but he was ready to pour money into any intellectual vessel, so long as it was an untried vessel. One of his hobbies was to wait for the American Shakespeare—a hobby more patient than angling. He admired Walt Whitman, but thought that Luke P. Tanner, of Paris, Pa., was more "progressive" than Whitman any day. He liked anything that he thought "progressive." He thought Valentin "progressive" thereby doing him a grave injustice.

The solid appearance of Julius K. Brayne in the room was as decisive as a dinner bell. He had this great quality, which very few of us can claim, that his presence was as big as his absence. He was a huge fellow, as fat as he was tall, clad in complete evening black, without so much relief as a watch-chain or a ring. His hair was white and well brushed back like a German's; his face was red, fierce and cherubic, with one dark tuft under the lower lip that threw up that otherwise infantile visage with an effect theatrical and even Mephistophelean. Not long, however, did that *salon* merely stare at the celebrated American; his lateness had already become a domestic problem, and he was sent with all speed into the dining-room with Lady Galloway on his arm.

Except on one point the Galloways were genial and casual

enough. So long as Lady Margaret did not take the arm of that adventurer O'Brien, her father was quite satisfied; and she had not done so, she had decorously gone in with Dr. Simon. Nevertheless, old Lord Galloway was restless and almost rude. He was diplomatic enough during dinner, but when, over the cigars, three of the younger men—Simon the doctor, Brown the priest, and the detrimental O'Brien, the exile in a foreign uniform—all melted away to mix with the ladies or smoke in the conservatory, then the English diplomatist grew very undiplomatic indeed. He was stung every sixty seconds with the thought that the scamp O'Brien might be signalling to Margaret somehow; he did not attempt to imagine how. He was left over the coffee with Brayne, the hoary Yankee who believed in all religions, and Valentin, the grizzled Frenchman who believed in none. They could argue with each other, but neither could appeal to him. After a time this "progressive" logomachy had reached a crisis of tedium; Lord Galloway got up also and sought the drawing-room. He lost his way in long passages for some six or eight minutes: till he heard the high-pitched, didatic voice of the doctor, and then the dull voice of the priest, followed by general laughter. They also, he thought with a curse, were probably arguing about "science and religion." But the instant he opened the *salon* door he saw only one thing—he saw what was not there. He saw that Commandant O'Brien was absent, and that Lady Margaret was absent too.

Rising impatiently from the drawing-room, as he had from the dining-room, he stamped along the passage once more. His notion of protecting his daughter from the Irish-Algerian n'er-do-well had become something central and even mad in his mind. As he went towards the back of the house, where was Valentin's study, he was surprised to meet his daughter, who swept past with a white scornful face, which was a second enigma. If she had been with O'Brien, where was O'Brien? If she had not been with O'Brien, where had she been? With a sort of senile and passionate suspicion he groped his way to the dark back parts of the mansion, and eventually found a servants' entrance that opened on to the garden. The moon with her scimitar had now ripped up and rolled away all the storm-wrack.

The argent light lit up all four corners of the garden. A tall figure in blue was striding across the lawn towards the study door; a glint of moonlit silver on his facings picked him out as Commandant O'Brien.

He vanished through the French windows into the house, leaving Lord Galloway in an indescribable temper, at once virulent and vague. The blue-and-silver garden, like a scene in a theatre, seemed to taunt him with all that tyrannic tenderness against which his worldly authority was at war. The length and grace of the Irishman's stride enraged him as if he were a rival instead of a father; the moonlight maddened him. He was trapped as if by magic into a garden of troubadours, a Watteau fairyland; and, willing to shake off such amorous imbecilities by speech, he stepped briskly after his enemy. As he did so he tripped over some tree or stone in the grass; looked down at it first with irritation and then a second time with curiosity. The next instant the moon and the tall poplars looked at an unusual sight—an elderly English diplomatist running hard and crying or bellowing as he ran.

His hoarse shouts brought a pale face to the study door, the beaming glasses and worried brow of Dr. Simon, who heard the nobleman's first clear words. Lord Galloway was crying: "A corpse in the grass—a blood-stained corpse." O'Brien at last had gone utterly out of his mind.

"We must tell Valentin at once," said the doctor, when the other had brokenly described all that he had dared to examine. "It is fortunate that he is here"; and even as he spoke the great detective entered the study, attracted by the cry. It was almost amusing to note his typical transformation; he had come with the common concern of a host and a gentleman, fearing that some guest or servant was ill. When he was told the gory fact, he turned with all his gravity instantly bright and businesslike; for this, however abrupt and awful, was his business.

"Strange, gentlemen," he said as they hurried out into the garden, "that I should have hunted mysteries all over the earth, and now one comes and settles in my own back-yard. But where is the place?" They crossed the lawn less easily, as a slight mist had begun to rise from the river, but under the guidance of the shaken Galloway they found the body sunken in deep grass—the body of a very tall and broad-shouldered man. He lay face downwards, so they could only see that his big shoulders were clad in black cloth, and that his big head was bald, except for a wisp or two of brown hair that clung to his skull like wet seaweed. A scarlet serpent of blood crawled from his fallen face.

"At least," said Simon, with a deep and singular intonation, "he is none of our party."

"Examine him, Doctor," cried Valentin rather sharply. "He may not be dead."

The doctor bent down. "He is not quite cold, but I am afraid he is dead enough," he answered. "Just help me to lift him up."

They lifted him carefully an inch from the ground, and all doubts as to his being really dead were settled at once and frightfully. The head fell away. It had been entirely sundered from the body; whoever had cut his throat had managed to sever the neck as well. Even Valentin was slightly shocked. "He must have been as strong as a gorilla," he muttered.

Not without a shiver, though he was used to anatomical abortions, Dr. Simon lifted the head. It was slightly slashed about the neck and jaw, but the face was substantially unhurt. It was a ponderous, yellow face, at once sunken and swollen, with a hawk-like nose and heavy lids—a face of a wicked Roman emperor, with, perhaps, a distant touch of a Chinese emperor. All present seemed to look at it with the coldest eye of ignorance. Nothing else could be noted about the man except that, as they had lifted his body, they had seen underneath it the white gleam of a shirt-front defaced with a red gleam of blood. As Dr. Simon said, the man had never been of their party. But he might very well have been trying to join it, for he had come dressed for such an occasion.

Valentin went down on his hands and knees and examined with his closest professional attention the grass and ground for some twenty yards round the body, in which he was assisted less skillfully by the doctor, and quite vaguely by the English lord. Nothing rewarded their grovellings except a few twigs, snapped or chopped into very small lengths, which Valentin lifted for an instant's examination and then tossed away.

"Twigs," he said gravely; "twigs, and a total stranger with his head cut off; that is all there is on this lawn."

There was an almost creepy stillness, and then the unnerved Galloway called out sharply:

"Who's that? Who's that over there by the garden wall?"

A small figure with a foolishly large head drew waveringly near them in the moonlit haze; looked for an instant like a goblin, but turned out to be the harmless little priest whom they had left in the drawing-room.

"I say," he said meekly, "there are no gates to this garden, do you know."

Valentin's black brows had come together somewhat crossly, as they did on principle at the sight of the cassock. But he was far too just a man to deny the relevance of the remark. "You are right," he said. "Before we find out how he came to be killed, we may have to find out how he came to be here. Now listen to me, gentlemen. If it can be done without prejudice to my position and duty, we shall all agree that certain distinguished names might well be kept out of this. There are ladies, gentlemen, and there is a foreign ambassador. If we must mark it down as a crime, then it must be followed up as a crime. But till then I can use my own discretion. I am the head of the police; I am so public that I can afford to be private. Please Heaven, I will clear everyone of my own guests before I call in my men to look for anybody else. Gentlemen, upon your honour, you will none of you leave the house till tomorrow at noon; there are bedrooms for all. Simon, I think you know where to find my man, Ivan, in the front hall; he is a confidential man. Tell him to leave another servant on guard and come to me at once. Lord Galloway, you are certainly the best person to tell the ladies what has happened, and prevent a panic. They also must stay. Father Brown and I will remain with the body."

When this spirit of the captain spoke in Valentin he was obeyed like a bugle. Dr. Simon went through to the armoury and routed out Ivan, the public detective's private detective. Galloway went to the drawing-room and told the terrible news tactfully enough, so that by the time the company assembled there the ladies were already startled and already soothed. Meanwhile the good priest and the good atheist stood at the head and foot of the dead man motionless in the moonlight, like symbolic statues of their two philosophies of death.

Ivan, the confidential man with the scar and the moustaches, came out of the house like a cannon ball, and came racing across the lawn to Valentin like a dog to his master. His livid face was quite lively with the glow of this domestic detective story, and it was with almost unpleasant eagerness that he asked his master's permission to examine the remains.

"Yes; look, if you like, Ivan," said Valentin, "but don't be long. We must go in and thrash this out in the house."

Ivan lifted the head, and then almost let it drop.

"Why," he gasped, "It's—no, it isn't; it can't be. Do you know this man, sir?"

"No," said Valentin indifferently; "we had better go inside."

Between them they carried the corpse to a sofa in the study, and then all made their way to the drawing-room.

The detective sat down at a desk quietly, and even without hesitation; but his eye was the iron eye of a judge at assize. He made a few rapid notes upon paper in front of him, and then said shortly: "Is everybody here?"

"Not Mr. Brayne," said the Duchess of Mont St. Michel, looking round.

"No," said Lord Galloway in a hoarse, harsh voice. "And not Mr. Neil O'Brien, I fancy. I saw that gentleman walking in the garden when the corpse was still warm."

"Ivan," said the detective, "go and fetch Commandant O'Brien and Mr. Brayne. Mr. Brayne, I know, is finishing a cigar in the dining-room; Commandant O'Brien, I think, is walking up and down the conservatory. I am not sure."

The faithful attendant flashed from the room, and before anyone could stir or speak Valentin went on with the same soldierly swiftness of exposition.

"Everyone here knows that a dead man has been found in the garden, his head cut clean from his body. Dr. Simon, you have examined it. Do you think that to cut a man's throat like that would need great force? Or, perhaps only a very sharp knife?"

"I should say that it could not be done with a knife at all," said the pale doctor.

"Have you any thought," resumed Valentin, "of a tool with which it could be done?"

"Speaking within modern probabilities, I really haven't," said the doctor, arching his painful brows. "It's not easy to hack a neck through even clumsily, and this was a very clean cut. It could be done with a battle-axe or an old headsman's axe, or an old two-handed sword."

"But, good heavens!" cried the Duchess, almost in hysterics, "there aren't any two-handed swords and battle-axes round here."

Valentin was still busy with the paper in front of him. "Tell me," he said, still writing rapidly, "could it have been done with a long French cavalry sabre?"

A low knocking came at the door, which for some unreasonable reason, curdled everyone's blood like the knocking in *Macbeth*. Amid that frozen silence Dr. Simon managed to say: "A sabre—yes, I suppose it could."

"Thank you," said Valentin. "Come in, Ivan."

The confidential Ivan opened the door and ushered in Commandant Neil O'Brien, whom he had found at last pacing the garden again.

The Irish officer stood up disordered and defiant on the threshold. "What do you want with me?" he cried.

"Please sit down," said Valentin in pleasant, level tones. "Why, you aren't wearing your sword. Where is it?"

"I let it on the library table," said O'Brien, his brogue deepening in his disturbed mood. "It was a nuisance, it was getting—"

"Ivan," said Valentin, "please go and get the Commandant's sword from the library." Then, as the servant vanished, "Lord Galloway says he saw you leaving the garden just before he found the corpse. What were you doing in the garden?"

The Commandant flung himself recklessly into a chair. "Oh," he cried in pure Irish, "admirin' the moon. Communing with Nature, me bhoy."

A heavy silence sank and endured, and at the end of it came

238

again that trivial and terrible knocking. Ivan reappeared, carrying an empty steel scabbard. "This is all I can find," he said.

"Put it on the table," said Valentin, without looking up.

There was an inhuman silence in the room, like that sea of inhuman silence round the dock of the condemned murderer. The Duchess's weak exclamations had long ago died away. Lord Galloway's swollen hatred was satisfied and even sobered. The voice that came was quite unexpected.

"I think I can tell you," cried Lady Margaret, in that clear, quivering voice with which a courageous woman speaks publicly. "I can tell you what Mr. O'Brien was doing in the garden, since he is bound to silence. He was asking me to marry him. I refused; I said in my family circumstances I could give him nothing but my respect. He was a little angry at that; he did not seem to think much of my respect. I wonder," she added, with rather a wan smile, "if he will care at all for it now. For I offer it him now. I will swear anywhere that he never did a thing like this."

Lord Galloway had edged up to his daughter, and was intimidating her in what he imagined to be an undertone. "Hold your tongue, Maggie," he said in a thunderous whisper. "Why should you shield the fellow? Where's his sword? Where's his confounded cavalry—"

He stopped because of the singular stare with which his daughter was regarding him, a look that was indeed a lurid magnet for the whole group.

"You old fool!" she said in a low voice without pretence of piety, "what do you suppose you are trying to prove? I tell you this man was innocent while with me. But if he wasn't innocent, he was still with me. If he murdered a man in the garden, who was it who must have seen—who must at least have known? Do you hate Neil so much as to put your own daughter—"

Lady Galloway screamed. Everyone else sat tingling at the touch of those satanic tragedies that have been between lovers before now. They saw the proud, white face of the Scotch aristocrat and her lover, the Irish adventurer, like old portraits in a dark house. The long silence was full of formless historical memories of murdered husbands and poisonous paramours.

In the centre of this morbid silence an innocent voice said: "Was it a very long cigar?"

The change of thought was so sharp that they had to look round to see who had spoken.

"I mean," said little Father Brown, from the corner of the room, "I mean that cigar Mr. Brayne is finishing. It seems nearly as long as a walking-stick."

Despite the irrelevance there was assent as well as irritation in Valentin's face as he lifted his head.

"Quite right," he remarked sharply. "Ivan, go and see about Mr. Brayne again, and bring him here at once."

The instant the factotum had closed the door, Valentin addressed the girl with an entirely new earnestness.

"Lady Margaret," he said, "we all feel, I am sure, both gratitude and admiration for your act in rising above your lower dignity and explaining the Commandant's conduct. But there is a hiatus still. Lord Galloway, I understand, met you passing from the study to the drawing-room, and it was only some minutes afterwards that he found the garden and the Commandant still walking there."

"You have to remember," replied Margaret, with a faint irony in her voice, "that I had just refused him, so we should scarcely have come back arm in arm. He is a gentleman, anyhow; and he loitered behind—and so got charged with murder."

"In those few moments," said Valentin gravely, "he might really—"

The knock came again, and Ivan put in his scarred face.

"Beg pardon, sir," he said, "but Mr. Brayne has left the house."

"Left!" cried Valentin, and rose for the first time to his feet.

"Gone. Scooted. Evaporated," replied Ivan in humorous French. "His hat and coat are gone, too, and I'll tell you something to cap it all. I ran outside the house to find any traces of him, and I found one, and a big trace, too."

"What do you mean?" asked Valentin.

"I'll show you," said his servant and reappeared with a flashing naked cavalry sabre, streaked with blood about the point and edge. Everyone in the room eyed it as if it were a thunderbolt; but the experienced Ivan went on quite quietly:

"I found this," he said, "flung among the bushes fifty yards up the road to Paris. In other words, I found it just where your respectable Mr. Brayne threw it when he ran away."

There was again a silence, but of a new sort. Valentin took the sabre, examined it, reflected with unaffected concentration of thought, and then turned a respectful face to O'Brien. "Commandant," he said, "we trust you will always produce this weapon if it is wanted for police examination. Meanwhile," he added, slapping the steel back in the ringing scabbard, "let me return you your sword."

At the military symbolism of the action the audience could hardly refrain from applause.

For Neil O'Brien, indeed, that gesture was the turning-point of existence. By the time he was wandering in the mysterious garden again in the colours of the morning the tragic futility of his ordinary mien had fallen from him; he was a man with many reasons for happiness. Lord Galloway was a gentleman, and had offered him an apology. Lady Margaret was something better than a lady, a woman at least, and had perhaps given him something better than an apology, as they drifted among the old flowerbeds before breakfast. The whole company was more light-hearted and humane, for though the riddle of the death remained, the load of suspicion was lifted off them all, and sent flying off to Paris with the strange millionaire—a man they hardly knew. The devil was cast out of the house—he had cast himself out.

Still, the riddle remained; and when O'Brien threw himself on a garden seat beside Dr. Simon, that keenly scientific person at once resumed it. He did not get much talk out of O'Brien, whose thoughts were on pleasanter things.

"I can't say it interests me much," said the Irishman frankly, "especially as it seems pretty plain now. Apparently Brayne hated this stranger for some reason; lured him into the garden, and killed him with my sword. Then he fled to the city, tossing the sword away as he went. By the way, Ivan tells me the dead man had a Yankee dollar in his pocket. So he was a countryman of Brayne's, and that seems to clinch it. I don't see any difficulties about the business."

"There are five colossal difficulties," said the doctor quietly; "like high walls within walls. Don't mistake me. I don't doubt that Brayne did it; his flight, I fancy, proves that. But as to how he did it. First difficulty: Why should a man kill another man with a great hulking sabre, when he can almost kill him with a pocket knife and put it back in his pocket? Second difficulty: Why was there no noise or outcry? Does a man commonly see another come up waving a scimitar and offer no remarks? Third difficulty: A servant watched the front door all the evening; and a rat cannot get into Valentin's garden anywhere. How did the dead man get into the garden? Fourth difficulty: Given the same conditions, how did Brayne get out of the garden?"

"And the fifth," said Neil with eyes fixed on the English priest who was coming slowly up the path.

"Is a trifle, I suppose," said the doctor, "but I think an odd one. When I first saw how the head had been slashed, I supposed the assassin had struck more than once. But on examination I found many cuts across the truncated section; in other words, they were struck *after* the head was off. Did Brayne hate his foe so fiendishly that he stood sabring the body in the moonlight?"

"Horrible!" said O'Brien and shuddered.

The little priest, Brown, had arrived while they were talking, and had waited, with characteristic shyness, till they had finished. Then he said awkwardly:

"I say, I'm sorry to interrupt. But I was sent to tell you the news!"

"News?" repeated Simon, and stared at him rather painfully through his glasses.

"Yes, I'm sorry," said Father Brown mildly. "There's been another murder, you know."

Both men on the seat sprang up, leaving it rocking.

"And, what's stranger still," continued the priest, with his dull eye on the rhododendrons, "it's the same disgusting sort; it's another beheading. They found the second head actually bleeding into the river, a few yards along Brayne's road to Paris; so they suppose that he—"

"Great Heaven!" cried O'Brien. "Is Brayne a monomaniac?"

"There are American vendettas," said the priest impassively.

Then he added: "They want you to come to the library and see it.

Commandant O'Brien followed the others towards the inquest, feeling decidedly sick. As a soldier, he loathed all this secretive carnage; where were these extravagant amputations going to stop? First one head was hacked off, and then another; in this case (he told himself bitterly) it was not true that two heads were better than one. As he crossed the study he almost staggered at a shocking coincidence. Upon Valentin's table lay the coloured picture of yet a third bleeding head; and it was the head of Valentin himself. A second glance showed him it was only a Nationalist paper, called *The Guillotine*, which every week showed one of its political opponents with rolling eyes and writhing features just after execution; for Valentin was an anti-clerical of some note. But O'Brien was an Irishman, with a kind of chastity even in his sins; and his gorge rose against that great brutality of the intellect which belongs only to France. He felt Paris as a whole, from the grotesques on the Gothic churches to the gross caricatures in the newspapers. He remembered the gigantic jests of the Revolution. He saw the whole city as one ugly energy, from the sanguinary sketch lying on Valentin's table up to where, above a mountain and forest of gargoyles, the great devil grins on Notre Dame.

The library was long, low, and dark; what light entered it shot from under low blinds and had still some of the ruddy tinge of morning. Valentin and his servant Ivan were waiting for them at the upper end of a long, slightly sloping desk, on which lay the mortal remains, looking enormous in the twilight. The big black figure and yellow face of the man found in the garden confronted them essentially unchanged. The second head, which had been fished from among the river reeds that morning, lay streaming and dripping beside it; Valentin's men were still seeking to recover the rest of this second corpse, which was supposed to be afloat. Father Brown, who did not seem to share O'Brien's sensibilities in the least, went up to the second head and examine it with his blinking care. It was little more than a mop of wet white hair, fringed with silver fire in the red and level morning light; the face, which seemed of an ugly, empurpled and perhaps criminal type, had been much battered against trees or stones as it tossed in the water.

"Good morning, Commandant O'Brien," said Valentin, with quiet cordiality. "You have heard of Brayne's last experiment in butchery, I suppose?"

Father Brown was still bending over the head with white hair, and he said, without looking up:

"I suppose it is quite certain that Brayne cut off this head, too."

"Well, it seems common sense," said Valentin, with his hands in his pockets. "Killed in the same way as the other, found within a few yards of the other. And sliced by the same weapon which we know he carried away."

"Yes, yes; I know," replied Father Brown submissively. "Yet, you know, I doubt whether Brayne could have cut off this head."

"Why not?" inquired Dr. Simon with a rational stare.

"Well, Doctor," said the priest, looking up blinking, "can a man cut off his own head? I don't know."

O'Brien felt an insane universe crashing about his ears; but the doctor sprang forward with impetuous practicality and pushed back the wet white hair.

"Oh, there's no doubt it's Brayne," said the priest quietly. "He had exactly that chip in the left ear."

The detective, who had been regarding the priest with steady and glittering eyes, opened his clenched mouth and said sharply: "You seem to know a lot about him, Father Brown."

"I do," said the little man simply. "I've been about with him for some weeks. He was thinking of joining our church."

The star of the fanatic sprang into Valentin's eyes; he strode towards the priest with clenched hands. "And, perhaps," he cried, with a blasting sneer, "perhaps he was also thinking of leaving all his money to your church."

"Perhaps he was," said Brown stolidly; "it is possible."

"In that case," cried Valentin, with a dreadful smile, "you may indeed know a great deal about him. About his life and about his—"

Commandant O'Brien laid a hand on Valentin's arm. "Drop that slanderous rubbish, Valentin," he said, "or there may be more swords yet."

But Valentin (under the steady, humble gaze of the priest) had already recovered himself. "Well," he said shortly, "people's private opinions can wait. You gentlemen are still bound by your promise to stay; you must enforce it on yourselves—and on each other. Ivan here will tell you anything more you want to know; I must get to business and write to the authorities. We can't keep this quiet any longer. I shall be writing in my study if there is any more news."

"Is there any more news, Ivan?" asked Dr. Simon, as the chief of police strode out of the room.

"Only one more thing, I think, sir," said Ivan, wrinkling up his grey old face, "but that's important, too, in its way. There's that old duffer you found on the lawn," and he pointed without pretence of reverence at the big black body with the yellow head. "We've found out who he is, anyhow."

"Indeed!" cried the astonished doctor, "and who is he?"

"His name was Arnold Becker," said the under-detective, "though he went by many aliases. He was a wandering sort of scamp, and is known to have been in America; so that was where Brayne got his knife into him. We didn't have much to do with him ourselves, for he worked mostly in Germany. We've communicated, of course, with the German police. But, oddly enough, there was a twin brother of his, named Louis Becker, whom we had a great deal to do with. In fact, we found it necessary to guillotine him only yesterday. Well, it's a rum thing, gentlemen, but when I saw that fellow flat on the lawn I had the greatest jump of my life. If I hadn't seen Louis Becker guillotined with my own eyes, I'd have sworn it was Louis Becker lying there in the grass. Then, of course, I remembered his twin brother in Germany, and following up the clue—"

The explanatory Ivan stopped, for the excellent reason that nobody was listening to him. The Commandant and the doctor were both staring at Father Brown, who had sprung stiffly to his feet, and was holding his temples tight like a man in sudden and violent pain.

"Stop, stop, stop!" he cried; "stop talking a minute, for I see half. Will God give me strength? Will my brain make the one jump and see all? Heaven help me! I used to be fairly good at thinking. I could paraphrase any page in Aquinas once. Will my head split—or will it see? I see half—I only see half."

He buried his head in his hands, and stood in a sort of rigid torture of thought or prayer, while the other three could only go on staring at this last prodigy of their wild twelve hours.

When Father Brown's hands fell they showed a face quite fresh and serious, like a child's. He heaved a huge sigh, and said: "Let us get this said and done with as quickly as possible. Look here, this will be the quickest way to convince you all of the truth." He turned to the doctor, "Dr. Simon," he said, "you have a strong head-piece, and I heard you this morning asking the five hardest questions about this business. Well, if you will ask them again, I will answer them."

Simon's pince-nez dropped from his nose in his doubt and wonder, but he answered at once. "Well, the first question, you know, is why a man should kill another with a clumsy sabre at all when a man can kill with a bodkin?"

"A man cannot behead with a bodkin," said Brown calmly, "and for *this* murder beheading was absolutely necessary."

"Why?" asked O'Brien, with interest.

"And the next question?" asked Father Brown.

"Well, why didn't the man cry out or anything?" asked the doctor; "sabres in gardens are certainly unusual."

"Twigs," said the priest gloomily, and turned to the window which looked on the scene of death. "No one saw the point of the twigs. Why should they lie on that lawn (look at it) so far from any tree? They were not snapped off; they were chopped off. The murderer occupied his enemy with some tricks with the sabre showing how he could cut a branch in mid-air, or what-not. Then, while his enemy bent down to see the result, a silent slash, and the head fell."

"Well," said the doctor slowly, "That seems plausible enough. But my next two questions will stump anyone."

The priest still stood looking critically out of the window and waited.

"You know how all the garden was sealed up like an airtight chamber," went on the doctor. "Well, how did the strange man get into the garden?"

Without turning round, the little priest answered: "There never was any strange man in the garden."

There was a silence, and then a sudden crackle of almost childish laughter relieved the strain. The absurdity of Brown's remark moved Ivan to open taunts.

"Oh!" he cried; "then we didn't lug a great fat corpse on to a sofa last night? He hadn't got into the garden, I suppose?"

"Got into the garden?" repeated Brown reflectively. "No, not entirely."

"Hang it all," cried Simon, "a man gets into a garden, or he doesn't."

"Not necessarily," said the priest, with a faint smile. "What is the next question, doctor?"

"I fancy you're ill," exclaimed Dr. Simon sharply; "but I'll ask the next question if you like. How did Brayne get out of the garden?"

"He didn't get out of the garden," said the priest, still looking out of the window.

"Didn't get out of the garden," exploded Simon.

"Not completely," said Father Brown.

Simon shook his fists in a frenzy of French logic. "A man gets out of a garden, or he doesn't," he cried.

"Not always," said Father Brown.

Dr. Simon sprang to his feet impatiently. "I have no time to spare on such senseless talk," he cried angrily. "If you can't understand a man being on one side of a wall or the other, I won't trouble you further."

"Doctor," said the cleric very gravely, "we have always got on very pleasantly together. If only for the sake of old friendship, stop and tell me your fifth question."

The impatient Simon sank into a chair by the door and said briefly: "The head and shoulders were cut about in a queer way. It seemed to be done after death."

"Yes," said the motionless priest, "it was done so as to make you assume exactly the one simple falsehood that you did assume. It was done to make you take for granted that the head belonged to the body."

The borderland of the brain, where all the monsters are made,

247

moved horribly in the Gaelic O'Brien. He felt the chaotic presence of all the horse-men and fish-women that man's unnatural fancy has begotten. A voice older than his first fathers seemed saying in his ear: "Keep out of the monstrous garden where grows the tree with the double fruit. Avoid the evil garden where died the man with two heads." Yet, while these shameful symbolic shapes passed across the ancient mirror of his Irish soul, his Frenchified intellect was quite alert, and was watching the odd priest as closely and incredulously as all the rest.

Father Brown had turned round at last, and stood against the window, with his face in dense shadow; but even in that shadow they could see it was pale as ashes. Nevertheless, he spoke quite sensibly, as if there were no Gaelic souls on earth.

"Gentlemen," he said, "you did not find the strange body of Becker in the garden. You did not find any strange body in the garden. In face of Dr. Simon's rationalism, I still affirm that Becker was only partly present. Look here!" (pointing to the black bulk of the mysterious corpse) "you never saw that man in your lives. Did you ever see this man?"

He rapidly rolled away the bald, yellow head of the unknown, and put in its place the white-maned head beside it. And there, complete, unified, unmistakable, lay Julius K. Brayne.

"The murderer," went on Brown quietly, "hacked off his enemy's head and flung the sword far over the wall. But he was too clever to fling the sword only. He flung the *head* over the wall also. Then he had only to clap on another head to the corpse, and (as he insisted on a private inquest) you all imagined a totally new man."

"Clap on another head!" said O'Brien, staring. "What other head? Heads don't grow on garden bushes, do they?"

"No," said Father Brown huskily, and looking at his boots; "there is only one place where they grow. They grow in the basket of the guillotine, beside which the chief of police, Aristide Valentin, was standing not an hour before the murder. Oh, my friends, hear me a minute more before you tear me in pieces. Valentin is an honest man, if being mad for an arguable cause is honesty. But did you never see in that cold, grey eye of his that he is mad? He would do anything, anything, to break what he calls the superstition of the Cross. He has fought for it and starved for it, and now he has murdered for it. Brayne's crazy millions had hitherto been scattered among so many sects that they did little to alter the balance of things. But Valentin heard a whisper that Brayne, like so many scatter-brained sceptics, was drifting to us; and that was quite a different thing. Brayne would pour supplies into the impoverished and pugnacious Church of France; he would support six Nationalist newspapers like *The Guillotine*. The battle was already balanced on a point, and the fanatic took flame at the risk. He resolved to destroy the millionaire, and he did it as one would expect the greatest of detectives to commit his only crime. He abstracted the severed head of Becker on some criminological excuse, and took it home in his official box. He had that last argument with Brayne, that Lord Galloway did not hear the end of; that failing, he led him out into the sealed garden, talked about swordsmanship, used twigs and a sabre for illustration, and—"

Ivan of the Scar sprang up. "You lunatic," he yelled; "you'll go to my master now, if I take you by—"

"Why, I was going there," said Brown heavily; "I must ask him to confess, and all that."

Driving the unhappy Brown before them like a hostage or sacrifice, they rushed together into the sudden stillness of Valentin's study.

The great detective sat at his desk apparently too occupied to hear their turbulent entrance. They paused a moment, and then something in the look of that upright and elegant back made the doctor run forward suddenly. A touch and a glance showed him that there was a small box of pills at Valentin's elbow, and that Valentin was dead in his chair; and on the blind face of the suicide was more than the pride of Cato.

MURDER
FOR
FINE
ART

BY JOHN BASYE PRICE

MY DEAR NIECE,

Now that I have reached the age of more than threescore, and my life draws to a close, I think it only right that you should know the real truth about my trouble with Pompeo—trouble that put me in the gravest danger of my life and nearly ended my career thirty years ago. Do not show this letter to anyone, but do not destroy it! Instead, wall it up in the new hall now being built at your convent, so that it may be found only after the building falls to ruins many hundred years hence.

It was in Rome in 1534, shortly after I had lost my position as Director of the Mint, that Pompeo approached me. I had known him for some time as a jeweller from Milan. He thought himself clever, but I regarded him as a pompous windbag, and (although he did not know it) as a secret enemy. However, I greeted him politely, and asked what he wanted.

"You would not call me an artist, would you?" he surprised me by asking.

"Well, hardly," I replied.

"And yet in half an hour I can make a better picture than the greatest artist can paint in a week."

"I have no time for jokes," I said, turning away in disgust.

He clutched my arm and took something out of his pouch. "Look at this!" he said.

I stared in amazement at a piece of parchment he held in his hand. On it was a picture of the Coliseum, but such a picture as I had never dreamed of. Except that the picture was in black and white, it was exactly as if an image from a mirror had been miraculously transferred to the parchment.

"Did *you* make this?" I gasped.

"I did, in half an hour, yesterday morning."

I looked and looked at the picture. I could not imagine what medium had been used. The picture had not been drawn by pencil or pen, nor painted with oil-paint or water-colours.

Pompeo stood by, with a smile on his face, watching my perplexity and wonder. Finally, I turned to him and asked, "But why do you show this to me, Pompeo?"

"The truth is," he said, "I need your help."

"*My* help?"

"Yes. I know that you are making some medals for Pope Clement (VII) and see him often. If you can get me an audience with his Holiness and will help persuade him to grant me a large reward for my new method of making pictures, it will make the fortunes of both of us, for I will give you one-tenth of all he gives me."

"But, Pompeo, you are closely related to Messer Trajano, the Pope's favourite servant. Why don't you approach his Holiness through him?"

"Unfortunately, an estrangement has arisen between us." This (I learned later) was true, and for a reason most discreditable to Pompeo. Under the circumstances I, of course, agreed to Pompeo's conditions. After he had sworn me to secrecy, he took me to his shop and revealed his secret.

No doubt you know, my dear niece, that with the right kind of lens it is possible to project a picture of the view outside on the wall of a darkened room. This is called a camera lucida. In brief, what Pompeo had done was to take a thick lens and place it at one end of a closed box, which thus acted as a small camera lucida. At the other end of the box he placed a plate of thin isinglass treated with chemicals (which I shall not name). The light of the image so affected the chemicals that they reproduced the outside scene on the isinglass in reversed black and white. Pompeo explained that it was necessary to fix the image by soaking the isinglass in other chemicals in a dark room to make the image permanent. Then with this plate exposed to sunlight he transferred the picture to chemically treated parchment.

I congratulated Pompeo on this great discovery, and told him to bring his sun-camera and chemicals to my house the next morning, from whence we would take them to show to the Pope.

I slept but ill that night, turning over and over in my mind two questions: first, where had Pompeo learned the secret of the sun-camera (for I was convinced that he was not capable of inventing such a thing by himself); and secondly, what was I to do in regard to the matter? It was not until the early hours that I reached an answer and a decision.

In the morning, Pompeo came to my house as arranged, but I greeted him with a long face. "I am sorry, Pompeo," I said, "but I have just heard that his Holiness was taken ill last night, and can see no one today. Let us hope that he will be recovered by tomorrow."

"I hadn't heard that," he said. (Neither had I, as a matter of fact, but I was determined that Pompeo should not see the Pope.)

I continued: "The news has just reached me, but come, it is too fine a day to sit here repining. I have a new gun, and the marshes are full of ducks and other fowl. Let's get on our horses and go out for a day of sport. Come, let us start."

"But what of the sun-camera and chemicals? I must take them home first."

"Not a bit of it!" I replied. "We can lock them up in my strong-box and they will be perfectly safe."

This was done, and we started off for the marshes. I was careful to find the most deserted spot imaginable. We tied our horses, and as we advanced towards the water I was holding the gun. It crossed my mind that anything falling into one of the nearby bogs would never be seen again. I looked all round, but no one was in sight, then I turned to Pompeo and said, "Now we are alone. Suppose this time you tell me the truth about the sun-camera. Who really discovered it?"

"As I told you before, I did."

"Oh, no Pompeo, you will never make me believe that a donkey like you could invent such a thing as the sun-camera . . . but never mind, I already know the answer. There is only one man who ever lived who was capable of making a discovery like that."

"Who do you mean?"

"That great artist, poet and scientist—Leonardo da Vinci."

"But, man—Leonardo has been dead for fifteen years!"

"Yes, but I was born in Florence myself, and I have heard that he left many unpublished note-books. You were in Florence a few months ago; no doubt you read them and stole the idea of the sun-camera."

"You are dreaming," said Pompeo; "but even if all that were true, what difference would it make? Leonardo is dead, and I have the sun-camera."

"No, you are wrong."

"What do you mean?"

"*I* have the sun-camera, Pompeo, locked up safe in my strong-box!"

"For the love of God, what's the matter with you? Surely you are not a thief? I thought you were my friend."

"You are no friend of mine, Pompeo. I know perfectly well that it was you, acting through Messer Trajano, who persuaded the Pope to deprive me of my position as Director of the Mint and to give the post to Fagiuolo instead."

"But that is an old story, why bring it up now?"

"Do you not understand, even yet? Here we are entirely alone; over there is a deep bog that would hide a body for ever; I am armed and you are not. In short, I am going to kill you, Pompeo!"

So saying, I cocked my gun. I had expected that he would attack me, but instead, he turned to run. Aiming the arquebus directly at him, I pulled the trigger; but by cursed ill-luck the gun misfired.

Dropping the gun, I drew my dagger and started after Pompeo. But in all my life, before or since, I have never seen anyone run as fast as he did. Fat as he was, he reached the horses first, flung himself astride, and galloped off as if the Devil were after him.

By chance or design Pompeo had taken the faster horse, but he weighed much more than I, so I had every prospect of over-taking him before we reached the city. But I lost him when he turned and took a short-cut through a field.

I set off for the city as fast as I could. By good luck I reached my house in time; I opened the strong-box and took out the sun-camera and the chemicals and hurried to the house of my best friend, Albertaccio del Bene, whom I knew I could trust. I left them with him for safe keeping and started back to my own house.

When I came in sight of it, as I had expected, I saw Pompeo in front of my door, and with him was the Bargello (sheriff) with his constables, some armed with pikes, some with arquebuses and some with two-handed swords.

I approached and called out, "Pompeo, are you feeling better now?"

He was taken back for an instant, and then shouted at the Bargello, "Arrest that man; he tried to kill me!"

"Kill you, my dear fellow!" I exclaimed in a tone of amazement. "Your mind is more disturbed than I thought."

Turning to the Bargello, I said, "Pompeo's mind has been affected for some time; and this morning, when he came to see me, it was evidently much worse. He talked in such a wild way that I tried to soothe him by taking him for a day's shooting in the marshes. But as soon as we got there, he lost his reason altogether. He screamed that he saw the Devil coming after him and galloped off. I followed as fast as I could, for I feared that in his state he would do himself some injury. I have just arrived."

"Lies, lies, lies!" screamed Pompeo; "I tell you, he tried to shoot me, and would have, but his gun misfired!"

"But, Pompeo, calm yourself; why should I want to kill you?"

"You know why; you want to steal my invention—my sun-camera."

"Sun-camera! What on earth do you mean? I never heard of such a thing."

This enraged Pompeo so much that he forgot his need for secrecy. Turning to the Bargello, he said, "I have invented a machine that can make a better picture in half an hour than the best artist can draw in a week."

"Do you mean that *you* can draw a picture in half an hour that is better than one made by a trained artist?" the Bargello asked in astonishment.

"No, I don't draw the picture myself. With my machine the

sun makes the picture for me. Just as if an image from a mirror had been transferred to parchment."

At this reply the Bargello's whole attitude changed. Turning to me, he said, "I beg your parden for doubting you for a moment. You are right, Pompeo has gone mad. There can be no doubt that he is insane."

"No, no, no!" screamed Pompeo, "I'm not crazy. I don't care, now, whether the Pope gives me a reward or not. I'll show you my sun-camera and you can see for yourself." Pointing at me he said, "he locked it in his strong-box this morning. Have him open it and I will prove it to you."

In silence I handed my keys to the Bargello, and we three entered my house. The Bargello opened my strong-box, but, naturally, there was nothing inside.

"There you are," I said. "I am very sorry for Pompeo; I happen to have a medicine which is very useful in cases of this kind. Let me give Pompeo a few drops and soon, no doubt, he will be more quiet."

"For the love of God, no!" screamed Pompeo. "He's trying to poison me!" He was so worked up that he foamed at the mouth and acted in such a manner that if the Bargello had had any remaining doubts they would have been dispelled. He and his constables marched Pompeo away and locked him up.

The next day I was summoned by Pope Clement, for the Bargello had reported the matter to him. In answer to his questions, I told him that there was no doubt that Pompeo was dangerously insane. Others had reported the same thing, so the Pope ordered Pompeo to be confined in an asylum until he should recover his wits.

If Pompeo had been at all clever he would have calmed down and stated that he now realized that his tale of a sun-camera was a delusion, and that his mind was now recovered. But, like the donkey he was, he kept insisting that everything he had said was true. (As a matter of fact it was, but only I knew that.)

For a time everything went well with me. The Pope was very pleased with some gold medals I had made for him, and promised me enough new work to make my fortune. Everything seemed to be going my way, with the Pope my patron and Pompeo in the insane asylum. But suddenly the Pope was taken ill. I had finished another medal, and took it to him; he was in bed and unable to see the medal clearly, even with his spectacles. Three days later Pope Clement died.

I knew I must be careful, for anything can happen in the anarchy which occurs after one Pope dies and before the new Pope is elected. On Clement's death, his order confining Pompeo to the asylum was annulled.

I learned this unexpectedly. I was sitting in the street with several friends watching the great commotion which always follows the death of a Pope, when a group of ten Neapolitan soldiers, very well armed, came up and stopped just opposite us. The ranks opened, and Pompeo stepped out from the centre of the group and hailed me.

"So, Pompeo," I said, "I am happy to see that you have recovered your wits again. Or have you? I see that you have hired these ten men as a bodyguard. No doubt to protect you from some fancied danger?"

Pompeo replied with a torrent of abuse, and called me every vile name he could think of. My companions expected me to draw my sword against him, but I saw that was just what Pompeo wanted. If I drew my sword it would give his hired soldiers an excuse to kill me. My friends and I were armed, but were outnumbered. And so I said in a loud voice to Albertaccio del Bene, at my side, "If any sane man were to talk to me like that it would be the last thing he would ever do on this earth; but poor Pompeo has not yet recovered from his madness, so I will just ignore him."

"This was too much for any of Pompeo's remaining caution, and he shouted when he should have kept silent. "We will see if I am crazy or not! Tomorrow, I will have another sun-camera ready; and this time the Bargello will believe *me*." So saying, Pompeo and his bodyguard marched off slowly towards the Chiavica.

Although I did not show it, Pompeo's last words had given me a tremendous shock. I had supposed that it would take him weeks to grind a new lens for the sun-camera (for an ordinary spectacle lens will not do). Was it possible that he had already made another lens beforehand? Pompeo was a liar and a boaster, but this time he might be telling the truth. I wished then that I had drawn my sword and led my friends against him, but it was too late now. How could I ask them to attack a man who I had just stated was not responsible for his actions?

Very uneasy, I followed Pompeo's party alone, taking care to keep out of his sight. When the group reached the corner of Chiavica, all my fears were confirmed, for Pompeo entered an apothocary's shop while his guards remained at the door. He had told me that he always bought fresh chemicals from this shop just before making a sun-picture.

I saw all my plans in ruins about me, and knew that I had not an instant to lose. Pompeo came out of the shop, and his soldiers opened their ranks and received him in their midst. Nerving myself, I drew my dagger, and taking everyone by complete surprise, I pushed into the midst of the group. Before they could draw their swords I seized Pompeo with my left hand and with the dagger in my other hand struck at his head. (I have always maintained, since, that I only meant to wound him, but this is not true.) I tried to kill him, and I did kill him, for as he turned away in fright, my dagger stabbed him just behind the ear and he fell stone-dead in the street.

Shifting the dagger to my left hand, I drew my sword to defend myself against odds of ten to one. However, these soldiers were so taken by surprise that they all ran to lift up the corpse, and before they could recover their wits and attack me, I had escaped alone through Strada Giulia.

You already know, my dear niece, what deadly danger I went through after the death of Pompeo. I had to go in hiding from the Bargello, who had orders to take me dead or alive. Worse still, Pompeo's family hired assassins with promises of great rewards if they would slay me. I had several very narrow escapes from being killed. Finally, I had to flee from Rome and take refuge in my native city of Florence.

After almost a year, my friends in Rome persuaded the new Pope Paul (III) to grant me the pardon of Our Lady's Feast in mid-August. I went to Rome under a safe-conduct, and presented myself to the Pope, who signed the pardon and had it registered at the Capitol. On the day appointed, I walked in penance in the procession, and so got clear of the murder at last.

And now, my dear niece, no doubt you are wondering why you have never heard anything about the sun-camera and its marvellous pictures. You will wonder why I did not use the invention and make a great fortune with it. To explain: Pompeo was wrong, that day on the marshes, when he thought that I wanted to steal the sun-camera for my own advantage. Murderer I have been, but never a thief. When I first realized that the discovery could only have been made by Leonardo da Vinci, I asked myself, "Why had not Leonardo given his discovery to the world?"

A little thought gave me the answer. Leonardo knew that artistic creation is the greatest glory of our human race. The past century has given us many great artists, and doubtless the next century will give us as many more. But suppose the secret of the sun-camera became known. Anyone and everyone, from Emperors down to common ploughboys, could make as accurate pictures as now only the greatest artists can make. Real artists no longer would be able to obtain patrons to order portraits, and would either starve or be forced into common labor. All the great artists of the future would be stifled in their youth. And artistic creation would be extinct.

And another matter. No doubt some artists with private means would continue painting for pure love of the work. But I fear that a group of quacks and charlatans without any artistic ability at all would paint pictures distorting things as they really are just for an effect of novelty. They might cover canvases with meaningless daubs of colour, and then try to persuade the ignorant and gullible that they were great pictures that common people couldn't understand.

Perhaps these "new artists" might even sneer at genuine artists doing honest painting, and say that their pictures only represented things as they are and were no better than sun-pictures.

The artists of centuries to come would thank me if they could know what I have done for them, even though it was necessary for me to murder my enemy, that thief Pompeo, to accomplish it.

I threw the camera into the Tiber, and I pray the Good Lord it may be three hundred years before someone else rediscovers its secret.

Your devoted uncle,
BENEVENUTO CELLINI